SUMMER MAGIC

SUMMER MAGIC

Edited by Sarah Brown
and Gil McNeil

BLOOMSBURY

First published 2003

Foreword copyright © J. K. Rowling 2003
Introduction copyright © Sarah Brown 2003

This collection copyright © PiggyBankKids Projects Limited 2003

The copyright of the individual contributions
remains with the respective authors

The moral right of the authors has been asserted

Bloomsbury Publishing Plc, 38 Soho Square, London WID 3HB

A CIP catalogue record for this book
is available from the British Library

ISBN 07475 6521X

10 9 8 7 6 5 4 3 2

Typeset by Hewer Text Ltd, Edinburgh
Printed by Clay Ltd, St Ives plc

Acknowledgements

OUR GRATITUDE goes to the authors who have contributed to this collection, and to their agents; to everyone at Bloomsbury, especially Liz Calder, Rosemary Davidson, Ruth Logan, Nigel Newton, Katie Collins and Minna Fry; everyone at One Parent Families for their hard work and enthusiasm; to their Ambassador, J. K. Rowling, for writing the Foreword; the PiggyBankKids Board of Trustees for their support for this project; and to Hugo Tagholm, Programme Director of PiggyBankKids, who has liaised with all the authors and agents.

Personal thanks are due to Gordon Brown; Joe McNeil; Jo Frank; Helen Scott Lidgett; Alan Parker and everyone at Brunswick; and Lord Evans of Watford.

CONTENTS

J. K. ROWLING

Foreword

WHEN YOU are bringing up children on your own, it can be a struggle. You can feel very isolated. Even today, when one in four families is headed by a lone parent, many still feel stigmatised. For over half of lone parents, the hardest thing of all is the daily struggle to make ends meet.

There are no quick and easy answers. But for single parents, it's so important to know that there is a 'professional friend' that is 100 per cent on your side. Someone you can turn to when you need it. One Parent Families is just that. It helps single parents from all walks of life: to tackle money and family problems; advising on how to get into work or education; and enabling parents to access local support.

Last year, One Parent Families helped over 30,000 single parents in England and Wales through its helpline and advice and information services. The charity has now joined forces with its 'sister' charity, One Parent Families Scotland. Together, they run Lone Parent Helpline: a free, confidential and independent service responding to the needs of parents across Britain who are bringing up children on their own.

What impressed me most of all about One Parent Families, and the reason I chose to become one of their

Ambassadors, is that as well as responding to lone parents' needs, to the daily crises that so many face, the charity also works to tackle the root causes of poverty and isolation. I support One Parent Families because they refuse to accept that any child should be disadvantaged simply because they live with one parent rather than two. It is possible to imagine a world where lone parents are not poor. It's not a magic wand we need, but determination and expertise and hard work. And, of course, money.

I am truly grateful to the wonderful writers who have so generously given their work to this brilliant collection. The writers have contributed their work out of the kindness of their hearts. I would also like to thank Bloomsbury for getting behind this magical idea. The inspiration for this book came from the Editors, Sarah Brown and Gil McNeil, who have also set up PiggyBankKids, to raise funds for children and young people in need. Their powers of persuasion are now legendary, and I am delighted that PiggyBank-Kids has chosen to support the work of One Parent Families and One Parent Families Scotland. I would also like to thank *you*. By buying this book, you are supporting their continuing efforts to provide lone parents in Britain with a brighter future. Enjoy *Summer Magic*.

If you would like to do more to help lone parents and their children, why not get in touch with One Parent Families today?

SARAH BROWN

Introduction

I HAVE ALWAYS loved short stories: they're the perfect way to immerse yourself in another world for a few moments – the ideal mini-break without packing a suitcase. *Summer Magic* is a wonderful anthology that can be dipped into and read in any order. And with such a rich variety of writers the book offers everyone the chance both to meet up with old friends and to discover someone new.

Twenty-four of Britain's most loved writers have contributed to this collection, and it has been a joy to work with them. They have all been very generous in writing their stories for this book and donating their royalties to PiggyBankKids.

I set up PiggyBankKids in 2002 in order to make a real difference to my existing charity commitments. Over the last few years, I've been very glad of the opportunity to host launches with Gordon at 11 Downing Street, and it has been a privilege to be a patron of a number of impressive charity initiatives that work, in their many different ways, to the benefit of children and young people most in need. Now, with Piggy-BankKids, I can support my favourite charities, together with some like-minded friends, who are equally passionate in their desire to help organisations that create valuable and lasting improvements in the lives of children and young people.

Last year, Gil McNeil and I edited *Magic*, our first volume of short stories, with all the royalties going to One Parent Families. The book was such a success that we were encouraged to create a new collection. This is one of the first projects for PiggyBankKids, and the charity will be donating all of the royalties, £1 on each copy sold, to One Parent Families and One Parent Families Scotland. If you would like more information about PiggyBankKids and One Parent Families you will find contact details at the end of this book.

I hope you enjoy reading these terrific stories, and whether you are reading them on a holiday beach, or the train to work, in blazing sunshine or pouring rain, I hope they weave a bit of Summer Magic for you.

CLAIRE CALMAN

Sheer Magic

Her:

TO BE honest, I wouldn't mind if I never had a relationship ever, ever again. Believe me, if you'd recently emerged from wasting over eighteen months of your life on a man – no, let's keep it factual – a thirty-three-year-old *boy* as infuriating as Mike Prior, you'd be looking forward to a lifetime of glorious singledom with eager anticipation. I can't enumerate the full encyclopaedia of Mike's many delightful qualities here, but just to give you a taster, this is a man who a) snores so loudly that I swear they're keeping an eye on him at the Earthquake Monitoring Station in San Francisco. No, he doesn't live there, his home turf is what estate agents describe as Dulwich Borders and the rest of us call Peckham; b) believes that, if he leaves a pair of socks on the floor or the stairs or the kitchen worktop, they will get up on their toes and skip merrily to the laundry basket of their own accord; and c) thinks that when a thirty-one-year-old woman wants to have a civilised and much-needed discussion about the future, she is 'rocking the boat'.

It's not that I'm bitter, OK, well, maybe a bit – it's not like I can get a refund on the last two years, is it? –

it's just that I feel stupid . . . and frustrated . . . and really, really pissed off.

And that's just with me.

I tried to be angry with him and I got up quite a head of steam at the time, but in the end how could I blame Mike for being Mike? He's no different from the way he's always been. He never lied about what he wanted, he never pretended to be someone else. The sad, pathetic fact is that *I* wanted him to be someone else and then, when I eventually realised that he wasn't the person I'd conjured up in my head, I felt incredibly disappointed in him. I started talking about commitment and where our relationship was heading even though if he had said yeah, let's go for it, babe, let's get spliced, I'd probably have run a mile; all I wanted was, I don't know, just to talk about it maybe, to look at it as a possibility rather than just staying exactly as we were then waking up one morning and finding I'm forty and still having a relationship that would suit a seventeen-year-old.

So what the hell was I doing with him in the first place? Well, he was tall and good-looking and kind of sexy for a start. Yes, yes, I know that's very shallow. He was super-confident, cocky as hell really, but that only made him more attractive. He wasn't exactly the brightest man I'd ever met, but he was quick and he could be funny on a good day in that brief spell after he'd had one or two pints but before he'd had four or five. Our relationship consisted of going down the pub/watching videos/having sex/getting takeaway Chinese. I didn't mind carrying on with all of these, but I also wanted to consider adding the following activities to our agenda: going on holiday/buying a place together/getting married/having babies – or rather I wanted them on my agenda and he was the person who happened to be in my life at the time so I mistakenly thought they might include him. So you could say that we didn't have enough interests in common. Oh, I forgot to say, the other main reason I was with Mike is that he was completely different from Anthony.

Where Mike was broad-shouldered and almost beefy, Anthony was sort of spindly – he looked like a sapling that might snap in a stiff breeze if you didn't hurry up and tie it to a good, strong stake. Mike thought the Elgin Marbles were actually marbles and couldn't see why the Greeks were getting themselves in such a sweat over wanting them back – why couldn't they just make a new set or something? Anthony had read Classics at Cambridge and had been known to read Pliny years after he left college for fun. *For Fun.* Mike wore a hip leather jacket and jeans that showed off his cute bum. Anthony wore a fleece and cords so baggy you couldn't tell if he even had a bum. Mike made me feel intelligent but embarrassed that I knew anything at all, so I found myself pretending to be more ditsy than I was because it was just easier and I wouldn't have to put up with Mike taking the piss out of me and saying, 'Ooh, clever clogs, listen to her!'

Anthony made me feel stupid and embarrassed that I could possibly be so ignorant in such a wide range of subjects, so I found myself nodding and saying 'Mmm' because it was just easier and I wouldn't have to put up with him smiling with that little frown crumpling his eyebrows and saying, 'But surely you must have known that? Sweetie? Surely, hmm?'

I was with Anthony through half of my twenties, nearly six years. Looking back, I have no idea how we could possibly have lasted that long. Perhaps we were subject to some sort of time warp or maybe I was in a coma for most of it? What I do know is that somehow the years slipped by in a vaguely companionable way: we went to films at the art-house cinema; we had holidays where we each took a suitcase stuffed with books so that, by the end of a week, we'd barely have accumulated more than half an hour's conversation; we made love about once a fortnight, which was perfectly nice in its way, sort of like watching a so-so programme on TV – you vaguely wonder if there might be something better on another channel but, hey, the remote's all the way over on the other side of the room and you can't be bothered to go and get it so this'll have to do.

You would have thought that, eventually, I'd have been swept off my feet by someone else and I'd have had to let Anthony down gently: 'I'm sorry, but . . .' But no. It was Anthony, Anthony who'd always been so judgemental about romance and love at first sight and all that 'sad, self-deluding fantasising, dressing up the fundamental need for human bonding as some sort of emotional and spiritual quest'. It was Anthony who um-ed and ah-ed one suppertime after work and stumbled over embarrassed explanations: 'This might sound rather ridiculous, Cathy, but I seem to have fallen in love . . .'

So Anthony moved out and within a month I'd hooked up with Mike and was counting myself lucky that I'd escaped the clutches of such a dry, tedious intellectual and had found myself someone who really knew how to have fun, who didn't mind getting pissed on a weeknight and was spontaneous enough to try and have sex on the stairs.

The problem with having sex on the stairs is that it's one of those things that sounds wild and adventurous but then, when you actually get down to it, you discover that it's unbelievably uncomfortable and, if you're the one underneath, your feet are the wrong way round to get a grip so you have to dig your heels into the carpet or clutch at the banister to stop yourself bump-bump-bumping down the steps like a Slinky, and then you get the edge of a step digging into your back, so while part of you is thinking: Wow, aren't we spontaneous and sexy – we couldn't even wait to get into the bedroom, another part of you is thinking: God, I wish he'd hurry up and come, this is doing my back in.

So now I'm not with Anthony and I'm not with Mike either. My best friend Jenny says I'm well shot of them both, they're not the only two men on the planet, after all, but then she's been with Roger for eleven years and so she's not Out There, having to face the whole dreadful business of dating and getting your hopes up and wondering: Is this it? Shortly to be followed by: No, it isn't.

Years ago, before I met Anthony, I used to have this long wish-list of how my perfect man would be: he'd be handsome but not vain, intelligent but not a show-off, a god in bed but very unselfish, he'd be naturally funny without trying too hard to make jokes, manly but not tediously macho, thoughtful but with a wild side, sensitive but not wet, interesting but not neurotic, kind to animals but not owning any slobbery dogs, on and on the list went. He should have an interesting job, but not so interesting that it was the focus of his life to the exclusion of all else including me; he should have enough good friends so that I'd know he was popular but not so many that he never had time for me; he should be reasonably fit but not a gym nut. On and on.

Then, after a few relationships, you start refining the list a bit. You think: Well, I could compromise on the looks and the dogs and the fitness thing . . . And you meet more men and you refine your list a bit more. I think I've got it down to something rather more manageable now; he needs to be:

1) Not gay.
2) Not bankrupt.
3) Not mad.

That just about covers it, I think.

No, what I really want – or what I *would* want if I were looking for somebody, which I'm not, obviously, because I'm not doing this stuff any more – what I would like theoretically is someone who would be my best friend, but I'd also fancy him. Is that really so much to ask? Ach, it's never going to happen, is it? I'm off to get myself a coffee. A large mochaccino from Café Bella. With plenty of foam and a sprinkling of cinnamon. If only you could order a man just the way you want him.

Him:

Why do we put ourselves through it? Is it just the sex, is that all it's for? The desperate, driving urge to spread our sperm as far and wide as possible? Tell me if that's all it's really about, no, really – please do, because that would make things a whole lot easier. Then I could just focus on having as much sex as possible, not at all a bad thing to focus on, and forget about – all that other stuff. Sometimes I get the feeling that there are men out there who know how it's done only no one's let me in on the secret. Maybe it's genetic – you're born with the Can Do Relationships gene and the Can Choose Good Woman gene and that's it, you're sorted. You'll find yourself a girlfriend and she won't be neurotic or have a cat that she speaks in a baby-voice to, she won't have a mother who puts her hand on your knee while you're there for Sunday lunch, she won't get pissed every Friday night so you end up holding back her hair over the toilet bowl at three o'clock in the bloody morning, she won't say things like, 'Ooh, you know ever such long words, you! Aren't you clever?', she won't keep her videos in covers masquerading as books, and – oh yes – she won't shag one of your mates on the bathroom floor at your own party. She'll be . . . normal. A nice person. Nice is one of those words that people take the piss out of, isn't it? Nice is supposed to be uncool and unsexy, but it isn't to me. I reckon it's underrated. I've sampled a fair old selection of not nice girlfriends, including the one who dumped me via Christmas card – classy! – the one who said, 'Sorry, Neil, I'm just finding it, like, really, really hard to get past the whole receding hairline thing,' and, straight in at Number One, Saskia, she of the penchant for playing Hide the Sausage on my bathroom floor with Terry. And I'd only just finished doing the bloody bathroom, that's what really gets me – that floor had only been down a week.

My mate Carl reckons I'm too soft, says you get walked over if you're too nice. Maybe I could get lessons in how to be a right bastard? My mum says it's just a matter of finding the right woman and I'll know her when I've found her and it'll all be worth the wait. Yeah, yeah, I could get run over by a truck tomorrow, I'd like someone while I'm still just about young enough to enjoy it. Actually, my gran got remarried when she was seventy-one, but at least she'd had a good run with my grandad for forty years before he keeled over, so it was more a getting her second wind kind of thing. They say the odds get better as you get older, because more blokes get killed in wars and from riding fast motorbikes. So, as long as I don't suddenly get overtaken by a wild urge to join the Army and stick to using my Tube pass, I should be giving myself an advantage, right? Then, when I'm seventy or so and most of the men have dropped dead, I should get my pick of the Sunnyside Home for the Elderly and Confused. Great. That's a real comfort, something to look forward to.

It's not that I'm hideous. At least, I don't think I am. Aside from the gripe about the insufficient quantities of hair, I've never had anyone make a formal complaint about my appearance. I change my socks and pants every day, I don't wear Scandinavian jumpers or bobble hats, I trim my nostril hair. The trouble is, I see a woman I like and then I get embarrassed and I don't know how to talk to her. Over the years, I have developed two cunning strategies to get round this problem: 1) Chat up women at parties after I've had a few and have got a bit more confidence. Down side: my judgement goes AWOL along with my nervousness. Result? Saskia, whose main interest in life turned out to be vast quantities of lager and, oh yeah, Terry's penis. 2) Chat up women I don't really fancy so I'm not remotely nervous. Clever, huh? Down side: er . . . you probably worked that out a whole lot faster than I did. Result: Katie, who was, like, rahlly rahlly Sloaney and rahlly rahlly boring and the only way I could stand it is if we went to parties or to a film so we wouldn't have to attempt conversation, which was painful, especially as her two favourite subjects were horses and clothes. She owned a massive total of eleven books, of which eight – I know because I was so bored I checked them out in detail – were from her childhood, or, now I come to think of it, maybe even her mother's child-hood, and had titles like *Marjorie Rides to Victory*. The other three included a book of 'Love is . . .' cartoons, the ones with the creepy little naked children being all smoochy, *The Equestrian Handbook* and *You and Your Golden Retriever*. And, no, she didn't have one, but her family had owned one when she was little so she'd bought the book because she knew she absolutely must, must, must have one as soon as she had her proper house in the country.

It's not as if I'm asking for too much. I've given it a lot of thought and I've modified my expectations. All I'm looking for now is someone who is:

1) Not unfaithful.
2) Not stupid.
3) Not bonkers.

I mean, how hard can it be? Ah, sod it, I'm going to go and drown my sorrows in a coffee. A large caffè latte should do the trick. And maybe a brownie, while I'm there. Whoo-hoo, now I'm really living it up.

The woman in front of me is ordering a mochaccino. Nice bum. Oops, hello, she's turning round. Nice eyes, too. She catches me looking at her and smiles. I turn away, peer into the chiller cabinet, pretend to be eyeing up the sandwich fillings, giving it serious thought. I sneak another look. She's standing there, slowly shaking cinnamon on to her drink, chatting away to one of the waitresses. I stand up straight, nod in what I hope is a debonair and sexy way, and smile. She tucks a strand of hair back behind one ear, puts her coffee down for a moment while she rummages in her bag for something, smiles back.

Hurry up, you idiot, I tell myself. Do something, anything, trip her up if necessary, knock her coffee over. Oh, good idea, Neil, scald the woman – that'll get her attention. She obviously hasn't found what she was looking for because her hand comes out of her bag empty. She zips up the bag and picks up her coffee again. God, that smile! Maybe she's smiling at some bloke behind me. Quick check. OK, no, right, action stations. She's moving towards the door.

I turn towards her. 'Excuse me, could you tell me which way the Tube is from here, please?'

Devastating. Witty. Clever. Possibly even brilliant in an understated sort of way. Dear God, why am I so hopeless at this? Not much of an opening gambit, is it?

She looks up at me and grants me another one of those smiles. 'Sure, it's just – actually, I'm going that way myself, I can show you if you like . . .'

If I like? I try not to nod too enthusiastically like an

over-excited puppy, but settle for looking down into her eyes, which are crinkling at the corners as her whole face lights up.

Magic. Sheer magic.

RUSSELL CELYN JONES

Political Education

I BELONG TO a family in crisis from which I choose to emerge like Atlantic swells travelling into shore from a storm. From the headland I watch these grey and purple waves march leeward in graceful step, as though at the beginning of a journey rather than the end of one. A swell has order but comes from disorder. Its source is always chaos. They turn up at my shore silent and chaste, wearing bridal headsets of pale spindrift. What the eye can't see is their fantastic propensity for violence.

I've got to get into the sea, that much is certain. The hair stiffening on the back of my neck tells me so. I run down to the beach, where my board is stowed inside a bamboo copse, leave my clothes where they fall and peel on a wetsuit. My stepfather works for IBM and tries to programme me. My being here on a school day proves just how unsuccessful he has been. The sea is all my own.

On the shore perspective changes again, and nothing makes clear sense any more. The sea smells of raw meat and the air is bruised. My earlier excitement turns to moroseness. The waves look far bigger, noisier and less organised than they did from above. The ground trembles from the power of dumping shorebreak. I look back to where I was standing ten minutes ago on the headland, which is now a jumble of gunsmoked gorges and cloud-filled plateaux. It seems far away and unreachable as history.

I spin my board in the wind. Cold water seeps through the neoprene and immediately begins to warm to my own body temperature. I rub sand into the waxed deck and study my destination, an outcrop of rocks exposed by an ebbing tide where the waves are excavating over shallow limestone shelf for the first time since beginning their voyage from the epicentre of the storm, hundreds of miles away. White water backs off and the waves reform over sandbars nearer to the shore. There they split into two, sweeping the bay at adjacent angles, creating a temporary channel of calmer water, a parting between the waves. I push my board forward and climb on.

Two hundred yards out on the sandbar a great foaming wall leaps towards me. It looks light and porous, but I know the difference and it hits me like a solid wall. I am knocked backwards and cling on to the board in the turbulence. There is a whole line of these burly waves to negotiate and makes me think of salmon climbing up rapids. Of fighting with my step-father. I make twenty yards and lose fifteen with each encounter.

I am climbing up a clean face, pushing the nose of my board through its lip and skidding down the backside into new morning light that is pink and misty with vapour. The wave shivers and cracks as it gives into gravity behind my back. Clear of the sandbars I alter course for the reef and circle in behind the rocks where the line is purest.

17

If the waves appeared silent from the headland, they are not silent here and make the sound of canvas ripping. The exposed rock is covered with sharp mussel and whelk shells, like a crown of broken glass. A place so obviously to be avoided, its enchantment is irresistible. Beneath me shipwrecks lie one upon the other. Buried under the sand are sacks of rice, bales of tobacco, herds of cattle, petrol casks, pianos, Panama hats, African slaves. It is spooky out here all alone with the sea creatures and ghosts of shipwrecked sailors hissing from the fissures in the rock.

There is a conflict of tensions: the sea in a state of flux and the rock rooted to the ground. Negotiating between these two elements is what I aim to do. There is no sweeter victory in this whole world than in conquering the narcissistic and vindictive rock. So why do I spend thirty minutes turning in the gyre of cross-currents without tackling a single wave? I am scared. I am respectful. I am fourteen years old. But these are not the only reasons. My mind is not yet clear of the recent past. I need to shake out of my head certain things in order to survive the present conditions. That recent past is not something I want to put into words. Things that were said to my mother by my stepfather that I overheard.

But to hell with all that. An irregularity on the horizon gives me due notice of ructions soon to come. A set banks around the beach head. There are always three waves in a set, a prime number. Each one is larger than its predecessor. I let the first one go to be greeted with the second of the set, feathering at the lip, shivering on the brink of collapse. The third wave will be closed out. I have to go now.

18

I slip my weight, spin around and stroke towards the rock. I see crabs creeping out of fissures, clawing at the elusive sky. The water beneath me is sucked up by the wave. My arms tangle in kelp as the stern is lifted and I begin to accelerate. I get to my feet in one move, crouching to lower my centre of gravity. I have put myself in maximum danger, taking off in front of the rock, with the intention of riding out of that danger. I drop down into the trough, turn and split open the right shoulder – a sheet of glass, scored with kelp and streaked with foam. In the deep hollow I begin to react intuitively to what the wave is doing, to its schedule of collapsing power.

It seems to be building itself higher and higher, peaking at two times my height. Five feet of board flaps in front of me, pushing back hard against the balls of my feet. The board shakes, travelling beyond its maximum speed. The lip snaps, curls and puts a roof over my head. For a moment I vanish inside a tunnel with a curtain of foam lifted off the wall by the exhaust of the breaking section. The tunnel collapsing at one end is building at the other, and filled with imprisoned sunlight. My face is close to its face. I hear two distinct sounds in counterpoint: the wave disembowelling itself against the limestone floor and the sizzling of a million air bubbles like a hive of bees.

My ride lasts no more than thirty seconds.

The appearance in the sea of two men with winter suntans and blond deadlocks fills me with rage. The rage disorientates me. As I am paddling back out, the first wave of a trinity lifts me skywards and seconds later, drenches me in a twenty-foot veil of spray as it takes a fairground ride over the rock. Pieces of limestone fly off into the air. There are spectrums in my eyes. One of the men scratches for the second wave of the set and the other guy takes off on the third one in. Their entries are so far left to seem reckless. But what they do from the moment they are up I have never seen any man do. Certainly no one from this tiny country can surf like that. If my rides are escapes, theirs are conquests. They carve up the wave as though their boards are knives, transform forces of nature into subservient forces of nature, reduce ten-foot killers into slaves.

They have atmosphere, like two tango dancers. Maybe they are gods, infused with the spirits of drowned seamen.

The first one to get back to the lineout speaks to admonish me. 'You surfing all alone?

His accent I cannot place. It sounds like beaten tin. 'Where you from?'

'South Africa. My *poes* is from California.'

The American joins us and we fight the rip together, shuttling around to stay in position. The American looks old enough to be my father, if he'd been fooling around with girls at my age, that is. He has bad skin for a Californian, the hallmarks of teenage acne, and the baby-sized teeth of an omnivore. Not one out of the mould. The other surfer is heavy-set, his big thighs straining the neoprene. Body hair sprouts out of his collar. His eyes are small and remote.

As the lull in the surf continues, the Californian gives me a look of seasoned suspicion. 'Shouldn't you be in school or something?'

'Shouldn't you be in work, or something?'

They both laugh at me. The Californian says, 'Something for sure.'

In the wilderness of sea that has no history, the American tells me he is dodging the draft. I think I understand what he means by that, but when he adds, 'to avoid going to Vietnam,' I don't.

'What is Vietnam?' I ask.

'A bad idea.'

The other guy says he is also avoiding a call-up, to fight in Angola with the South African Defence Force. Now I am really lost. 'Angola . . . is that a bad idea too?'

'Very bad vibe,' the South African says.

'You're very good surfers,' I add.

'We were on the ASP circuit, until we cut loose in Biarritz on the French leg of the tour.'

'I want to surf professionally.'

'You could do it, kid. We saw you earlier. You've got the potential.'

'Why is Angola a bad vibe?' I ask the South African.

'Because it's a civil war and because the Defence Force, who shouldn't be in there at all, are helping Unita fight the communists.'

'So Angola's a place?'

'Yeah,' the American chips in, 'like Vietnam's a place.'

I have never heard of Vietnam or Angola but I have heard of Jeffries Bay where the South African comes from, and the names Windandsea, Huntington, Trestles that the Californian mentions. These places I've internalised from the pages of *Surfer Magazine*. I've lived vicariously in all the surf hot spots around the world, while never going more than twenty miles in my life. I've never left Wales. London remains a place on the map I looked at one time when I was considering running away from home.

A set comes in and I let them have their pick. I can't wait to tell Pixie, Shirt, Chalkie, Brush and the rest of my mates about these two gladiators. The things they've missed by going to school! I bet they haven't heard of Vietnam either.

Between rides they tell me how they eke out an existence on the run from their wars. They live in an old VW van bought for a song in Earls Court and drive around in it without insurance or road tax. The South African is particularly proud of forging the tax disc, by cutting out the expired month with a razor blade and putting a future number in its place. Every morning they steal breakfast from doorsteps – the yoghurts and the milk. They take the odd job for a couple of days when they need petrol or beer. The last time they saw a vegetable was in late March. I want to invite them home so my mother can cook them a meal fit for heroes, but I abort that idea fast.

'My father was in the army, but I don't see him any more. My stepfather is a drunk.'

'Alcoholism is like Vietnam, know what I mean? Guys go there and never return. Others come back haunted.'

In the morning light the waves make beautiful purple forms against a blood-red sky. Cormorants slide by, skimming the surface of the sea. The tide has gone past its lowest ebb and is creeping back over the reef. The wind has slackened and the sea has gained a certain moderacy. Although less hollow now, the waves are exhilarating in a different way, spectral and enigmatic.

When I take my next wave I am thinking too much about everything. A liquid roof encloses me and the best I can be is nonchalant. I reappear on to the shoulder, shift my back foot to the left gunwale and cut back into the turbine, the nerve centre. I am heading for the rock, about to lasso me in the kelp. A 180-degree turn brings me round again and a second roof forms over my head. As the wave is about to collapse down its entire length I cut out the back.

Normally the blueprint of that wave would already be filed away in my head. But I can remember nothing about it. It's a lost moment. As a rule I can recollect waves I've ridden two or more years ago. Each one is different, like intense characters encountered briefly in the street. Like the human face, no two are exactly alike.

We are three surfers riding waves out of trouble. And *away* from trouble. We have our woes, but get everything in perspective out here. The desired potion we work hard to acquire is adrenalin, never emotion. In the smoke and unreason of the surf we aim to become the sum of our nerve endings. The past is the wave we cut out from; the future the next one thundering in.

But in terms of escaping trouble, these two draft dodgers are clearly further up the food chain than me. Over the next two hours I learn a lot more than I would in a whole month at school. I listen to them say to one another things they already know, for my benefit. They talk about the crimes and barbarities that have been committed in the name of communism being no different from the crimes and barbarities committed throughout history in the name of the best intentions. Like the Dutch Reformed Church leaders of South Africa who built the Apartheid State. Or the American Christian Democrats who sacrifice thousands of men in Vietnam for a doctrine which is its opposite; a doctrine that promises freedom with compassion.

Upheavals in world politics have thrown up upon my beach these footwork geniuses, exotic wave sculptors. Surfers as good as them have to be right about Vietnam and Angola. 'When the world is a lunatic asylum,' the Californian says, 'the only thing to do is surf. Surfers harm no one. Why we should be on the run is a fucking mystery to me.'

'My stepfather thinks surfing is for losers.'

'He probably wants you to play football.'

'I can identify with that,' the South African says. 'But the sport chooses you, *poes*.'

'Don't you want to go home one day?' I ask them.

The South African shakes his head and exhales as though smoking a cigarette. 'When you drive a car out there you have to use certain tactics. For instance, you get into the car, first you know, you shut the door, lock your door, check the mirrors just to see there's nobody crawling on the ground right next to you. If you go to the shop, before you get out you do the same. In the shop, is there anyone in the shop that is a potential terrorist? Are the people walking around carrying weapons? Because you don't know what's going to happen next in that country.'

'What about California, the Pacific Ocean . . .' The words made me feel delirious just mouthing them.

'I'd like to go home someday, sure,' the American says. 'The surf rolls in all day long over the reefs because the tides are negligible. In summer you never see a single cloud blemish the sky. We sleep in wrecked Olds, all sorts of smashed palaces under Bill Durham signboards, just to get the early morning waves. Some of us live in caravans with no roofs. No rain, so no roof required. Sometimes we camp in the foothills of the Mesa Peak alongside the religion freaks and all live off fruit from the trees. Olives, lemons, oranges growing wild. Trouble bears down on you, man . . . you just hit the water.'

I recall my stepfather's red and tumefying face. 'I'd like to go to California. Maybe I can go with you when you leave.'

'If I ever go back, sure.'

My head is full of drums beating and it spoils me for more time surfing out here. My stepfather, what he said to my mother was, If it wasn't for the kid we'd be better off. And my mother crying I can still hear now. He complained I was disruptive and a big pain in the arse generally. I walk around the streets with no shoes on my feet like some hobo. He wants to trace my father and send me away. I don't even remember what my father looks like. He said all this worry was making it harder for him to stop drinking. Why is he worried? His business is with my mother not me. But he feels he has to point out things to me like, Who do we thank for this supper? and makes me say grace. I've never been to church in my life before this guy turned up and tells me I'm going to hell unless I pray for my hot dog that my mum got out of a can. Not even my father did that before he upped and left us.

25

I should not push my luck and go in now, but I want to try this insecure structure approaching. But it's an avalanche of trouble. I turn the board, fall across the deck, and feel so angry. My take-off is late. Tons of water follow me down the face where I turn too fast in response to desperate conditions. I pull round and the fin pops out. The board spins, returns me back up the face, to meet head-on the sheet of free-falling water. I lose it all in less than a second and drop over the falls, separated from my transport.

The following seconds are unbearable ones. The wave won't let me up. The turbulence of tons of collapsing water buffets me. There is nothing I can do except journey at its discretion and preserve oxygen as best I can. To escape the violence above I have to sink deeper into ever darkening folds of cold water. I hit the rock and feel myself glowing hot. I am bounced against the rock and the oxygen goes in an instant. There is kelp all around and I snatch at clumps of it. The wave makes one final attack and then churns inexorably on. The water drains off the rock and leaves me beached. In that great expanse of air I have trouble breathing. The next wave in the train is close enough for me to touch. I tighten my hold on the kelp and inhale.

The wave comes down with a long whistling howl. The kelp rips out of my hand and I ricochet off peaks in the rock. I feel a tremendous tearing of my limbs. What an act of self-love is parenting. My foot catches in the weed. The water drains off the rock once again and I gulp the air while fighting to release my foot from the kelp. Another wave approaches at twenty miles an hour, trembling in anticipation of its little

26

human snack. My board has gone. My wet-suit jacket has gone too, ripped off my back. I free my foot just in time and dive off the rock into deep water.

I am swimming in the sea without protection and can't make any headway. The only way in is to body surf, but I haven't the strength. With nothing left to give I allow myself to drift on the swell. Time owns me as the current sweeps me out to sea. My mind wanders as men's minds wander in the desert. I see someone standing up on the headland watching me. He could be my stepfather, and I feel hit by confused feelings. I'd like it to be my stepfather. I'd not like it if it is.

My head is lifted manually on to a fibreglass deck. It is the American, with the South African riding shot-gun. They are my bothers and they are in my corner. They know the score without having to ask. As we make our way to shore, two-up on the American's board, I hear a disembodied voice impart the advice: 'One day, kid, you'll be bigger than your stepfather.'

The sea is a wilderness that makes no judgements. It has an ego that never overwhelms with its love. However violent the waves, they will always deliver you safely on to shore.

MARINA WARNER

The Birthday Party

THE TWINS' birthday fell in November, so it was dark and dank the afternoon of their party even though it was starting at four-thirty. My father drove me there through gleaming ooze and black splashes of fen water, and we found the house after stopping to ask in the village shop: the woman behind the counter laughed when we said, The Old Mill, as if she knew something about the family. I didn't know the girls who were turning fifteen, but Daddy had met the parents and so it was arranged that I should be invited, even though I was a full two years younger.

There was a side path through to the riverbank where the house stood, and it was slithery with fallen leaves; but the front door was lit invitingly, with candles in little pots on the lintel, they danced in the sharp air almost keeping time with the sluicing and slapping of the millstream you could hear but not see, moving in the empty dark near by.

One of the twins opened the door. 'I'm being a boy tonight,' she said. 'Cos we haven't enough coming.' She was wearing an outsize black-tie outfit, with a top hat thrust back on her head so she looked like a ragamuffin from a play. 'I'm Olympia, by the way. Cleo is being a girl. Like you.'

Daddy bustled in to find the parents and lots of loud talk followed about the time I should be collected. I was pretending not to listen, and hopping around on the stone floor as I pulled off my gum boots to change into my ballet slippers; they were in fashion, especially with big tulle multi-layered petticoats that were also the latest thing. I'd begged and wheedled for one for my own birthday.

I could see other guests in a room beyond, clumped by the mantelpiece, for there was a fire in the grate and the cold was severe. They were stiff and quiet, waiting for the party to begin. I hovered, afraid to move towards them, feeling with the billows of my skirt around me that I was being blown off course on to uncharted reefs.

When the front door closed on the disappearing bulk of my father, Olympia held out a glass and asked me, 'Ginger beer, lemonade or Chablis?'

I had never been to a birthday party where wine was on offer, and the sight of Olympia in drag, pointing towards a bottle in that airy way, in front of her parents and all her friends, really made me tremble all over with excitement, I can tell you. And that was only the beginning.

Olympia and Cleo began the dancing, Olympia holding her sister formally, and now and then bending her back till she laughed and fell over. They had a little portable turntable, and lots of EPs and 45s with numbers like 'Great Balls of Fire' and 'Let's Twist Again' and tracks like Dave Brubeck's 'Take Five'. Olympia and Cleo had an older sister, called some- thing like Allegra, who joined in with some of her friends from university who were even more unspeakably sophisticated: I didn't mind at all that I was gawping like a tadpole whose jam jar has suddenly been moved from the shelf of Miss Travers' class to a tropical aquarium. They were the most extraordinary crowd I'd ever seen, and even though since that time, reading magazines and biographies and novels and seeing films and, even occasionally, direct contact, have inured me to glitterati glamour and upper-crust Bohemia, I can still feel the awe, the bliss, the wonder of Olympia and Cleo as they tangled their arms together in their sitting room and made us all a party to their family spell.

Sasha and Henri, as the twins called their parents – again making my eyes roll at this unspeakable progressiveness – did not show themselves until time came for food, when we were all called into the kitchen. By this time I knew I wasn't moving on plotlines I'd ever met before, so I was expecting the unexpected, and was even able to withhold a blink of surprise that we weren't faced with a heap of sausage rolls, sticks of pineapple chunks and cheddar, pâté and cheese biscuits and Twiglets. I didn't find out then what we were eating, as I didn't want to reveal the full depths of my bumpkin ignorance, and I suspect that the twins' friends didn't know either. Of course, I can recognise in retrospect that this was my first Indian takeaway, with poppadoms and chicken tikka: the Taj Mahal, the trailblazer, opened in Cambridge in the mid-fifties, and the Lucketts had established their custom early.

'It's turmeric that gives it that lovely earth colour,' Cleo was saying to me as I nibbled at a skewer. I nodded eagerly.

Henrietta put out the light and then Allegra brought

in the cake, which she had made: it was chocolate, and shaped like a palette, with the names of the twins in different coloured icing where blobs of paint would appear, and candles making the number 15. But soon after it was shared out, when we were all beginning to drift back to the other room to play some more music, Sasha appeared and followed us in; he was carrying a candle in a candlestick with a handle, and he told us to sit down on the floor and turn off all the lights in that room as well, as he was going to tell us a story.

Henrietta and Allegra and the twins handed round cushions, and Sasha held the candle under his chin so that the flame made strange hollows in his face and blotted out his eyes; his voice made it bob and so his features became lopsided and glowed reddish in the light. He had a long face, with swept-back grey hair ('too long, over the collar', I'd heard Daddy comment more than once). I was sitting just to his left, almost under him, so the candle even made his nostrils trans-lucent and rosy and cast the long beak of his nose against his other cheek. I was thrilled, slightly tipsy on my first glass of wine, and I held tight on to the hand of the boy who'd eaten birthday cake from the same plate as me, even though I thought he was scraggy and would have preferred to hold Olympia's in her boy's costume.

Sasha began:

'My elder brother, Gawain, though we all called him Gully – we're one of those affectionate, large groups of kin who develop secret languages and nick-names and private jokes – you know the sort of thing . . .'

I didn't, but I longed to.

'Gully was gifted. He had second sight. It runs on the male side, not the female, unlike what people expect. He knew, for example, the moment when one of our cousins died climbing a mountain in the Pyrenees before the war. The telegram only came two days later. Gully suffered from his gift. And from sleep-walking, nightmares, and precognition – in another time, he would have been a Daniel in Pharaoh's court, called to interpret the dreams of the great . . . but in the respectable shires of England, he had to keep quiet. Still, one day while walking, he wandered a little farther than usual, and he came across a lake he didn't remember was there, and on the shore of the lake, he met a fairy . . .

'You might scorn the idea, you sophisticated youth of today, with your mopeds and your coffee houses. This was a fairy child, specially light on her feet. Her skin was almost the colour of mother-of-pearl, and she had wispy, pale hair like spindrift, and her eyes were wild.'

Sasha lifted his eyes and demonstrated how the fairy's eyes rolled in her head.

'But she also looked like a human girl, in almost every way.' His glance came to rest on his daughter Olympia's face and he said, 'She was a little like you . . .' Then his eyes swept over to Cleo, who was of course Olympia's identical twin, and he repeated the phrase. He continued to scan our faces as we gazed up at him, and I was longing that he should say the same to me, even though I didn't look in the least like his amazing daughters, but he passed me by and he went on:

'Gully talked to her that day, and she told him to

come back at the same time the next evening, and she would be able then to tell him her secret. So it went on, he said, for a few days. He told me about it, and I wanted to go with him, because I was frightened for him, but also because I was envious, and I wanted to see the fairy and talk with her and . . . perhaps, like my brother, feel her pale skin and touch her burning cheek.'

This was excruciating; I was now clutching the boy's hand and our palms were soaking wet, horrible but somehow inextricable.

'The fairy was a captive under the hill, in the secret commonwealth of the elves and goblins, where an enchanter held her in his enchanted castle: she really was a human girl and she needed a knight, as all such enchanted maidens always do, to set her free. Gully said she was more beautiful than the day itself, that she was sweet to smell as newly baked bread, that she was soft to touch as a peach, and she had chosen him for the task.

'He had to gather together all kinds of things. Some of them I helped him with: an owl's droppings, a ball of orange string, a white rose with dew from the night of a full moon, the tarsi of a cock, the breastbone of a badger – Oh, I don't remember all the ingredients.

'Then he set out.'

Sasha stopped at this point, and told us to get up and stretch our legs and fill our glasses and help ourselves to some nuts and dates and other fruit next door in the kitchen.

He had us in the palm of his hand, as we obeyed him but came rushing back.

'Gully went, with the amulets she had carefully listed, into the fairy hill to fetch her back.'

Pause. We sat quietly, in the dark room, with only the candle and the light of the fire in the grate.

'He never returned.

'We looked high and low, we put out searches, we advertised for knowledge of Gawain Luckett, but there was never a trace.

'He had been taken by the fairies. And he wasn't the first.'

Sasha sighed, and dropped his big head into his cupped hands, and began again, muffled, mournful. I tingled with the horror and the wonder of it. I wanted to whisper to Olympia, Is it true? I looked across at her, at Cleo, and their heads were bowed, and they were smiling. I turned back, reassured, to listen to their father's story.

Sasha opened his hands, and announced, in a big voice now:

'But Gully did come back to see me. I knew he would. He was my brother, my companion, my double. It happened like this.

'It was late, very late, and I was staying up reading in my study in the house Henri and I had when we were first married, and Allegra had just been born. I kept irregular hours because of the baby's rhythm, and I was relishing a quiet moment all to myself, when Gully appeared.

'He was gaunt and haggard, and his hair had grown very long in the years he'd been gone, and he said that he had entered the enchanter's garden protected from his magic with the charms the fairy had told him, but when he moved towards her, holding the bundle in front of him to ward off danger, looking neither to right nor left, as she had told him, making towards her,

34

he felt his flesh turn to ice and a black mist came down in front of his eyes and his memory of who he was and how he should escape that awful place – all, fled!

'She had forgotten one of the essential ingredients – a hoopoe's tail, I think he said.'

At this Sasha got up with his eyes fixed straight ahead, as if sleepwalking, and imitated his brother, swinging his arms left and right, and stumbled a little in the room, till he spun around and bent down and pulled me up into his grasp, and I felt the strength and girth of his body as he brought me closer to him, and walking backwards, returned to his seat with his arms encircling me.

'He held her fast, like I am holding you, and then he tried to move, but found he could not. Like the girl with her wild eyes, he too was now captive in fairyland.

'He told me that he would be able to return only one more time out of the fairy hill, for the christening of Allegra – he had prevailed on the enchanter to make a pact that if he could find someone to be his champion in this world, he would release him.

' "Sasha," he said, "There is only one way you can be my champion and free me from that evil magician and his fairy child . . ." '

At this Sasha held me even more tightly so that I remember thinking he would leave a print of his big hands on my dress and I would never wash it so that I would always know that this thing that was happening, whatever it was, had truly happened.

'Gully went on, his words spilling out feverishly from his wan, white face: "You must take a knife with you to the church, Sasha," he said. "A kitchen knife you'd use for carving. Sharpen it well on the whetstone beforehand and hide it about yourself. Then, when I appear and call out to you, you must raise the knife and strike at my heart. It is only if someone who loves me pierces my stolen heart that I'll be free from the fairy's fatal love, and you are the only one who can.

' "Then I'll be able to come back to the land of the living, out of the fairy hill." '

'When the day of Allegra's christening came, I did take a knife from the kitchen drawer, even though I thought that I too was suffering from hallucinations in the night. But sure enough, as the priest began saying those words about renouncing the devil, Gully appeared, clearer than any of you in this darkness, and he held out his arms to me and opened his mouth silently as if pleading with me.

'But I was foolish then, and slow and weak, as all men are, and I stood amazed. I failed to pull the knife from my pocket where it lay wrapped in a handkerchief, and I missed the moment, and had to watch as Gully's wraith faded into the stones of that country church with a terrible cry.'

At this, Sasha bent over the candle flame and blew it out.

'Aaaoww!' he howled into the dark, 'Aaaoooooow!'

Then, beneath the shrieks and squeals of his daughters and their friends that rose in the darkened room, he pulled me closer to him and kissed me on my forehead and with his winy breath, murmured in my ear, 'He was with La Belle Dame sans Merci, my dear. D'ye think he wanted to be set free?'

SUSAN CROSLAND

The Flamingo

Topsy was the only child of Arthur Fairweather III, who was third-generation rich. The first Arthur made his money out of a Pittsburgh steel foundry, and his fortune grew and grew like Topsy, thus accounting for his great-granddaughter's name. When she wed Francis Randolph, he brought with him money of his own and one of the oldest names in Virginia. It was what Virginians call a 'good marriage'.

They lived in the country just outside Alexandria and made a striking couple when they rode to hounds, she side-saddle on her bay, he astride a gelding from the same dam, his huntsman's horn fastened by a chain around his neck. It was obvious that Topsy was besotted with her black-haired, blue-eyed husband, amused by his brusque pomposity rather than annoyed.

Three daughters were born within five years, and after a four-year lull, Topsy was pregnant again. The baby boy who emerged was a small version of his father, straight black hair and eyes the same china blue. Christened Charleston, for a while he was the pet of his sisters, and Minnie, the youngest girl, gave him the name by which he was known. As soon as Charlie could talk it was evident that he had his father's mix of charm and self-importance. Father and son were indulged by Topsy.

The children were raised largely by a nanny. When home for the evening, Francis and Topsy dined alone, she seated on his right so she could be near him. Sometimes she reached out and ran a finger over the back of his hand, pushing up the little black hairs. Her passion for him was unabated. Nonetheless they made some time each day for their offspring. This took place soon after Francis got home from the Randolph family bank.

In order of their age, the children went into the library one by one to have fifteen minutes each with their parents. Few things were allowed to interfere with 'family hour'. At least once a week the children agreed in advance that Horatia, the eldest, should ask to see the elephant-size folio of Audubon's *Birds of America*. These hand-coloured engravings, each bird life-size, shared an enclosure with other immensely valuable books, the metal grille kept under lock and key. Francis would lug this huge folio to a table where the pages could be opened wide. What Minnie found magical was that the largest birds, whatever their shape, somehow fitted within the borders of the page.

Horatia's favourite was the cruel-beaked owl. Laura preferred the Carolina turtle dove feeding its young. Minnie loved the flamingo best, its neck bent like a croquet hoop so it would fit; her father said that was the way flamingos stood in real life. Ritually she said to him: 'I still think it's magic that he fits perfectly. When I grow up, may I have the flamingo to hang above my fireplace?' Charlie chose the turkey cock, its tail erect.

Francis and Topsy continued their habit of keeping their mounts close together when riding to hounds. This day they were almost side by side as they galloped at a stone wall fronted by a brook. Topsy's bay sailed over. Francis's mount fell heavily. His wife pulled up and turned back to where the gelding staggered to its feet. Even before she leapt from her saddle, she saw how her beloved lay. He was forty-two.

For a long long time she remained unbalanced by grief. When eventually she resumed family hour in the library, Minnie noticed a sweet rich fragrance was added to the room's musty scent of parchment and leather.

'What's that nice smell coming from Mummy?' she asked Horatia later.

'Bourbon,' Horatia replied shortly.

Twenty years later, by which time her siblings had married and produced children of their own, Horatia's severe nature had hardened into the certitude of many single women. She continued to live in the big family house with her mother. Two of the servants slept in – the cook and her husband who doubled as butler and chauffeur. While Topsy still rode daily, for much of the afternoon she rested in her bedroom. When she joined Horatia at the dinner table, the aroma of bourbon soon scented the room.

On the whole, Topsy was even-tempered, if a little vague. She remained witty. When Laura or Minnie included her in their dinner parties, she was an amusing guest. She preferred going to Minnie's house, because her youngest daughter showed no unease at her mother's fondness for bourbon. Laura, however, fussed about it. In her home, the old-fashioned cocktail handed to her mother was paler than were the others, and though of course Topsy knew water had been added, she did not remark upon it. Before everyone else was even halfway through their drinks, Topsy had finished hers and put her glass back on the table. In a minute or two she picked it up again, looked into it hopefully, gave it a little shake so the ice rattled, then put it to her lips in case a drop remained.

'Would you like a freshener, Mother?' asked Laura's husband.

'Why, that would be very nice, dear,' replied Topsy, and her son-in-law took away her glass, returning it with an inch of still paler bourbon.

At table, Topsy's wine glass was never filled as much as the others, and Laura watched closely when a servant came round with the decanter. If Topsy became over-animated, Laura and her husband exchanged a look. One evening on the way back to their drawing room for coffee, Topsy caught her heel on the door sill; only the quick help of a guest kept her from falling.

'Are you all right, Mummy?' Laura asked in an anxious voice, and when Topsy assured her she was, Laura pressed her lips.

Charlie avoided the whole situation by seeing his mother on his own, which suited Topsy admirably as she'd never much cared for Charlie's wife. Now that he was United States Senator for Virginia, he was disapproving of his mother's drinking habits.

'You talk as if she falls down drunk,' Minnie said reproachfully to her brother. 'Mummy never loses her dignity. And she's always amusing. My friends love it when I ask her to dinner with them.'

'Your idea of dignity is not mine, Minnie,' Charlie replied in his self-important baritone.

He was the one who proposed that all the adults in the immediate family gather for a conference with Topsy. 'It's for her own good,' Charlie stated.

Horatia agreed readily. 'As long as Mummy lives at home, not a day goes by when I don't worry about her.'

Laura was uncertain about this scheme but said she would go along with it if Charlie really thought it best. 'Mummy still thinks of you as her "golden boy",' she added, the familiar phrase rankling as she said it.

Only Minnie was adamantly against the whole thing. 'What right have you, Charlie, to make Mummy give up one of the few things that have comforted her since Daddy died? I'll have no part of it.'

'You're just being a sentimentalist!' shouted Charlie, suddenly furious.

'What you're doing, Minnie,' said Horatia in her I-know-about-these-things voice, 'is taking the easy way out. You're leaving the rest of us to take the difficult decision, even though you'll benefit from it too.'

'How will I benefit from your bossy decision to push Mummy around?'

'Let me handle this, Horatia,' said Charlie. 'Look, Minnie, I'll get my secretary to find a couple of places that would be suitable. Then I'll discuss it with Horatia and Laura, and they can check them out. You needn't lift a finger. But once we've settled on a clinic' – his voice hardened ominously – 'you damn well better not chicken out.'

'But she's not doing anyone any harm by living as she likes in her own home, for God's sake,' Minnie answered.

'Each day and night she is risking her health,' Horatia intoned solemnly. 'If she falls and breaks a hip, her brain could be permanently affected by the shock. As it is, all that whisky can't be doing her brain any good.'

'I was there last week when the lawyer came to see her about some changes in her will,' retorted Minnie. 'He said she had a perfectly sound grasp of her financial affairs. She's scarcely touched her capital.'

'*Our* capital one day,' said Charlie. 'Do you know what changes she made?'

'She wanted to make sure that each of the servants received a bequest.'

'Not too big a one, I trust,' Charlie muttered with a chuckle.

'Oh Charlie, you mustn't be so greedy,' Laura chided him. 'There's more than enough money coming our way in time.'

'I think everyone should wait on telling her about the clinic,' said Minnie. 'She'll hate the idea, and I don't want to see her bullied into it.'

Horatia looked her sternest. 'It's not bullying, Minnie. It's persuading.'

'There's to be no backsliding on our decision,' Charlie declared fiercely. 'We've all got to stand together – and be seen to stand together – on this. Daddy would want it that way, I have no doubt. Once the plan is settled, I shall make a point of getting away early from Capitol Hill.

Damned inconvenient, but it must be done for our mother's sake. The rest of you can have no excuse not to attend. Spouses must be present as well.'

Not many weeks afterwards, Topsy returned to her room as usual after lunch. Later in the afternoon, Horatia knocked at the bedroom door.

'Mummy, come down and join us in the library. You look fine in your dressing gown. We're all there except Charlie. His secretary just phoned to say he's had to go off unexpectedly with five other senators on a fact-finding trip to Mexico. Otherwise he would have been here with us. And that goose of a wife of his won't do anything without him. Your children love you, Mummy, and we all need to talk with you about something serious.'

When Topsy entered the library, Laura and Minnie as well as their husbands rose as if a coffin had been carried in. Laura's eldest daughter was there too, looking uncomfortable. Laura came forward with her eyes slightly averted and hugged her mother.

'You know we're only thinking of you, Mummy,' she said.

Minnie stayed where she was, her face pale and drawn. Her husband stepped forward to put a hand on Topsy's arm.

'Hi, Mother,' he said heartily.

Topsy saw the stranger amongst them, his dank mouse-coloured hair faultlessly parted, dark suit soberly cut, shirt whiter than white. She thought of an undertaker.

'Topsy.' He addressed her in a strong melodious voice, taking her hand in his and pressing it reassuringly. 'My name is Stanley Hunter. Horatia invited me to join the family today. Why don't you come and sit down?' he said, as if he were the host.

Instead of settling back comfortably into her usual armchair, Topsy sat very straight upon its seat. The library was so spacious that eight people made little impact on it, yet she felt she was pressed in by a crowd.

'Now who's going to speak first?' said the stranger called Hunter.

Horatia began. 'Mummy, we want you to be happy. And no one who regularly drinks too much can possibly be happy.'

'We want you to be safe,' said Laura. 'You almost fell at my house not long ago. You would have fractured your hip. Everyone knows how dangerous that is for a lady of your years. We want to protect you from that danger.'

Minnie looked utterly miserable.

'You are the loveliest mother anyone could have,' she said in a tearful voice. 'It's just when you have too much bourbon that you're not always your best. And that's when some of us grow a little anxious,' she added, choosing her words carefully so as not to be disloyal to her siblings.

'I take it I embarrass you, Minnie,' Topsy replied.

'Oh Mummy, don't say that,' cried Minnie, tears starting from her eyes.

Even the young granddaughter had her say, speaking like an actress who had over-rehearsed her lines. She too painted a benign picture of her grandmother – 'when you are yourself, not that different person you sometimes become' – though Topsy rarely when drunk was other than benign.

Horatia put a hand on her mother's cheek and kissed the top of her head. 'It's entirely up to you, Mummy. Mr Hunter has his car out front. If you like, he could take you to the clinic now.'

A light flickered in Topsy's brown eyes. Then they darkened until they were nearly black. She seemed to sit even more erect on her chair.

'I thank you for your observations,' she said in a constricted voice. But it cleared as she went on: 'I have looked after my affairs since your father died. I intend to continue to do so.' She rose to her feet. 'You will all be going now, I expect.' She left the room.

In the morning she phoned the lawyer, and later that day he rang the doorbell. Horatia went to her mother's bedroom to tell her who had arrived unexpectedly.

'He came at my bidding,' said Topsy. 'Please have him come upstairs. I shall receive him here. Alone.'

Less than a week later, when starting down to dinner, Topsy caught her heel at the top of the stairs. She pitched head first to the bottom. At the noise, Horatia and the servants came running into the hall to find her lying with her neck at a strange angle.

After the funeral, the family gathered once more in the library. This time Charlie and his wife were present. As some years ago Topsy had shown her children her original will, they knew she intended dividing her estate equally between them, along with the contents of the house. With a typical Topsy touch, the will had specified that the elephant folio of Audubon's *Birds of America* could be broken up as her children wished, 'so long as Horatia Randolph receives the owl, and Laura Randolph Easton receives the Carolina turtle dove, and Minnie Randolph Bartlett receives the flamingo "to hang over her fireplace", and Senator Charleston Randolph receives the turkey cock'.

Clearing his throat, his face impassive, the lawyer read out the final version of the will. Inserted after its date were words he said were expressly stipulated by Topsy: 'the day following Mr Hunter's unheralded visit'. Apart from bequests to the staff, it cancelled the previous will. Instead it directed that the entire estate should be left to Senator Charleston Randolph, 'the only one of my four children who declined to take part in their mother being carted away like a sack of potatoes by Mr Hunter'. The contents of the house were also to go to Senator Charleston Randolph 'with the exception of Audubon's *Birds of America*'.

Minnie put her hand to her throat.

'This elephant folio is bequeathed,' the lawyer continued, 'in its entirety, pristine and intact, to the Public Library of Pittsburgh.'

The silence that followed was broken at last by the sound of Minnie sobbing.

HOWARD JACOBSON

My Father the Wizard

Y OU CAN read and talk about magic all you like, some of us have had to live it. My father was a wizard. Sometimes he called himself a magician, sometimes an illusionist, and sometimes, when feeling modest, a children's entertainer – Uncle Max. But a wizard was what he was. Or at least – if there's a hierarchy of these things – a wizard was what he became. I observed this wizardry first hand. He almost defied death with it. And even that's not entirely fair to him. In fact he did defy death with his wizardry, he just didn't defy it for long enough. But you have to start somewhere.

What made my father popular, both as a man and as an illusionist, was that he accepted his limitations cheerfully. The man part was easy. In imperfect times there are advantages in letting your imperfections show. People like you to have weaknesses. For an illusionist, though, imperfection is more problematic. An illusion either works or it doesn't. It's true that you can pretend to fail while you're actually succeeding, as Tommy Cooper did, but that's an illusion within an illusion, masking the fact that everything's actually working out as planned. Whereas many of my father's illusions failed full stop.

Take his levitation trick, in which a mysterious entity – in reality a blow-up doll wearing old clothes belonging to my mother – was meant to appear from what looked like an empty bed, and then rise two feet in the air with no visible means of support, as my father proved, or intended to prove, by passing a steel hoop over and under the body. No matter what he did, my father was never able to get this eerie resemblance to my mother to levitate more than an inch, and even when it levitated that far it did so for no longer than a hundredth of a second, which is too quick for the human eye to discern. Part of the problem – and I hope this isn't to explain away too much of my father's mystery – was getting sufficient air fast enough into the doll. What my father had been using for this was one of those low-tech creaking foot-pumps with which balloon salesmen blow up their stock. At last he realised that only an industrial pump, something that inflates airships or puts air into the wheels of a pantechnicon – adapted for the stage, of course – would do the trick. Fill the doll with a great inflatus of gas and floating like a dirigible would be its only option. Except that it wasn't. The other option was for it to burst. Which it did on its very first public outing.

'And now,' announced my father, spreading his cloak, fluttering his fingers over the empty bed, throwing the switch to the pump, and mixing up his allusions, 'the great Svengali will create life out of chaos, not Frankenstein but Frankenstein's wife! – abracadabra, hocus pocus, who's a liar . . .'

Whereupon, with the noise of a river bursting its banks, the hitherto invisible doll filled with a mixture of nitrogen and heaven knows what else, leapt beyond my father's grasp, soared into the roof of the auditorium and then exploded, scattering far and wide my mother's old clothes – shoes, stockings, dress, handbag – on to an audience hysterical with delight.

They liked him, you see. They liked him more for getting it wrong than they would ever have liked him had he got it right. I think it must have been the size of his ambition they admired. And of course the gap between that ambition and his performance. Aim big, come unstuck big.

It also helped that he had an easy manner and saw the joke of his own incompetence. Failure is a shame and a humiliation to some of us: our effects misfire and we have no recourse but to flee human society for ever as a consequence. Not my father. He laughed, shrugged his shoulders, and tried to do it better the next time.

There was one trick in particular with which he battled unsuccessfully all his life. Don't ask me exactly what was meant to happen because I don't understand tricks and, what is more, had never seen this one work. But essentially, as far I could fathom it, the idea was to borrow a ring from a member of the audience, wrap it up in a handkerchief, return it to its owner who would then put it in his or her pocket, only to discover subsequently that it wasn't there after all, that the handkerchief was empty, whereupon, but only after much deliberately confusing business which included introducing a glass and a sheet of blotting paper, my father would, as it were, recover the ring from the nowhere land of magician's space, have it come hurtling invisibly towards him in a series of loops which he would follow comically with his head until it landed, with a chinking of gold and no disturbance of the blotting paper, into the glass. That, I think, was the intention, anyway. Usually the ring got lost, wiping a smile that was already sickly from the owner's face, until it turned up later in the evening either in my father's sleeve or in one of his trouser turnups. A reasonable trick in itself, I always thought, but not what my father was after.

I remember this attempted illusion from my childhood. Whether my father abandoned it in later years or made a decision not to go on trying while I was around I don't know. But the last time I saw him do it – the last time I saw him do any trick – I felt that the years had unpeeled, that I was a child again, and, what is more, that so was he.

He was desperately ill. I had spent the previous night at the hospital with him, holding his hand, trying to stay awake, afraid that if I nodded off his fingers would instantly turn cold in mine. Any time now, the doctors said. Maybe that morning, maybe that afternoon. My father guessed the same.

'What, am I still here?' he woke at six and asked. Not relief, not disappointment, just surprise at his own persistence.

But since he'd made it through the night, it was important to him to appear smart for the morning's visitors. A nurse he liked bathed him in his bed, trimmed his beard, combed his hair.

'You look a handsome devil today, Max,' she told him, and though he knew he was wasted he chose to believe her.

Why not? He was still here, which he was not supposed to be, so why shouldn't he still be his old handsome self? There were bigger miracles. He had an eye for women, my father. That could partly explain his desire to be a magician: he wanted – no, he needed – to amaze women. He wanted to see them hold their breath, to wonder, to be a little afraid, and then to smile when it was all over. He wanted – no, he needed – to take them on that great adventure from apprehension to relief. And afterwards, of course, to receive their applause.

Who doesn't? And in the case of the nurse who was bathing and complimenting him, every man would have wished himself a magician. How she combined her aura of competence and authority with the atmosphere of conviviality not to say complaisance she gave off, I have no idea. But she bewitched the whole ward, animating even the despairing old men who day and night trudged back and forth between their beds and the toilets, clutching those egg-boxes into which, like a magician yourself, you try to make water. She was lovely to look at, a quick, lithe presence, with golden skin, intelligent brown eyes, and the gift of laughter. My father prized laughter in women above everything else. So how could he not, I now see – given that he was on stolen time, given that he had nothing to lose for everything was as good as lost – how could he not want to hear that gasp of laughter once more?

He whispered something in her ear as she was plumping his pillows.

She threw her head back.

'Max!' she said. It was almost a reproach. 'Max, are you sure you've got the strength?'

Yes, he was sure.

So she did as he had asked and went looking in his

bedside table, not for the pills or the pyjamas or the letters or the photographs or the bibles which other dying men keep by them. But for his props. His magic. In this instance a glass, a handkerchief and a sheet of blotting paper.

No, Dad, I thought. Not the ring trick. Not here. Not today. Not ever.

But the ring trick it was. Perhaps he wanted to see up close if his nurse was wearing any rings. Perhaps he wanted to find out, the old fool, if she was married. Perhaps he wanted to slide the ring off her finger himself. He had the ring off her fast enough, anyway, and then into a handkerchief which went into her pocket. Stethoscope, thermometer, morphine, ring in magic handkerchief, everything you need for raising or relieving the dead. And he had her attention, half sitting on the edge of his bed, her head tilted slightly as though ready for any shock, her lips pursed in amusement and appreciation. Ah, those, those. Amusement and appreciation. Magic in themselves. Magic enough to send the blood running through my father's emaciated fingers at any rate, and to create in him a quality of dexterity I had never seen when he was well, when his fingers were each the thickness of a banana. Deftness.

Amazing but true: on the morning he was not meant to be alive, my father discovered deftness.

Everything he now did, he did exquisitely. Normally what my father palmed, the short-sighted child on the back row could see sticking out of his fist. Today he conjured the invisible spirits of the air. Normally when my father employed diversionary tactics, they were so obvious you blushed for him. 'You've put it down your shirt!' the kids would shout from another room. Today he was as subtle as a sneak-thief. To her horror, when she checked the handkerchief in her pocket, the nurse discovered it was empty. Engrossed, she followed the movement of my father's head as he charted the ring's loops through the stratosphere. Amazed, she heard it tear through the blotting paper, though the blotting paper remained intact – figure that! – and then settle with a chink at the bottom of the glass. And with astonishment, when it was returned to her, did she confirm it was hers.

Applause for my father from those fellow-inmates who had found the strength to gather round his bed. From the nurse a hug, a kiss, and best of all her laughter.

'Max, how did you do that?'

'Aha!' my father said, all smiles himself now. 'Aha!'

Which presumably meant he didn't know how he'd done it either.

The following day he was discharged from hospital. Not cured. Magic can perform wonders but not miracles. But well enough to live, hear voices, laugh and talk another month, and well enough – if I may put it like this – to die in his own bed.

I wasn't with him when he did die. I was in another country. But I was satisfied that I had been with him when he all but died the first time, when he died a layman's death, and had been present at his resurrection. Because I am a sentimentalist I am also grateful that the last piece of wizardry he ever performed, he performed perfectly. And that I saw it.

MAVIS CHEEK

Sheep's Eyes

I F SALLY PARKER'S next-door neighbours were surprised that she accepted their invitation, their surprise was as nothing to her own. One minute she was standing in the back garden thinking sun-lounger, the next she was nodding. Worse, she was also nodding to Peter Beales' solemn undertaking to supply her with an adequate anorak should it be necessary. 'Can't trust June,' he said. For a moment she thought he had broken out and was telling her something wicked and interesting about a floosie – but no – it was only the usual British thing about weather. 'Just a little picnic for some pals,' said Jennifer, 'because Granny's having the children.'

Pals, thought Sally, was pushing it. Neighbours, yes. For while Sally had flown the world the Beales had produced two noisy children and never the twain were likely to meet. They were the sort of couple who put a pond and trickling hosepipe in their back garden and ever after referred to it as a water feature.

The friendliest gesture Sally ever made towards them was to stuff earplugs in on Sunday mornings when she finally took the ground job, and not complain about the bloodcurdling screams that were, apparently, family fun. Which made her think that passing on marriage and motherhood, despite everyone else telling her what she was missing, was no bad thing. Besides, she was still trying to settle down to life on the ground. Life *single* on the ground. And truth was that she enjoyed the peace of it all. But certain people kept issuing her with warnings . . .

Certain people like Val. Sally's old boss and a couple of years her senior. 'Since I stopped flying I haven't smiled into a man's eyes – except my dad's and he's senile – for three years,' she said. 'You think the high life is going to last and then – well – I tell you, Sal my girl, *never* turn anything down . . .'

Sally smiled and nodded and said that she wouldn't. But she was unconvinced. For Sally, who had worked for airlines since she left school, dating men went with the job – from London to Karachi, New York to Moscow – never a shortage. In the last year it all began to wear a bit thin: after seventeen years chasing around exotic Hotspots and Nitespots Sally found that her home, and her small garden, and the neat row of houses quietly placed by the river, were seductions enough. Besides, if you were used to the flashing gold teeth of a handsome silk-seller from Karachi – or the wicked smile of a jazz man in New Orleans, Peter Beales' anorak held few charms.

Maybe, she argued, she needed a little time to adjust.

Val just rolled her eyes. 'While you're getting adjusted, dear,' she said, 'others will pounce.'

It was a touch too chilling. A touch too close to the ancestral jungle of the predator. Sally imagined all these women holed up in trees, skulking at the mouths of caves and hiding in undergrowth with their talons sharpened and their teeth bared, ready to fight to the last for the one potent male. Fortunately the image of Peter Beale as a husband went some way to dealing with such fantastical imagining.

She did try. But she was still unused to the unattached male opening conversations with the wetness of the weather instead of the delightful silliness of how beautiful her eyes were (the Karachi silk-seller) or that he could read her soul (the jazz man). Romance, she felt, was wanting.

'You'll be lucky,' said Val. 'Just make do.'

Which was unedifyingly like her mother's view of the world. But at least she was trying. Peter Beales' anorak or not, she would go.

The day dawned clear-skied. Nevertheless she dutifully put her wellingtons into the Beales' hatchback and they set off to meet the rest of the party somewhere 'in the wilds of Oxfordshire', as Jennifer Beales put it. It all looked remarkably tame to Sally. She had, after all, driven a jeep into the Gobi Desert. But she kept quiet about that.

'This is Sally,' said Jennifer to everyone, 'our next-door neighbour. She's only just come back to England for good.' The subtext was that they must All Be Very Kind To Her . . .

She did not disgrace herself during the lengthy stomping over hill and dale as the colourful, slightly absurd (and she included herself in this) party made their way along the Ridgeway. She managed to look deeply interested in one father's remarkable child, someone's husband's detailed plans for early retirement, and she even counselled one bright-faced mother

56

puffing up a hill beside her about girls and languages and a career in the air.

'Obviously it's not all being a glorified waitress,' she said firmly. 'It's more like being everyone's multi-lingual mother and a few other things besides.' She did not say what these might be. The puffing mother looked anxious enough already.

There was, of course, a single male of the party. And much like children who have been brought along by their parents to be introduced because 'they'll get on so well together' both she and the single male avoided each other like the plague. But at the highest point of Hickpen Hill Jennifer announced that it was lunch-time. Sally and the single man, called Bill, were given a flask of coffee to share and a Tupperware box of assorted crustless triangles. What the Beales' children took to school every day, Sally guessed. She and Bill smiled awkwardly. Jennifer said, 'Bill's an actor.' And with the somewhat desperate suggestion that they admire the view, which was mostly sheep, she left them to it.

'I always do what my sister-in-law tells me,' he said, turning to look over the fence and holding out his hand to a curious sheep. The sheep came closer.

She assumed he was being ironic and laughed. 'I'll bet!' she said roguishly.

He looked back over his shoulder, puzzled and frowning.

Oh, she thought, he *means* it – he really means it.

'Nice –' She tried to think what could possibly be nice. 'Um – nice to have someone so – capable – to tell you what to do.'

'Yes,' he said.

57

He returned his gaze to the dim-looking ram and threw a bit of sandwich. It bounced off its nose. To no effect. 'She's certainly knocked my brother into shape.'

'Yes,' said Sally, feeling stupid in the face of such admiration.

He turned back again and smiled. 'She's trying it on me now.'

Sally shut her mouth. Personally she couldn't think of anything worse.

'Making a good job of it, too,' he said.

'Lovely,' she replied.

She studied him as he tried to entice the sheep with a bit of sandwich. He was short and squat and kind-faced – but not at all attractive. Well, not in a flashing-gold-teeth sense. Also he was wearing a beige anorak. Actually, she thought, it's worse than that – it's a car coat. Still – an actor had possibilities. He would be perfectly acceptable if he was wearing something else. A shirt and jeans or a sweater and cords – or anything really. She heard Val's voice . . . 'Never turn down an opportunity.' Plough on, girl, she thought. She leaned against the fence and held out a piece of sandwich. Another daft-looking sheep approached. Followed by all the others, knocking into each other and looking – well – cretinous.

'Nice things, sheep,' said Bill. 'Don't you think? Attractive animals.'

Could he be serious? He was. Oh well, she decided, it shows that he has a nice nature. She looked at the bobbing heads, a couple of dozen with one thought between them. But she put the brightest of smiles on her face. Now or never.

'Oh yes,' she said. 'My favourites.'

One of them made a baa-ing noise at her as if it knew. She stared back at it and just about managed to stop herself, with the aid of a little cheese-filled, crustless triangle shoved strategically into her treacherous mouth, from adding, 'Rosemary, garlic and mint sauce, yum yum.'

Later, at home, stretching her aching limbs in the warm bathwater and sipping a glass of sherry, she decided that she had acquitted herself very well. (Perhaps there was something in this star-sign stuff. She was, after all, a two-sided Gemini). Bill and she had managed the rest of the afternoon's walking very amicably, with conversations ranging from teaching drama (which is what, it transpired, he did) to his moment of truth after being in *Crossroads* and thinking he had made it, and being dropped six months later when his character was made to run off with the owner's amnesiac aunt.

'My job was a bit like acting,' she said.

'Really?' he replied.

'Mmm. I had to get on that plane and wow them no matter what. I rather liked it, actually.'

'I'm not that keen on flying,' he said.

'Well, I'm not now,' she said brightly. Her face was beginning to ache with the effort.

Val came early to the party. 'Before the hordes arrive,' she said, and whipped out a chilled bottle of champagne.

'Hardly hordes,' laughed Sally. 'Only the neighbours and that walking crowd – and you.'

She opened the bottle and they sat there in the garden in the waning sunlight enjoying that special moment before a party really begins.

'I just announced it up there on the top of a hill. God knows why. Bravado maybe. I was surrounded by a load of sheep and something made me want to assert my human qualities. Partying used to be one of them . . .' She sighed.

'Do you miss flying?'

'Oh don't *you* start,' said Sally.

Val stared at her. 'Sorry,' she said. 'It reminds me of having face-ache, that's all.' Val stared at her even harder. Best change the subject. Steam might appear at any moment from those ears. Sally was extremely wound up. 'So then – who else is coming?'

Sally drained her glass. Amazing the courage a glass of bubbles can give you on an almost empty stomach, she thought, and boy, if she was going to carry this thing through, did she need it.

Out loud she said, as casually as possible, 'Oh – and Bill's coming.' She giggled. 'My beau in beige.'

'Lucky you,' said Val. 'Give me half a chance. I wouldn't care if he wore sky-blue pink with spots on. Or taupe.' She too sighed into her glass.

Sally refilled it. 'Cheer up,' she said brightly. Taupe is beige.' After two glasses of good champagne she felt considerably better. Or was it resigned?

Jennifer, Peter and Bill arrived first.

'Don't mind if we're early, do you?' said Jennifer in the voice of one who is utterly confident. She leaned towards Sally and hissed much too loudly, 'But Bill couldn't wait any longer.'

He did not look like a man who could be impatient for anything – well, not in that shade of turtle-neck anyway. Stop it, she counselled, stop it . . .

'Bill,' she said, smiling with every tooth in her head,

and she held out her hand. He looked relieved as he shook it.

'Tush,' she heard Jennifer say behind her. 'Peter – the present.'

Peter Beale, in a fetching royal-blue handknit, stepped forward and handed Sally a bottle of sparkling white wine. With a pink bow on top. He – or someone – obviously thought they should make up for Bill's complete lack of colour. Actors, she decided kindly, needed to be self-effacing for their profession. Sally put the bottle down next to the half-full bottle of Veuve Cliquot. The Widow. The Black Widow. The champagne appeared (or was Sally imagining it) to turn up its dainty, grieving nose.

'Thank you so much,' she said.

'Bill?' said Jennifer, as if she was marshalling troops.

Bill stepped so smartly forward that Sally nearly saluted. Then with his two hands he proferred a heavy and oddly disjointed parcel. He presented it to Sally as if he were laying a wreath. It was wrapped in very jolly paper with smiling clowns all over it and had yet another bow. An enticing egg-yolk yellow.

'How lovely,' she said, bright as ever. There was something about Bill that made you want (if not yearn) to be *bright*. 'You really shouldn't have.'

The label said it would remind her of their walk.

'Aah,' she cooed in a voice she did not know she owned.

She unwrapped the gift slowly letting the paper drift to the floor, from where Peter Beales immediately bent down and picked it up and began smoothing and folding it. She watched him, mesmerised for a moment, and then turned back to what she now held, unwrapped, in her hands. And then she gasped. It was a pottery sheep. But no ordinary pottery sheep – a pottery sheep of most peculiar dimensions and perspective – with a very small head and two little dots for very-close-together eyes, making a remarkably silly face – anthropomorphically not unlike some anxious politician – with a body that ballooned out into a huge and weirdly disproportionate size. Some foolish craft notion of 'modern'. Very foolish.

She remembered the cave paintings of animals in the Levant, the Hindi carvings of oxen and bison, the modern marble and alabaster sheep in a crib in Southern Italy. Beautiful shapes, unburdened by any need for realism but perfect in their essential rightness. This, in her hand, was very bad art. In art terms, actually, she thought, it's the equivalent of taupe.

'I hope you like it,' he said.

She opened her mouth to be bright. For a moment there was silence.

Then Val, sitting there so demurely, her glass quite empty again, said genuinely, 'Oh how lovely – and so unusual.' Val never was any good at artistic things.

Bill looked at her gratefully.

Sally looked at her even more gratefully.

Suddenly she saw again those silly sheep in that Oxfordshire field, hustling for something they neither understood nor wanted. She handed the pottery sheep to her friend.

'Val loves things like this,' she said. 'Don't you, Val?'

Val looked startled, but game.

'She collects them.'

Val nodded vigorously. She did now.

62

'And this –' Sally gave Bill's sleeve a pat and winked at him, 'is – curiously enough – her favourite colour.'

Then she turned to the bottle of sparkling wine, removed the pink bow, which she also dropped on the floor, giving Peter Beale an 'I dare you' look, and opened it with a satisfactory pop for her guests.

'Lovely,' they all said.

'Lovely,' she replied.

And then she picked up the remaining Veuve Cliquot and took it back out into the garden and she called over her shoulder that anyone who wished to join her would be most welcome. They followed. All except Val and Bill who were left examining and delighting over the curious sheep.

As they sat at her little round table (brought back from Isfahan) she put her finger to her lips and said, 'Shush. If you listen hard you can just hear the sound of your water feature.'

They all concentrated for ages before Jennifer Beale suddenly said, 'But I don't think it's turned on.'

It was a strain, but she pulled through, and Val, at least, went off happy. Thank God for the Veuve Cliquot, thought Sally afterwards, as she yawned herself into bed. Because – just for once (and this time she did laugh out loud) – a couple of glasses of that, and she *wasn't* anybody's.

CAITLIN DAVIES

Snake Girl

O NCE UPON a time there was a little girl called
Mighty. Her real name was Maitumelo, but
everyone called her Mighty. She was a strong girl,
as fresh and fit as the oil-fried fat cakes she so loved to
eat.

Mighty grew up in a small village just west of the
vast Okavango Delta. There was a river some few
kilometres from her home and, in the past, when the
wind blew, there was so much water that the people
got wet. But these days it was a dry, quiet place.
Mostly the villagers were farmers, yet the only crop
that could be relied on was watermelons.

Mighty attended the local primary school where she
quickly learnt to read and write, to sing songs to God,
and to keep her classroom clean. She was a popular
girl with beautiful fish-shaped eyes, and lips that were
always turned up in a smile, whether she was feeling
happy or not. She lived with her mother and brother in
a thatched house that was cool in summer and warm
in winter.

At the age of fourteen Mighty was accepted into
junior school and it was then that her troubles started.
One day, walking home along the sand pathways of
the village, a man called to her.

'Hey, Mighty,' said the man. 'Come here.'

'*Ee, Rra*,' said Mighty respectfully, hanging her head a little as was proper when being addressed by an elder.

'Are you well?'

'*Ee, Rra.*'

'I have a message for you, from my brother Mr Wright.'

Mighty waited.

'Well, this message is that my brother is looking for a friend . . . a special friend. You might even say he's looking for a wife.'

Mighty's lips turned up in a smile, though she felt fearful.

'Yes,' said the man. 'I think he would like to marry you. Of course, the proper channels will be followed. We will approach your family and so forth. But I am being kind and I am telling you this now. So in the meantime just keep quiet,' and he mimed zipping his lips shut.

Mighty nodded.

'So, you agree?' said the man a little impatiently.

'No,' said Mighty, nervously. 'I do not.' She did not want to marry, she wanted to go to school and become a pilot.

The man was outraged and he even took a step backwards as if he had just avoided something dangerous.

'How can you not want to marry my brother?' he asked, breaking off a branch from a nearby marula tree as if he were about to beat her.

Mighty didn't know what to say. She knew Mr Wright, of course; he was the most successful man in

65

the village. He was short and fat and it was said he hadn't seen his feet since 1985, which was the year he had opened his first shop.

'Run home,' said the man. 'I don't know why I am even bothering to talk to you.'

The following morning Mighty woke up with a strange feeling. She lifted her T-shirt and to her surprise she saw a soft piece of red string tied around her stomach. She quickly pulled her T-shirt back down and then she lifted it again.

'Bashi,' she whispered to her elder brother, who was busy admiring himself in a tiny slice of broken mirror.

'What?'

'Look,' said Mighty, showing him the string.

Bashi laughed. 'You look like a baby! Why do you want to tie string around yourself like a baby?'

'I didn't do it,' protested Mighty. 'I just woke up and it was there.'

'Oh, you're talking rubbish,' said Bashi, and he went back to admiring himself in the mirror.

Two days later Mighty woke up to find more red string tied around her stomach. On the third morning she woke to find she couldn't move her arms.

'Bashi,' she called to her brother, who was trying to pierce his ear with a matchstick.

'What now?'

'My arms, see, I can't move them. They feel as if, as if . . .'

'As if what?'

'Well, they are heavy but there is something *moving* inside . . .'

Bashi came to where his sister lay on the bed. He looked down at Mighty's left arm and just then the

66

arm, or something within the arm, shivered like the skin of a dreaming dog. Then the skin just above Mighty's armpit swelled up and it rolled right down to her wrist like the wind rippling through a washed sheet hanging on a tree branch to dry.

'Oh my God!' shouted Bashi. 'You've got a snake in your arm!'

The following weekend the family held a meeting. By this time there were snakes moving up and down Mighty's arms almost all the time. The family decided to approach a traditional doctor, for the elders said only Setswana medicine would work. Their child, they said, had been bewitched.

Mighty didn't know what to believe and, anyway, no one consulted her. Mighty stayed away from school and she lay inside the house on the bed, except for the visit to the doctor. The doctor said indeed someone had bewitched the girl, and the family received some medicine. They paid for the treatment with a goat.

But the snakes didn't leave Mighty, they just increased. Soon she spent most of her time in bed and she could barely remember what it was like to go to school. The family approached two more traditional doctors, and one had a speaking pot which also said Mighty had been bewitched. By the end of the visits the family didn't have any livestock left to pay for any more medication. So then they went to the clinic. The clinic nurse said the problem was blood pressure, that bewitchment was in the mind of the beholder, and she gave Mighty some medicine for free.

But still the snakes continued, and now they moved to Mighty's legs as well. Some people in the village said

Mighty had been cursed by God. When, occasionally, she went outside, to gather firewood or to the stand-pipe to get water, people whispered, 'There goes the girl with snakes in her leg.' Even her old schoolfriends wouldn't look at her in the eyes any more. So she lay down on her bed, her body and face covered with a blanket, and she wept. When the snakes started up, Mighty's whole body began to shake and so did the bed she was lying on.

Six months after the snakes first appeared in Mighty's arms a journalist named Phillip came to the village. Phillip worked for a newspaper down in Maun and he had heard several rumours about a snake girl. He had even brought his camera with him. Phillip was an odd-looking man with a very long forehead as if a parti-cularly bad-tempered midwife had used a little too much force with the forceps during his mother's la-bour. He was from Francistown originally and he was ignorant of the rural areas and also a little afraid.

'Get a picture of the snake girl,' his editor had told him.

His editor was a white man from England and he said he didn't believe in witchcraft, but he thought the story would sell well.

'It's a real *African* story,' said the editor. 'And we've all had enough of lions and AIDS.'

Phillip talked with Mighty's family, who thought he might be able to help them in some way, and they told him everything that had happened. The journalist went away and wrote a big story about the snake girl.

Two months later Phillip came back. He said the snake girl was now famous. The doctors at the private hospital in Gaborone were willing to treat Mighty, and the President had heard of her plight and wanted to meet her as well.

When Bashi heard this he was jealous.

'You are just doing this to get attention,' he hissed at his sister.

But she had her blanket over her head and she didn't reply.

'Mr Wright is looking for you,' said Bashi in a singsong voice as both Mighty and the bed began to shake. 'He sent his brother here this morning. You know what people are saying? That you rejected Mr Wright. Why? You don't want this family to improve itself?'

A few weeks later Mighty's sister arrived from Gaborone. She was as fresh and fit as her little sister used to be and she carried a smell of baby cream about her.

'Mighty,' said Neo when she arrived.

She crouched down by her sister's bed and in her hands she cradled a box of damp Kentucky Fried Chicken. It was impossible to get fast food like this in the village so the box was a sign that Neo was now a city woman. She worked as a radio presenter in the capital, but she never abandoned her roots and always came home during public holidays and for funerals and suchlike.

'Sit up and tell me everything that has been going on,' Neo urged her sister. 'These people here are talking like crazy. I know they talk nonsense most of the time, but what's wrong? You tell me what's wrong.'

But Mighty hadn't been talking to anyone for a long time and she didn't know what to say.

'Little one,' said Neo, and she carefully peeled down the blanket. 'Look at you! You're so thin. You don't want Kentucky Fried Chicken? Are you sick? What's going on?'

Mighty sat up on the bed. She held out her arms for her sister to see. They were rigid and still and then, suddenly, something started pulsing under the skin. It rippled from just above her armpit right down to her wrist.

'*Mme we*!' cried Neo. 'Is it painful? Does it hurt? My sister, when did this start and why?'

'No, it doesn't really hurt,' said Mighty. 'But I'm so afraid I . . .' and she burst into tears.

That evening Neo took a stroll through the village, on her way to Mr Wright's house. She left her mother in the family compound preparing supper, hacking away at two cabbages with a rusty old knife. It had rained a few hours earlier and, as Neo walked, the air was full of the sound of frogs breathing in and out, purring like a huge mechanical cat. Neo walked quickly, as she always did, her fingers picking away as she went. She was going to tell Mr Wright that she knew exactly what was going on and she rolled some angry words around in her head.

Who did he think he was that he could just choose some young girl to be his wife? This was exactly what had happened to Neo and Mighty's own mother. She had been taken out of school and married off to an old man. After a few years the man had begun going out with other girlfriends, saying he needed someone educated to talk with.

Neo was not afraid of Mr Wright and she knew that would be her strength. She was sure that he would argue that the issue was one of culture and that a man had the right to choose his own wife. But culture, thought Neo, was like an elastic band. Sometimes it was small and round and encompassed very little. Other times it was stretched so far that it included things that had never been a part of anyone's culture at all.

As Neo neared Mr Wright's house, the largest concrete house in the village, she slowed her pace. Perhaps she shouldn't go in fighting, she thought, for Mr Wright was a powerful individual. Suddenly she pictured her mother as she had left her in the compound and it came to her that her own mind was like the cabbages being prepared for supper, the outer leaves limp and dirty like old thoughts. So Neo began mentally to peel off the leaves until she reached the freshness of a new thought. Her sister Mighty had said the journalist from Maun wanted to put her on television and now Neo thought this could be a good idea.

The crew from Botswana Television arrived in the village just two days later. They were not used to working on assignment in the rural areas; usually they just took their cameras to a conference hall to film whichever government minister was making a speech that day. But Neo had convinced them that if they came to the village they would be able to do a whole feature on the snake girl. 'You know what these rural people are like,' said Neo, playing on their prejudice.

The BTV driver stopped on the main tar road into the village and asked for directions. He explained he was looking for the compound where the snake girl lived. The woman he asked for directions sucked her teeth. This girl Mighty liked fame, thought the woman, just why did she think she was so special? But she told the men where to find her.

When the TV crew got to the compound it was late morning and there were a lot of people sitting in the yard. Mighty sat half bent by the reed wall, her face mostly covered by her hands, a woollen hat on her head though the sun was blazing. Next to her sat her mother, along with several other relatives on the sand. A little way away sat a large man with a slippery forehead, his legs splayed apart on a white plastic chair. His cheeks were plump and shiny as if he had recently eaten a large amount of money.

Mr Wright waited for the TV people to greet him. He was excited to be on television but he kept a sombre expression. Neo had explained that there was to be a feature on the most successful man in every village in the Okavango Delta and so Mr Wright was not at all surprised that he had been chosen. Now those big shots down in Gaborone would see him on the evening news.

The television crew set up their equipment and then had a break for some tea and freshly cooked fat cakes.

'Are you going to start, or what?' Neo asked them.

'*Ee, ee*, we're starting,' said the cameraman.

The interviewer threw away his cigarette and smoothed down his hair.

'Roving reporter Dumelang Batho, BTV, here in the Okavango Delta,' he began. He believed his name was the most important thing so he always started with that. 'Here in this tiny village, we have a young girl they call the snake girl . . .' The interviewer paused for effect. 'This girl has been plagued with *snakes* in her arms, in her legs, they are *moving*, ladies and gentlemen, all over the place . . .'

The cameraman zoomed in on Mighty who still sat by the reed wall.

'And I am her sister,' said Neo, striding forward and putting herself in front of the camera.

'Ah, my little sister has really been suffering. We can't know who has done this to us. But do you know, I think there are some funny things going on in this village. Because right here . . .' And she pointed to where Mr Wright sat on the white plastic chair. 'Is a man with bees in his buttocks . . .'

Mr Wright frowned. He didn't think he could have heard right. He thought the programme was to be about successful businessmen.

'Stop!' he said, putting his hand up. 'I refuse . . .' And he leant forward. And then he stopped, for, as he shifted his generous buttocks on the white plastic chair, there was a distinct sound of buzzing. He shifted again, and now everyone could hear the buzzing noise.

'Film in on him,' said Neo quickly to the cameraman. 'Look, the man with bees in his buttocks!'

By the side of the reed wall, Mighty looked up and, opposite her, Bashi began to giggle. Mighty looked at Mr Wright and she looked at her sister and she smiled the first real smile she had smiled for a very long time. She stood up then and felt as if she were flying, for the moving in her arms had completely stopped and she

73

felt as light and fresh as a butterfly. She waved her limbs around a bit, smiled at her mother who had begun to cry, and then she thought she would go and find her school uniform and give it a good wash before school tomorrow.

PHIL HOGAN

Whitebait

I T'S LATE in the afternoon when Julie rings. Aidan can't take calls at the office and Julie knows it, but his mobile starts vibrating in his trouser pocket so he has to go off to the rest room to ring her back. There was unfavourable publicity last year, according to Frank, in the papers and then on some consumer-affairs show on the radio. After that, the company caved in and said you could go to the rest room as often as you needed to, though not to smoke or read a magazine or have customers hanging on the line listening to the Classic Gold Collection while your wife brings you up to speed on what kind of a day she's having. No, there's still a crackdown on that. So Donna, the supervisor for his section, sees the little flag go up on his station and registers with a nod as he stands and untangles his ear from the wire on the headphone. Donna is Spanish but speaks perfect English. She does have a moustache, though, which Aidan finds himself fascinated by when he's listening to her questions about closures or follow-ups. Aidan's section is property – house and contents. One thing he has learnt in his five months here is that he should be on motor. Or, better, mortgage and loans. Frank is on m & l and is running round in a late-model Audi with alloy wheels.

Aidan knows even before she speaks that Julie is ringing to remind him about calling in at the supermarket on the way home to buy fish for her lunch party tomorrow with Marie and Nicqui: some white fish – cod, or even hoki or whiting, she said, remembering the options given in the recipe – and a 'medley' of seafood. She has the baby and can't drive out to the supermarket now that Aidan uses the car to get to the station, and she needs to cook ahead so she's not in a big flap tomorrow. Five-star fish pie, she's decided on. Once it's ready, you can reheat the next day. She's seen it whipped up in fifteen minutes by one of the TV chefs. Aidan is supposed to pick the car up as usual off the train but then drive to the Sainsbury's in Dedston. At least three sorts of seafood, she reminds him, including prawns.

'Ask at the counter what's fresh,' she says.

'Won't it all be fresh?' Aidan can't stop himself saying.

'Just ask,' she says.

Hunkered down in the cubicle, sitting on the closed toilet lid, he wants to keep this brief. He wants to remind Julie not to call him at work, but he knows the baby is keeping her awake nights, and that having a lunch party is her way of showing that babies are just part of life and therefore needn't be a bar to *having* a life, so he bites his tongue and nods. Marie, who lives in a new boxy house identical to theirs on the estate, has already hosted a lunch party and Billy is only a few weeks older than little Jade. They call it a party but it's just the three of them and the three babies.

Aidan is feeling the late August heat in here, away from the air-conditioned office and corridors. As Julie talks, he looks at his watch and makes an impatient face as though he's dropping a hint.

'Funny how you can't take calls in a call centre,' she jokes, as if reading his mind but then ignoring what it says.

'Mmm,' he says. *Mmm.* He speaks so quietly it could be the light buzzing outside above the wash-basins.

'The baby's been fine,' she's saying, warming up to talk more.

'*Gooood . . .*' he says, just breathing the word, not moving his lips.

Aidan is busy with his hands under the dryer when Frank comes swinging in. He sniffs at the air as if urine is his thing.

'Big night for your boys, Adie,' he says.

Frank has one of these Scottish accents with the edges sanded down to make him sound less threatening to English people. Like most of the staff at MLF Direct, he is from somewhere else, in his case Aberdeen. He is talking about tonight's Uefa qualifier in the Ukraine against Kiev.

'Seven o'clock kick-off,' Aidan grins, and his heart beats giddily at the thought, as if Julie is still listening. Julie doesn't know about the game and doesn't need to. In his mind, for a split second, he sees the white of the team strip glowing against the radioactive green of the pitch as it appears on TV and hears that shifting noise that crowds make, rearing and sliding way like waves on rocks.

'Karen's just outside,' Frank warns over his shoulder. 'Talking to Richard.' Shit. Aidan goes out, covering the shape of the phone in his pocket as he passes the two of them in the corridor, and feels his ears glowing. He catches the scent of Karen McPhaill's perfume, hears her brisk, serious voice and the click of her expensive shoes on the floor tiles as she steps back to let him through. Richard, nodding in agreement with his eyebrows pinched together, is her number two. Donna is one of eight number threes. Aidan and Frank are two of 128 number fours. That's the hierarchy. Karen catches his glance, he thinks, but no, she's looking right through him, distracted by what Richard is saying. Karen wasn't always brisk and serious. Five months ago she sat in on Aidan's interview, and for a while afterwards would ask in a friendly way how things were going, how he was settling in. But gradually, as he did settle in, she stopped asking, and now Aidan belongs to the cast of assimilated number fours that time has made too familiar to notice. His view of her, too, has lost the sharpness of actual experience and become the same as everyone else's. She seems up there somewhere, and the less she talks to him now the more it alarms him when she does. He'd bet Karen is no more than three or four years older than himself but, in the way she moves and handles things, and speaks in that brisk and serious manner without needing to think about it first, she inhabits a world where working is no harder than breathing. He has seen her on the train once, sitting in the blue plush of business class, her laptop on the little coffee table.

Donna watches Aidan coming back to the floor. Everyone else is too busy to notice, all talking at once, like bees buzzing with their own tasks. Put a smile in your voice is the first thing you learn. He gives Donna his phone smile now and eases himself into the blue swivel chair.

Inside the smile, though, is a bigger smile of satisfaction, and is to do with the fish for Julie's lunch party, which is in a long, shallow polystyrene box packed with ice under his desk. It has been there since just after lunchtime. The fishman comes Wednesdays and Fridays to the market near the office. He has a white hat and coat and sells out of a white trailer that opens up at the side. Aidan explained to him it was for a five-star fish pie. Well, the fishman said, you couldn't beat cod, which flaked well while retaining its firmness and succulence. He only had tiger prawns but you could chop them up, or keep some whole and chop the rest for variety. He had some nice baby squid too, he said, and whelks, freshly boiled. Aidan was anxious about the whelks as he paid and took the polystyrene box, and hurried awkwardly back to the office with it, the sun beating down on his back. In the lift, the sweat was cold on the inside of his shirt. Would Jamie Oliver use whelks in a five-star fish pie? Might the shells be a hindering factor? Julie hadn't said anything about shells. And then, when he got to the kitchen, the fridge was full. Not crammed full – just the usual yoghurts and bottles of mineral water and Fantas and Snickers bars squirrelled away for afternoon breaks – but too full to get his box in without rearranging things. So he carried the box to his desk. Packed with ice it would be fine. He sniffed at the polystyrene. Perhaps just the faintest smell, probably from the fishman's hands. No one remarked on it.

*　　*　　*

79

Julie likes to have Aidan home by seven to help with the baby. Before little Jade came along – the days when he was back in his old job at Whinnick's, the estate agents on the high street – he might stop off for a couple of beers after work. No problem. Now, working in an office block in the East End, he'll call Julie from the train to say he's on his way. That's the routine. But you could reasonably add forty-five minutes for a trip to the supermarket – perhaps more, he thinks now, if he rings Julie to say there are no prawns at the Sainsbury's in Dedston and that he'll have to try the big Tesco on the bypass. Thinking about it, he has seen two Tesco carrier bags in the office kitchen he can use, which now makes it seem less like a deceit and more like fate almost. This way, Julie gets her fish, he gets to watch at least the first half of United versus Kiev at the Cooper's Arms and no one gets hurt. The Cooper's has a widescreen TV and it's right next to the station car-park. He'll drink Coke, which leaves no trace of wrongdoing. Then, when he gets home, he'll mention the whelks in an excited, favourable way. He'll emphasise their freshness. Perhaps he'll tell Julie that the only alternative was whitebait, and isn't that the one with the little crunchy bones left in? That would be a nice touch. Whitebait is where the idea of small fry comes from, he thinks. Little fish are eaten by bigger fish and so on. Sure, whelks have got shells, but he figures they have to be better than whitebait.

The sun slants through the windows here on the fifth floor and Donna has to get up and lower the blind, just as she did yesterday and Monday. Amazing it's so hot, with September just around the corner. He's feeling lucky now. He fills his lungs with the cool, conditioned air and hits a button under the row of blinking lights, leaning back in his chair to speak. '*Hell-oo*, my name's Aidan, could I take your *postcode* please . . .' It helps to put a little run-up and a bounce in your voice as well as a smile, like a TV commentator he remembers as a kid calling out darts scores to a studio audience. One hundred and *eighty*.

At six, Aidan takes the bus to the station. He has transferred the fish now from the awkward box to the Tesco carrier bag, or rather two bags – one inside the other, both knotted. In the kitchen, he hadn't thought what to do about the ice, but, fuck it – he decided to rinse the whole lot down the sink and double-wrap the fish to seal in the smell. Then he washed his hands in the rest room. But on the crowded bus, it's hard not to notice the whiff rising from the bag squatting between his feet, and it's still in the air as he comes down the escalator into the station and makes his way across the boomy concourse to platform twelve, the bag swinging softly and heavily at his side. It's like a bag of something sodden wet – towels, or hanks of seaweed, maybe, with the soft rasp of the shells.

His train is in and he gets into the carriage next to business class. The window seats are taken and he stands for a moment wondering what to do with the bag, before eventually pushing it on to the overhead rack. There's a bunch of flowers up there and a rolled-up mac. The carrier bag feels cold and squashy and the smell comes to him more strongly now, as if it's in there breathing out at him through the pores of the blue-and-white-striped polythene. It's hot in the carriage and, as he loosens his tie and takes a seat next to the aisle, he sniffs discreetly. The smell is right under his nose somewhere, perhaps on his tie. There's a fat man next to the window glancing sideways from his newspaper, his nostrils twitching, and a girl sitting across from the man who looks up from her book of puzzles. Both of them can smell it. Aidan wonders if he should say something – make a joke maybe.

He thinks about going to wash his hands again but other passengers are making their way down the carriage now, looking for seats as the train sets off. The seating is arranged in sets of twos and threes. Aidan is aware of someone settling himself into the middle seat next to the girl, and when he looks up there's Richard's big panting face right in front of him. He is wearing a sort of goofy, triumphant look – the kind you have when you've had to hurry for the train and managed to bag a seat. Richard isn't looking at Aidan but is gesturing excitedly and goofily over his head to someone else, and before Aidan can open his mouth, *Karen* has arrived and is sidling into the space next to Richard. She is laughing and saying something about the scramble for seats when she notices Aidan.

'Oh – HELLO!' Aidan says, getting his surprised voice in first.

'Hey . . .' she says, in her old friendly way, the way he remembers from his first days at MLF. 'Adrian, isn't it?'

'Yes. Well, Aidan actually.' He grins. 'Strictly speaking.'

'Aidan, of course, sorry. Richard, you know Aidan – motor, isn't it?'

'Property,' Aidan says. 'For my sins,' he hears himself add.

Richard has a less friendly look about him. Perhaps

he resents being seen looking goofy and excitable by a subordinate. 'I started in property,' he says, folding his arms. 'It was good enough for me.'

'No, no, it's fine really. It's great,' Aidan says. He can see a silvery smear of fish scales on his hand. Still grinning and looking at them both, he wipes it on the seat.

'Excellent,' Karen is saying. 'I'm glad you're settling in. How long is it now – two, three months?'

'Yes, about that. Five, I think.'

Richard, feeling the heat, pulls at the knot of his tie. 'What on *earth* is that smell?' he says.

'Fish, I'd say,' Karen says, looking round, sniffing.

Aidan opens his mouth to own up – perhaps beg their indulgence with a goofy look of his own – but, seeing Richard's twisted features, he hesitates and instead starts gesturing with his eyes towards the man by the window, who is now asleep with his head back and his mouth open and half his newspaper on the floor. Aidan raises his eyebrows to indicate the offending carrier bag squashed on to the rack.

'Ah . . .' Karen mouths, and gives a faint, knowing smile.

Richard, still making the sour face, gets up and strains to open the window, but it refuses to budge. A flap of his shirt has escaped his waistband, showing his bulging stomach, the skin pale and matted with wiry hair. There's something about this failed effort and the smell of fish and Richard's belly on view that makes Aidan not want to look. Richard sits down with exaggerated heaviness. 'Bloody thing's stuck,' he says. He's sweating. The girl next to Richard looks up at the stuck window and glances at Aidan. He avoids her eye.

An inspector comes down the aisle asking to see tickets. Karen shows a business-class ticket but Richard's is the same as Aidan's. Perhaps she bumped into Richard on the platform and didn't want to seem rude going off into the business-class carriage while he got into standard class. Or, hang on, Aidan thinks, maybe they're having an affair.

The inspector sniffs the air and gives a comic frown as he stamps each ticket in turn. 'We know what *someone's* having for dinner,' he announces.

There are tight smiles all round, except for the girl with the puzzle book, who purses her lips. The inspector leans across and touches the fat man's arm. 'Excuse me, sir . . .'

For an awful moment Aidan has a feeling he will ask about the carrier bag, but the fat man just wakes and starts fumbling in his pocket for his ticket. He is flustered at being caught asleep with his mouth open and wipes a creamy fleck of spit from the corner of his mouth and hastens to retrieve his newspaper from the floor. The inspector moves on and the man starts to read, but after a minute his eyes droop with the motion of the train and his head lolls back again. A moment later he is snoring.

'How far do you have to go?' Karen asks Aidan.

'South Walsey,' he tells her. 'Three stops.' His eyes wander up to the Tesco stripes of the fish bag, and he suddenly realises that he needs to know where Karen gets off.

She has seen him look at the bag because she directs her eyes at the snoring man and, crinkling her nose, says in a low voice, 'Let's hope he doesn't miss *his* stop.'

Aidan is feeling the heat himself now, and even Karen has a few beads of sweat on her upper lip, like a dewy version of Donna's moustache. Shuttling back and forth in the sun all day has made an oven of the train and the odour of cod and whelks and baby squid has expanded in the heat and filled the carriage like a poisonous gas. Richard, scowling and muttering, stands up again, leans across the girl with the puzzle book and tugs repeatedly at the window until at last it gives. 'Ah!' he says. Other passengers, some of whom have managed to open windows of their own, peer over their newspapers approvingly.

Aidan's phone starts vibrating in his pocket. That will be Julie making sure he's on time. It occurs to him now that he might have gained an extra five or ten minutes of the match for a delay but he can't say they're stuck in a tunnel with Karen sitting here. He leaves the phone to ring out while a goods train of container wagons thunders by on the other track. The violent clatter of it goes on and on but then disappears, leaving their own carriage in silence, like a saloon in the old cowboy films that goes quiet when a stranger comes to the bar.

After a moment Karen starts asking him about the business of the day, so he slips into his sales personality and talks about 'traffic' and 'responses'. He tells her about the woman who rang this morning needing flood cover for her horse, worried about a repeat of last September's weather.

'Are you sure she didn't say "house"?' Karen laughs.

'That's what I thought,' Aidan says, laughing too.

Richard says nothing; just sits there with his arms folded.

The train pulls into Hernlea and lets people off. A foursome – two girls and two men – are from their carriage and as the train moves away Aidan can see their relief at being off the train, with the heat and the fish.

'There must be seats up there in the next carriage now,' Richard says to Karen, half standing to look over Aidan's shoulder. Maybe he's annoyed that Aidan is here, cramping his style.

'I wouldn't bother,' Karen says. 'It's not far now.'

If Aidan hadn't been here, she and Richard might have moved to the next carriage. Maybe Karen senses that it would be awkward to leave him alone with the smell, having now established a 'rapport', as they put it in commercial training. On the other hand, it would feel odd to invite him to move to another carriage with them, as though they were a proper threesome. It reminds him of when he and Julie had someone in to wallpaper the landing and stairs when Julie was going through her nest-building phase; how, as lunchtime approached, they'd started to feel uncomfortable. Should they offer the man some of the cabbage and bacon soup Julie had made? Would he be embarrassed to be asked? In they end they just quietly closed the kitchen door.

'So . . .' Aidan says, but the word evaporates in the air as Richard starts to talk privately with Karen. Aidan catches something about 'numbers' and then 'Bristol' and 'Leeds'. Richard says something and chuckles deeply.

But then Karen turns to Aidan. 'Richard and I have

a working dinner tonight for senior management. Do you know Astley Hall?'

Aidan hasn't a clue, but pretends to think about whether he knows or not.

'It's a country hotel,' Karen continues, 'so the managers from out of town can stay overnight. I live near enough to get home, but poor Richard has to go all the way back to London. Midnight train.'

Richard looks aggrieved now, presumably because Karen has let Aidan in on their deliberations and because he's been made the butt of her amusement. But Aidan can see how clever she's being. She doesn't want Aidan getting the wrong end of the stick and blabbing an embroidered story round the office about her whispering on a train with Richard's tongue in her ear when all they're doing is going to some uninteresting management dinner. Aidan notices now that she has changed out of the clothes she had on earlier. By contrast, Richard is starting to look more clammy and more unkempt, as if the presence of the fish up there in the rack is silently working on him, infiltrating his open pores with its indelible tang, sticking his hair to his forehead with its whelky glue. He seems to need a shave. His thighs seem to have grown too big for his suit trousers. One of his fly buttons is undone.

The train is approaching a station. The signs on the platform pass too quickly to read but it must be Ambrook. Two more stops. Karen murmurs something to Richard that Aidan doesn't hear. Perhaps she's telling him they're getting off at the next one. He hopes so. But what if they don't? What is he supposed to do about the fish?

Then something catches his eye. Something just

dripped, he's certain of it. It's the bag. The bag is leaking – no, it's *sweating*. Another drop of water is forming on the putty-coloured metal grid above the sleeping fat man. Aidan's heart stops for a second as he watches it fall, splashing the edge of the man's suit collar. He looks away quickly, but now the girl opposite is clearing her throat and closing her puzzle book. She starts to get up. Aidan is certain she will say something as a parting shot – perhaps remind him not to forget his stinking *fish* – but no, thank God, she just squeezes past and goes to stand near the doors. But now his heart is thudding and the phone starts to vibrate again in his pocket. He ignores it. Karen's eye catches his and he smiles and raises his eyebrows, as if it's a phone ringing somewhere that they can both hear. She smiles back but seems to have decided to stop talking now. Richard, too, is mute, with his head back, pink-cheeked, and his eyes closed in resignation, as if waiting for something to end.

Aidan looks at his watch. Kick-off in fifteen minutes. OK, he thinks, if – *if* – he has to get off before them and take the fish with him, what's the worst that could happen? It would be a minor embarrassment, nothing more. At worst, it might make him seem something of a weirdo. Or a fraud. Or a clown. Nothing you could get fired for but things you might be remembered for the next time there was an opening in mortgage and loans for a bright, ambitious sales executive with highly developed communications skills.

The train is slowing for the next station but Karen has opened her briefcase and is studying something. No one is making a move.

Aidan takes a breath and leans forward. 'Where did you say you get off?'

Karen looks up, surprised. 'It's the stop after yours,' she says. 'Buttling?'

Aidan nods. He thinks. Yes, he could abandon the fish, cut his losses and drive to the supermarket in Dedston and miss the match. Or he could abandon the fish, *watch* the match and then tell Julie that both supermarkets had run out of fish of every conceivable kind. Neither of these options is fully satisfying. OK. He could abandon the fish but then race after the train in the car to Buttling (driving at unheard of speeds for a Nissan Micra), wait for Karen and Richard to get off the train, sneak on, grab the fish off the rack, jump off before the doors close, then drive at a similar speed of light back to the Cooper's Arms to catch the second half of the first half of the match and the first half of the second, remembering to ring Julie with the excuse about there being no prawns at Sainsbury's and having to try the big Tesco on the bypass. Or, no . . . he could *pretend* to get off at his own stop but then sneak back on to the train one carriage down, *wait* for Karen and Richard to get up from their seats at Buttling, creeping in at the last minute – under cover of everyone else who would be getting off there – snatch the fish, back-track into the other carriage and jump off the train before the doors close. But, then, how would he get back to the Cooper's? He could be waiting ages for a train the other way. A taxi was a possibility, but how much would that cost? Ten quid? That was more than a bagful of replacement fish would cost at the supermarket, but at least – worst scenario and all else being feasible – he'd get to see the first half of the second half of the match.

But as the train slows down for his station, he starts to see only the non-feasible aspect of things, sees that the coward's way out is the only one that offers both dignity and stable employment. This is it. The platform signs flick by and he glances at the sweating Tesco bag as he prepares to disown it for good. 'Well,' he says, getting up, 'this is me.' He grips the back of the seat. 'Hope you guys have a good evening.'

Karen moves to let him out. 'Yes, you too.'

Richard nods grudgingly. Aidan hesitates, then, nodding too, goes to stand by the far doors, waiting, not looking at the fish on the rack. The platform signs are going by slowly now, more slowly, until at last the train pulls to a halt – though not smoothly this time but with an unexpected abruptness, making everyone lurch with it. Aidan sees the fat man wake with the jolt and look quickly out of the window, his confused, bulging eyes registering in panic the name of the station. He leaps from his seat, grabbing the mac and flowers from the rack, and runs, stumbling, towards the middle doors as they open. Richard is shouting after him ('Excuse me, *hello* . . .') and is reaching up to the rack, but the man doesn't hear, is already on the platform, walking quickly, adjusting his belongings and gathering his wits and dignity, feeling an idiot for thinking the train was about to pull out like that when it had just pulled in. Other people are getting off. Aidan has about ten seconds.

'Give it to me!' he hears himself shout. Suddenly he's taking the bag from Richard's outstretched hand. 'I'll catch him up.'

'Good *man*,' Richard says, red-faced and exhilarated.

Aidan feels the bag sway with the weight as he takes it and hears the doors beeping their warning as he dashes back down the aisle, giving a last wave to Karen and Richard, their faces animated by the unexpected drama. The doors hiss shut as he hits the platform and starts to run in the direction the man has taken, out into the booking hall, past the news-stand and the key-cutter's, where he slows up. He turns to see the train moving off.

Yes! He punches the air, whooping under his breath. He stands for a second, savouring the moment before hurrying out, inhaling deeply, overtaking the fat man with his bunch of flowers and other passengers at the cab stand. From the bridge he can see the Micra, and just beyond the car-park the white stucco of the Cooper's Arms. He is running by the time he gets to the steps at the other side, seeing the TV flickering in the bar. He still has a few minutes to dump the fish in the boot and then to settle himself in the pub. He finds his keys just as the phone goes. Julie.

'Aidan, I've been trying to *call* you. Where are you?'

'Sorry, babe, we must have been in a tunnel. Everything OK?'

'You haven't got the fish yet?'

'No, course not, I'm just on my way now.'

'Oh, thank God.'

'Why, what's up?'

'Marie rang about half an hour ago. Little Billy's got a fever, so we've decided to postpone till next week. Which is better anyway. When I'm in less of a panic. Jade's just woken up too.'

Aidan doesn't know what to say. His mind is turning but there's nothing left to work with, like one of those cement mixers he sometimes sees left rumbling emptily in the gardens of the new houses on the estate. 'But . . .' he stutters, 'why don't I get some fish anyway? We could have some tonight.'

'No, no, I'll just stir-fry some chicken. If you could just come home quick and give me a hand, that'd be great. I'm exhausted. Thanks for offering, though, hon. You must be tired yourself.'

'I am a bit,' he says.

He looks at the chalky walls of the Cooper's and imagines again the white of United's strip against the turf and the ebbing noise of the crowd. He loves Julie and little Jade and their boxy little house with a stir-fry in the wok. But here, heavy-footed with the dead weight of fish and the clinging dampness inside his shirt and the sun winding all the clocks down as they speak, something feels like shame and defeat.

In his response, and the silence that follows, maybe Julie senses it too and softens her voice. 'So is that OK then – chicken?'

He smiles, thinking about this story of the fish that he won't be able to tell her when he gets back, even though, of all the people he knows, she'd be the best person to tell.

'That sounds great,' he finds himself saying. 'I can almost smell it now.'

JOANNA TROLLOPE

Star Rubbish

D O YOU remember the moment when you're about
fourteen and you look round the table at your
family and you think: I really, really do not belong to
this lot? And then you think: Do I? And then you
think: Well, if I didn't come from them, where did I
come from?

I suppose that for a lot of kids that thought is pretty
exciting. I mean, if you're secure enough in your family
to be bored by them, you've got the confidence to
think you could have come from anywhere; you could
have had billionaire parents, or a world-class footbal-
ling father, or a mother who was a runaway princess.
You'd be the sort of person who could look in the
mirror and see all kinds of possibilities, instead of a
face that bore absolutely no resemblance to the person
who was actually trapped behind it. You'd give yourself a high five and a big wink and you'd go, '*Yes*!'

There were a couple of girls in my class, when I was
fourteen, who were like that. They talked about their
families as if they were sad misfits who weren't going
to be *allowed* – these girls were in charge, you see – to
impede our heroines' meteoric rise to their real and
wonderful identities. The families, stuck fast in ban-
ality and ridiculousness, were going to stand gawping

on the sidelines while their changeling swan daughters glided past them into their natural habitats of glamour and fame and – of course – beauty. The families had had, it was implied, the amazing good fortune to be lent these glorious beings for early nurture – a bit, I suppose, like being a wet-nurse to royalty – and must surrender them in time with grace and gratitude. It was only natural, after all.

What was natural to *me* was rather different. What was natural to me wasn't so much that I thought I was really the daughter of a White Russian prince as that I couldn't somehow see I was the daughter of anybody much. When I looked in the mirror, it always gave me a fright. What I saw was never what I expected to see: the public face of my private self. I looked at somebody I didn't recognise, every time, and it made me feel that I was an outsider. Not an exotic alien, not a mysterious mooncalf, but just someone who didn't belong. And it wasn't just that I didn't belong to my family, it was more that I didn't feel I belonged to *myself*.

The therapist they sent me to when my mother left us wanted me to acknowledge that I was grieving, so that I could reconcile myself to the end of one stage of my relationship with my mother, and start more fruitfully (for us both) on the next. I didn't want to be fruitful. I sat in the therapist's cream-painted room with the flower prints on the walls and the kind of half-comfortable chairs that try and suggest a bit of home and a bit of hospital and glared at him. He wanted me to try and empathise with my mother, to try and imagine – 'You are fourteen, after all,' he said. 'You have feelings, emotional feelings' – how strongly she must have felt to leave her family for a man the other side of the world, in Australia.

My brother Nat had said bitterly, flicking Coco Pops at the wall with his knife, 'She said she'd die if she couldn't be with him.'

'And if she *had* to?'

'She'd feel,' said my father from behind the newspaper, 'like we do now.'

'Like bloody rubbish.'

'Don't say bloody —'

'Like bloody, *bloody* rubbish,' Nat said, and threw his knife after the Coco Pops.

'I don't want to imagine that,' I said to the therapist.

'You don't want to feel better?' said the therapist in his calm, knowing voice. 'You don't want to try to understand in case it makes you feel better?'

'Right,' I said.

He looked out of the window. He'd asked to see a picture of my mother, and since he'd seen it, he'd started wanting me to be generous, to do the giving. It was the effect my mother had on most people. It was the effect, presumably, that she'd had on the man in Australia.

After four sessions, I told my father I wasn't going to see the therapist any more.

He sighed. He sighed a lot back then, as if he'd always expected life to be disappointing, and oh boy, it hadn't let him down. He said, 'Isn't it helpful to talk to someone?'

'No,' I said. 'It's *un*helpful.'

'Would you like to talk to me?'

'No, thanks,' I said.

'Could – could you explain why?'

I looked at him. I looked at someone who had been around all my life but to whom I couldn't honestly feel much sense of belonging.

I said, 'I don't know you very well,' and then I looked at him again, and I said, 'Sorry,' and then I said, 'I don't know myself very well, either,' because of the expression on his face.

He did his best, I know he did. He took the fourth chair away from the kitchen table, and tried to make a life designed exclusively for three people, three people who had chosen this life deliberately, and not by default. He didn't try and take my mother's place, he just tried to squeeze shut the gap she'd left. I don't blame him. In his place, I'd probably have tried to do the same, and it would have taken so much effort and energy that I wouldn't have noticed, either, that my son and my daughter, in all respects but the physical, were living on the moon.

I don't think, to be truthful, that my brother stared in the bathroom mirror (always smeared with shaving foam and toothpaste) and thought: Who he? I don't think that's how his separateness worked; in fact, I doubt he ever looked in the mirror except when he was interested in some new girl and was checking for spots. Instead, he took himself off to a world where arbitrary painful human things didn't happen, worlds like astrology or botany. His astrology phase lasted ages, months of string theories and obsessions with amounts of time and space and light. He was passionate about time, how little the whole history of the world had had, how if you set out to walk from New York to San Francisco, and only took a step every two and a half thousand years, after five steps you'd have covered all known existence. He sat on the edge of my bed while I was trying to unscramble a Yeats poem and told me all this as excitedly as if he'd discovered the wheel.

I said, 'You're really lucky, Nat.'

'Lucky?' he said. 'Lucky? What's luck got to do with it?'

I put my Yeats poetry book upside down on my stomach.

'Do you,' I said, 'think Dad is our real dad?'

The light died out of Nat's eyes.

'Oh yeah.'

'Why oh yeah?'

'Well,' Nat said, in the flat voice he used for most of ordinary life, 'he would be, wouldn't he?'

'Why?'

'Because that's what dads are like, aren't they? That's how they are. You don't get surprises, with dads.'

I looked past him.

'Just with mothers.'

He got up. He walked to the door of my bedroom.

'Thanks for the time-machine lesson,' I said.

When he'd gone, I got off my bed and looked in the mirror my father had screwed to the wall when I was eight and wanted to see how my hair looked, in bunches. I had to stoop to look in it now. I saw the usual unexpected face, the face my father and my brother thought represented me, the face that my mother, writing from Australia, said she had framed beside her bed. I went back to my own bed and picked up the Yeats book, and then I threw it across the room. Who could live all winter on nine stupid beans rows anyway?

*   *   *

We lived like that, I suppose, for two years or so. Well, if you can call that living. We got up and went to bed, and shouted at each other about the bathroom, and argued with each other about duties and responsibilities, about tea bags and lavatory paper and ironing. My father took us on cold holidays to Northumberland and tried – half-heatedly – to make us go on hot ones to Australia, and we went to clubs and the cinema and not-quite-right restaurants on our birthdays. We let the garden grow into a jungle, and the paint peel on the window frames, and one year, the Christmas tree stood gathering dust and despondency in the front-room window until April, when our next-door neighbour came round to make sure that our father hadn't left us too.

It mightn't have been a thrilling life, but it wasn't a bad one either in its messy, low-key way. We didn't really argue much, except about trivia, and there was a familiarity which was, I suppose, looking back, reassuring. But I had a sense of waiting, just as I always had a sense – on good days – that one day I might look in the mirror and find that I had become someone I could relate to, that even if I was always going to be an outsider, I would at least have myself for company. I was waiting for that to happen, just as I was waiting for life to become something – or indeed allow me to turn it into something – that made me feel I had at last got to the beginning of my story, instead of being stuck in an eternal prologue.

You can't, can you, tell anyone about this kind of stuff. If you think it as a child, you're told you'll grow out of it. If you think it as an adult, you're told you've succumbed to the victim culture and instructed to get a life. If you think it as a teenager – well, forget it. No wonder teenagers talk only to each other. No one else will *listen*.

Then something happened. When it first happened, neither Nat nor I took much notice because it all looked so unlikely, weird even. I suppose, even if we had never allowed the thought anywhere near our lips, we had vaguely sort of considered the notion that our father would find someone else. No. Let me pull myself together. Even people of sixteen and seventeen, sunk in self-absorption, are not going to expect a man of forty-two to live without a woman for ever. Not even us.

But *this* woman? This noisy, not young, red-haired woman in jeans, and big awful jumpers with pictures on the front, banging round our kitchen and making prawn jambalaya? This – well, this *fat* woman? Who didn't seem afraid of us or made awkward by us and whom our father watched with the expression of a little kid opening something on Christmas morning and finding he'd got exactly what he'd been hoping for?

We were stunned. We were too stunned, I think, even to know what our reaction was to her, to him, to them. She was called Shirley. Sometimes, she skewered her hair up on top of her head with what looked suspiciously like swizzle sticks nicked from the pub, and sometimes she let it hang down her back and sometimes she tied it back with a bit of purple tinsel. As with everything, she didn't seem to notice what she did, she didn't seem to *care*, and nor, did it seem to me, did she care whether we liked her or not.

'I'm not here to mother you,' she said to me. 'You've got a perfectly good mother of your own to do that.'

I was bent over looking into the fridge hoping, as you do, to see something that would catch my stomach's eye. I muttered into the fridge, 'Except she *isn't* perfectly good.'

'You wait till you're a mother,' Shirley said from across the kitchen. 'You wait to see what a picnic it is.'

I straightened up, holding a cold sausage. There were never any cold sausages, before Shirley . . .

'*You're* not a mother,' I said rudely.

'I'm a teacher,' she said. 'Next best thing. It gives you a view of mothering.'

I took my sausage upstairs. I was beginning to re-visit some of the feelings I'd had when the therapist had encouraged me to be generous, had wanted me to see that joining the rest of the human race in terms of emotional intelligence might benefit me in the long run. I bent to look at myself in my bedroom mirror, chewing my sausage.

'Hello, stranger,' I said to myself with my mouth full. 'Don't let them *near* you.'

Shirley moved in. She painted her and my father's bedroom yellow and shunted the kitchen around so that the table was somehow in the middle and not crammed in a corner with its wall end stacked with sliding piles of newspapers. Then she said those were all the changes she proposed making. But of course they weren't. There were changes everywhere, in every aspect. I don't mean stuff like her passion-fruit shampoo in the shower, but timetables and food and atmosphere and requirements to live with a communal conscience instead of in three sealed units. Naturally, I looked to my father and my brother to resist all these unspoken but irresistible changes, but I looked in vain. It was plain from the very beginning that my father and brother, thankfully surrendering any domestic initiative, actually *liked* it.

I spent a long time that first summer Shirley was with us in front of my mirror – long, sticky afternoons persuading myself that my separateness was some kind of distinction, that by not joining this new merry-go-round of clean towels and meals at table, I was somehow upholding a kind of noble principle. There were moments, I have to admit, when the thought did sneak across my brain that maybe this kind of behaviour wasn't the last word in maturity for someone of sixteen, but my old habits of setting myself apart were so deep in me that it would have seemed a gross betrayal to let them go. Especially faced with Shirley.

She took over the kitchen. She made huge highly coloured meals and Nat's friends began to come round and share them. Shirley'd stand there, over some great pot of curry, or gumbo, with a ladle, and the boys would shove each other around and my father would get beers out of the fridge as if he'd been doing it all his life instead of learning how only three months ago. I'd go down and get my plate and answer back to Nat's friends and take my plate up to my mirror and my little shrivelled world, now no bigger than a walnut but as precious as a pearl. Nobody tried to stop me. Nobody even asked me if I'd like to stay. I'd only have said no, wouldn't I?

I don't know why I went out into the garden that evening. I can't honestly remember why I suddenly couldn't stand my room another minute and the sight of the early autumn evening sky outside my window looked so desirable that I couldn't bear not to be out under it, under all those sharp little stars polishing themselves up for the equinox. I went downstairs and deliberately walked through the kitchen where Shirley and Dad and Nat and Nat's friend Dutch (he wasn't, he was Welsh) were eating moussaka, and out of the door that led straight into the garden. I let it bang behind me, hard.

It was clear and coldish outside; not cold enough to crunch the grass, but cold enough to make the air taste clean. I stepped carefully into the middle of our shaggy lawn, and then I lay down, pulling my sweater sleeves over my hands. I stared upwards. The sky, even with the red night haze from the town, was as clear as an illustration from one of Nat's astronomy books. I blinked. I couldn't remember the names. Or rather, I couldn't remember which name fitted which pattern of stars. I blinked again. It was a stupid thing, a stupid not remembering thing to get worked up about, but I had an awful feeling, lying there on the damp, dark grass, that I might be about to cry.

The kitchen door opened. I didn't move. I waited for Nat to call out and ask me what I thought I was doing. But he didn't. Instead, a fat, dim shape moved very quietly out from the house towards me and lay down parallel, about three feet away.

I held my breath.

'What,' Shirley said, 'do you know about stars?'

I grunted.

'I don't know much,' Shirley said. 'Not my subject. But I know one thing.'

I said nothing. I didn't look her way, but I could sense the mound of her on the grass, all the same.

'We're all made of the same stuff, you see.'

'Rubbish,' I said, not meaning to.

'Exactly.'

I turned my head a fraction.

'What?'

'We're made of the same rubbish. We're made of the same particles. We're made of star rubbish.' She paused, and then she said, 'So we're all related, them, you, me. We can't be unrelated, even if we wanted to, because of *matter*. Matter links us, whether we like it or not.'

I sat up, very slowly. I glanced quickly sideways. Shirley was lying with her plump arms behind her head and her plump ankles crossed and her blue jersey with the jokey sheep all over it, rising over the hill of her breasts and belly.

'Has it ever occurred to you,' Shirley said in exactly the same voice, 'that inside what you see there is someone quite different?'

I was startled.

'What?' I said.

'Would it surprise you,' Shirley said, 'to know that inside this fat redhead lives a bony brunette? She's been there all my life and she's never got out.'

I bent my head. I wanted, for some reason, to say sorry, but couldn't seem to say anything.

'We're all the same, and we're all different,' Shirley said. 'If we weren't, we'd die of boredom. If you thought you were just like everyone else, you'd want to cut your throat. We've got our star side and we've got our earth side and it's up to us which side we choose to encourage.'

I tipped my head up, and stared upwards. The stars were glittering.

'Nat said that when they run out of fuel they'll die.'

'Yes.'

'But by then, enough dust particles will have gathered to make new ones.'

'Yes.'

I said unsteadily, 'I'm not sure I'm ready to make a new one.'

'Maybe not –'

'Then –'

'You could just think about it. Just consider it.'

'Suppose I don't feel like joining –'

'You're joined already,' Shirley said. 'We all are. Us and our dreams. Me and this skinny cow who never gets a look-in. You and those stars.'

I got up very slowly, flexing my knees. Then I went across to where Shirley lay and looked down at her. She wasn't looking back, and she appeared completely peaceful. I could see that the fronds of hair round her forehead were beginning to wire up in the night air, as if they had a life of their own. I bent a bit closer and put my hand down towards her.

'You'd better get up,' I said. 'That grass is damp.'

MALCOLM PRYCE

The King Canute of Lard

IF HE HAD been born two hundred years ago he would probably have been a chimney sweep and died of cancer of the scrotum. Or he would have worked in a match factory and the phosphorous would have eaten away his jaw. But he was born in 1962 and worked in advertising as an art director and one day he died from sleeping sickness caught while shooting a cigarette ad in Africa. All ages have their hazardous professions.

I shared an office with Semtex for seven years. It was his job to look after the visual side of things. Together we would think up the idea, and then he would take it away and oversee the design: the layout, the type, the photography. This was the dangerous bit. Most of it would be in the tropics, you see. I suppose if you spend half a lifetime there something's bound to get you eventually. Normally sleeping sickness is curable if caught early enough but the symptoms of mental dullness, apathy, and profound sleepiness are so indistinguishable from his normal self that we didn't notice. Sleeping was one of his favourite pastimes, actually. Although no one ever told him it was dangerous. And, of course, you don't expect it to crop up in the home counties, do you? The doctor thought he must have caught it at the zoo.

I wouldn't say he was a tragic figure – he's not someone you would mention up alongside the Thane of Cawdor. But there was a tragic dimension to his death in the sense that his struggle with the ravages of disease has overshadowed his other, more heroic struggle. The one that occupied him throughout his life and that is likely to be his true legacy. I mean his private war against the logo.

No one knows exactly what it is about art directors and the logo. To most of us this humble little corporate squiggle simply tells us which company paid for the ad. But to an art director a logo is an aesthetic crime that must always be reduced to near invisibility on any ad. Anyone who has ever worked in an agency knows about this. No phrase is uttered more, nor ignored more than the eternal, 'Make the logo bigger.' To an art director an acceptable size for a logo is about the size of a bacillus. And to a client . . . well, it's all he has in the world. You know what the logo is to the client? It's the Alamo.

Of all the combatants in this never-ending war, the adversary who had locked horns most frequently and most passionately with Semtex was our client Bill Trumpton. He was the eternal foe; the Joker to Semtex's Batman. Or since we are talking about defending the Alamo, you'd have to say he was Davy Crockett. Although you wouldn't think so to look at him. A portly, self-made businessman with an MBA from the University of Life, he was a man who prided himself on his canny knowledge of the world and believed advertising creatives were descended from the tailors who created the Emperor's new robes. He was a man with absolutely no time for 'nonsense' and there was no more extreme example of it, in his book, than the nonsense about the logo. To him it was self-evident that since this was the part that told everyone who had spent all the money (i.e. him), you made damn sure everyone could read it. It was Trumpton, actually, who christened Semtex years ago when Bernie said he couldn't ask him to make the logo any bigger because he might 'go off'. 'Go off!' shouted Trumpton. 'Is he made of bloody Semtex or something?' He was also the one who seriously threatened to have him shot.

I expect you probably already know about Trumpton's Lard. Your mum used to cook your tea with it but she doesn't any more because she now uses extra-virgin olive oil, even though she doesn't quite know why. Not that I'm getting at your mum, because none of us knows why, and this is really the root of Bill Trumpton's despair. He's the King Canute of Lard, commanding the olive oil to go back. An expert on lost causes.

Over the years he had fought and lost every battle there was with Semtex. He had surrendered the right to have a say in the creation of his ad; he had given up the hope that the concept would refer, no matter how obliquely, to his product. He had even abandoned the expectation that it would make sense. Until after a life spent in miserable retreat he found himself besieged in an outpost at the bottom right-hand corner of the ad, wearing a racoon-skin hat.

The most celebrated campaign in this war, the one everyone still talks about, began, paradoxically, the one time Bill Trumpton didn't say the magic words, 'Make the logo bigger.' He had just re-designed the pack of his mainstream brand, Trumpton's Original. And he naturally wanted to run an ad in the local paper to announce the new pack design. It was not a major change, just a bit of design tweaking – the sort of graphic 'housekeeping' that all products undergo from time to time to stop them looking dated. It was really the sort of thing their in-house studio should have done, but they didn't have one. So the job came to me and Semtex and, since it was a tiny, black-and-white ad we naturally considered it beneath our dignity and devoted exactly four seconds to it. A picture of the new pack and some silly pun that I can't even remember. Semtex scribbled a quick layout of the ad and gave it to Bernie. And that should have been the end of it.

Bernie took the layout and presented it to Trumpton in the pub. And for once, perhaps for the first time ever, there was no initial skirmishing. For once, the guns were silent. Because this was just a pack shot and the logo was emblazoned right across the front of the pack and since there was nothing else in the ad at all except a stupid headline, the logo was almost obscenely big. So big, in fact, that even Bill Trumpton had to admit there was nothing to complain about. Bernie gave a silent inward cheer and that's when Bill Trumpton threw down his thunderbolt.

He took out an envelope and slapped some black-and-white photos down on the table. They were shots of the new pack. Except, they couldn't be because Semtex hadn't commissioned a photographer to shoot it yet. So where could they have come from? Trumpton told him. 'I got one of our chaps in Wigan to knock them off. He's cheaper than these London johnnies, and we need to keep costs down, don't we?' Bernie was thunderstruck. The shots on the table were a clear violation of the code Semtex lived his life by, known as The Art Director's Creed, Article 26 of which states that existing photography is never good enough for use in an ad. All photography has to be specially commissioned.

Bernie's heart was in his boots when he went back to the agency. Existing photography, for God's sake! How was he going to explain this to Semtex? He could hardly trot out the 'keep costs down' line because of Article 31: In the construction of an ad nothing should be undertaken on the grounds that it saves money. Semtex had never once breached it in his entire career.

Bernie didn't waste his breath trying to explain; he knew from long bitter experience there was no point. He just walked in, put the shots down on the desk, and then took out a leather belt and lashed himself to the mast. Then waited for the typhoon. He didn't have to wait long. There was a slight pause, a half-second's silence and then Semtex did a passably good impression of someone who is strapped into Old Sparky and being electrocuted. He clutched the chair arms so fiercely his fingers went white; his eyes bulged and he began to smoke.

'What's this?!' he demanded. He knew what it was, of course – it was quite obviously shots of the new pack, but at the same time that was impossible because he hadn't chosen a photographer yet. There were only two possible explanations: either he was hallucinating or the victim of treachery. He turned to me to test the first hypothesis. 'Is it me?' he asked. 'Is there something wrong with my eyesight?'

And then he did what the military version of Semtex does when it gets rattled. He went off. For ten minutes he raged with all the theatricality of an Italian bus driver, as if using existing photography to save money was the thin end of a wedge that ends with all art directors being murdered in their beds.

When the storm finally subsided, Bernie asked Semtex if he could give him a reasonable explanation that he could take back to Bill Trumpton as to why we couldn't use the shots. Semtex was never very good at rational explanations. His was an instinctive, conceptual, non-verbal trade that relied more on gut instinct such as the unshakeable conviction that only London photographers with two assistants and a Range Rover can shoot ads. Anyone else is a wedding photographer, which is a generic term of abuse for anyone who falls outside the anointed category. All the same, he knew he had to try. So far, the only evidence he had produced against the photographer from Wigan – and even this was supposition – was that he wore a cloth cap.

Eventually he pounced on the assertion that we were about to ruin the ship for a ha'p'orth of tar. To back this up he weeps tears for the client that would have shamed a crocodile. Tears for Trumpton whom he normally refers to as 'that bastard from Wigan'. He points out that since he is one of our biggest accounts he is effectively bankrolling the agency and paying all our salaries. Therefore we owe it to him to do the best possible job and not skimp. This argument among all of them is the one that sticks in Bernie's craw the most and almost gives the poor guy a heart attack. Because it is precisely this argument that he has used to absolutely no effect on numerous occasions in the past and to which Semtex normally retorts that he can't work with a gun to his head. And now Semtex is throwing it back at him. Bernie naturally sneers at him for this, who wouldn't? And Semtex sneers back and shouts, 'Suits! You're all the bloody same. All you ever think about is saving money!' Which obviously isn't a charge that you could lay at Semtex's door. But despite the rank implausibility of Semtex's new-found conscience, Bernie knows he has a problem here. Because it almost sounds plausible. The bogus integrity, the pretence that he is doing this out of the workman's pride in a job well done, and a responsibility to the agency never to do anything less than excellent. If it were true it would be beautiful. And though Bernie is not stupid enough to fall for it, there is someone who is. Mr Crowmere.

Ah! yes, Crowmere, the dear old chairman, the doddery white-haired founding father of the agency. The great thing about Crowmere is this: though hailing from the account-service side he likes to think of himself as 'artistic' – a guy who loves and understands the creative process, a man with a reputation for knowing a good ad when he sees one. He doesn't, of course, but that is neither here nor there. He signals this aspect of his personality by affecting mild eccentricity and a slightly bohemian air, both of which are symbolised by the sartorial shorthand of a bow-tie. Mention the ha'p'orth of tar argument to him and you're in clover.

That's how we came to be wasting fifteen thousand

quid on commissioning new shots at Semtex's insistence, even though there was nothing wrong with the ones we already had, and which cost nothing. Semtex gives the job to one of London's foremost (i.e. most expensive) car photographers, and although the guy in Wigan shot the whole thing in half a morning, it turns out that half a morning is nowhere near enough time in London. It seems it's a far more complicated shoot than anyone imagined and Semtex and the snapper meet up a few days before to have lunch at Bill Trumpton's expense to discuss strategy. Of course Bill doesn't know he's paying because it appears on his final bill as 'bikes and couriers'. You need a lot of couriers when you are shooting a pack of lard, most of them shuttling back and forth to Oddbins.

Part of the difficulty was to do with the lighting and it is decided to have a 'pre-light', whatever that is, which adds to the expense because it means another day. But sacrifices have to be made when you're avoiding the ha'p'orth-of-tar dilemma. Soon we have enough tar to caulk an armada.

After the lunch Semtex comes back in buoyant mood – i.e. pissed – and proceeds to tell me what a knockout job they are going to do on this. Oh good, I think. In fact, he says, it's going to poke my eye out. Oh really, I think. Then he sits down with the pained concentration of a man trying to conceal the fact that he is drunk and says casually, 'You know, I was speaking to Jeff about it and we reckon on this one we might use a red filter.'

How fascinating, I think.

'Sort of beef up the contrast,' he adds.

I nod absent-mindedly.

'Because we need to beef up the contrast.'

Of course.

A look of pious determination appears on his face. 'Trumpton's our oldest client. He's been good to us. Damned good. All this we owe to him.' He raises a magisterial hand like an aristocrat indicating his extensive parks and grounds. 'We take it for granted a lot of the time, but it does us good to be reminded now and then. I really want to do something great for the guy. It's all about being professional, really.'

This new-found interest in Trumpton's welfare is too touching for me and I have to leave the room. And I know the reason for it, too. He's feeling exposed because the realisation is starting to dawn in his breast that in commissioning fifteen grand's worth of pointless photography for a pack of lard he may have overstepped the mark.

The shoot itself is an unremarkable day. I try ringing Semtex at the studio about some unrelated matter at ten and he's not there. So I try again at ten-thirty and at eleven. Then at eleven-thirty he calls me and says they've been hard at it all morning. In the next hour he rings three times, each time, seemingly, to tell me the shot is going to poke my eye out. And then the phone goes dead between the hours of twelve-thirty and four. After that Semtex rings in and tells me in a slurred voice that they've seen the test shots and they are fantastic. Red filter, that's the way to go, he adds.

Next day, he turns up in the office before ten – which is unusual – and we're all waiting for him. Me, Nobby, Gillian the account executive and Bernie. There is a mild air of anticipation in the room, as there usually is on such occasions, but I stolidly refuse to get involved and keep my eye buried in my magazine. Semtex strides in doing a reasonable impression of the cat that got the cream and throws an envelope of shots down on the desk. 'There you are,' he says. 'Red filter. You want a packshot to poke your eye out? Come to me, mate. Fucking red filter, that's the way.'

Bernie takes the shots out and I risk a sly peep over my magazine. The stuff looks OK as far as I can see, but there is a limit to how fantastic you can make a black-and-white shot of a pack of lard look and he certainly hasn't transcended these limitations, even with London's foremost car photographer. Semtex struts around like a peacock and Nobby is leafing through the shots. Nobby is the guy from the production department who takes charge of all the messy inky print and production stuff. You know the sort – sheepskin jacket in summer as well as winter, fingers stained with nicotine, a rolled-up copy of the *Daily Mirror* in his jacket pocket with all the horses marked up for the afternoon. Basically there is nothing under the sun that he doesn't know about print and production. And as Semtex keeps banging on about him being the man to show us all how to do a proper pack shot, Nobby says something. What he actually says, I don't know, because no one can hear. It's one of those situations where there is a lot going on and the general ambient noise drowns out what Nobby says. But it's a funny thing. Sometimes a word can make its presence felt even when you don't actually hear what the word is. And this happens here. A second or so after he speaks we all stop talking and turn to him.

'What?'

And he says with the casual air of one enquiring about the going at Doncaster, 'Where's the logo?'

The people in the room display a remarkable degree of synchronicity in their reactions to this. At exactly the same time we all do the following: turn and nod at the pack shot. Begin vocalisation of the phrase: 'There it is, on the . . .' Abruptly abort the vocalisation. Shoot open eyes, drop jaws. Make ? sound. Bend forward at the hip and look more closely at the pack. Make ! sound. Look round at Semtex.

Laugh.

It seems that a red filter, though being excellent for beefing up contrast, can also make your client's logo – if like Trumpton's it happens to be red – disappear.

There was something strangely appropriate in an advertising sense about the laughter that followed. Do you remember the commercials for Cadbury's Smash in the seventies featuring the Martians? The spot where the one Martian says to the other in his metallic robotic voice, 'On your last trip to Earth, did you discover what the Earthlings eat?' And the answer turns out to be potatoes and they all fall about laughing? That's exactly the sort of laughter that happened next. It went on for five minutes.

The reason the laughter eventually petered out was simple: we knew the best bit was still to come. What on earth is Semtex – who is normally such a cocksure smart arse – going to say? He's not looking happy, that's for sure. His brow is red and glistening and he has put the palm of one hand inside his shirt collar and is rubbing his neck. He composes himself, aware that there is a roomful of people waiting for his response. A roomful of people who are themselves aware that this is very probably the finest moment they will enjoy in advertising. A day on which it is a privilege to be alive. He waves a dismissive hand at the shots and says, 'These are just a few we knocked off as an experiment. I'll call Jeff and get him to send over the others.' He picks up the phone with a noticeably shaking hand and rings. He explains what has happened and then listens, all eyes on his face. It clouds over and gets darker and darker as he listens. And then he says simply, 'I see. Thank you.' Then he puts the phone down, looks at us with a sort of wheedling expression and says, 'That was the assistant. Apparently Jeff is doing a recce' in Monte Carlo for the rest of this week.' He then makes a little scoffing sound in the back of his throat and adds, 'All right for some, eh!'

This joking reference to the lavish lifestyle of photographers – one in which until recently he was an enthusiastic participant – is obviously a desperate attempt to switch allegiances; to smuggle himself out of the doomed citadel and across the border. But one look at our faces tells him the frontier is closed and likely to remain so for quite some time.

The muscles of our faces are, in fact, straining like the rigging of a ship in a gale, struggling to hold back the grins, which are ballooning out like spinnakers. Semtex gives his head a slight jerk as if complaining about a plumber and says, 'The fucking idiot used a red filter on them all!'

The hawsers snap and the laughter explodes with such violence that it sweeps all the paper on the desk into the air. It might have gone on for ever but it gradually subsides to give way to an even more delicious sensation: the thrill of horror as we contemplate the abyss in which Bernie now finds himself. Bernie is due to fly up north after lunch to present the shots to Trumpton. Even if you overlook the fact of the missing logo they did not look to the untrained eye any different to the ones that the cloth-cap-wearing wedding photographer had knocked off in half a morning. And yet we'd just spent fifteen grand and taken three days to do them.

At this point, Nobby assumes command. He takes the phone off Semtex and calls the studio. He asks the assistant if the packs are still there. They are. Good. Then he asks, 'How long have you been assisting Jeff? Two weeks. OK. But you know how to load film, right? OK, go to the fridge, look for the packs of five-four . . .' Basically Nobby gives the novice assistant step-by-step instructions on how to do a re-shoot in under an hour. It is the photographic equivalent of those scenes in the movies where the pilot is dead and a passenger sits at the controls and they talk him down. He tells him what lens to use, what film stock to load, what lights to use. Then he organises a courier – a real one this time as opposed to a bottle of Sancerre – and arranges to collect the film. Shortly after lunch the shots are here – rushed out by one of the numerous labs that owe Nobby a favour. And they're not bad. Not fifteen grand's worth, perhaps, but enough to get Bernie out of a hole. And we all agree. (All except Semtex who thought they could have done with a bit more contrast.) Soon Bernie is on a plane heading north and we all live to see another day.

Like most people I initially misunderstood the symbolism of this episode and regarded it as a great humiliation for Semtex. But with time I have come to realise it was nothing of the sort. It was actually his finest hour.

The day he finally took the Alamo.

NICHOLA McAULIFFE

The Nurglar

LEN WAS eighty-seven when he decided he didn't want to be eighty-eight. There weren't many pleasures left in life since giving up smoking at the age of eighty-three. It wasn't his lungs, they were as robust as the rest of him, no, it was his failing sight. He'd got to the point where he was setting fire to his fingers more often than his pipe.

His daughter was relieved when he did finally give up as she was tired of cleaning ash out of the bath.

But even bathing was difficult now, despite the shiny chrome bars and pulleys his son-in-law had put in with a remarkable amount of swearing and the air of a much tried martyr.

After his eldest daughter had married, unexpectedly, he'd moved in with his youngest. She was a busy woman, always on the move, ready to criticise, no children, no pets. Though she shared his name she had few of his values and almost none of his genes.

Now he sat at the back door, waiting for the robin to pick up the crumbs from his breakfast, waiting for the snooker to start on telly, waiting for some sort of reward for not giving up and shuffling off when his wife died thirty-one years before.

One morning, February it was, depressing month,

damp and dark, no place for an old man whose advice no one wanted and whose skills were now beyond his strength, Len put on his coat and hat and started out for church.

It wasn't far but now he hugged the privet hedges, was careful at kerbstones and always took his stick. His daughter had come into his sitting room last week and found him painstakingly wrapping white electrical tape around it.

If he wanted a white stick, she'd said, they'd get him one. She'd taken his stick away and replaced it with a foldaway state-of-the-art white wand.

It had taken him most of a morning to find where she'd put his stick. It was in the bin. Maybe it was revenge for his throwing her Humpty Dumpty away after she'd dropped it in the po.

His intention, as he walked up to church avoiding the main road, was to start saying his goodbyes. The priest would understand his readiness for death. Len had put a great deal of childlike faith in his prayers over the years and still knelt by his tall bed each night to say them.

'Hello, mister.'

Len had to turn to see who was speaking, the retinas at the back of his eyes were deteriorating. Quite normal in geriatrics apparently. But he knew who it was, the little boy who lived round the corner, and once ran after him when he dropped his bus pass.

'Hello? Is that you?'

He hadn't lost his Welsh accent after sixty years in London.

'Yeah. It's me again. I gotta be off school cos I've got lice.'

Len felt for the wall the boy was sitting on and lowered himself carefully on to it. Everything he did now was careful.

'Not nits this time then?'

The boy laughed, like nits were for babies.

'No. I had nits. I still got the stuff for me 'ead.'

'Ah,' said Len, nodding and reaching for his tobacco pouch. He remembered he didn't smoke any more and put both hands on the warm wooden curve of his walking stick.

'So you're home annoying your mam then.'

His hearing was more acute now his sight was poor and he heard the false bravado in the boy's voice.

'Nah . . . she's at work. I don't need her. I'm nearly ten, right? Dad says she just cramps me style.'

Len nodded. The boy's dad was doing seven years for GBH. Anything he said would, Len knew, carry weight.

'You're on your own then.'

'Yeah,' the boy said.

They sat considering this for a few moments.

'But don't tell no one or they'll put me in care.'

Len made a sound that was neither no nor yes but reassured the boy.

Behind them the dog started barking. It barked like a fog bell in the channel.

The dog had been there longer than most of its newly arrived Volvo-driving neighbours, as had the rundown, scaffolding-clad building it lived in, but that didn't stop the complaints. The boy lived above the dog. The council were keen to remove them all and sell at a profit. Untreated subsidence might well give the excuse.

'So what you up to then?' asked Len out of the companionable silence between them.

'Gonna watch *Robot Wars* when Mum gets home. I can't get in till then cos I set fire to the curtains last time I was on me own.'

Len thought of asking the boy back to his daughter's house but the idea of her finding lice on the carpet discouraged him.

'So what's *Robot Wars* then?'

The boy was suddenly enthusiastic.

'Oh, like it's wicked, you know? Everybody gets to build a robot, yeah? And they're like controlled with a remote thing, like the telly is, then they fight. And the ones on the side, right? They can get your robot if it goes too close, they're like policemen, only they can push you down the hole with the fire or hit you with a big hammer or anything.' The boy was running out of vocabulary. 'It's like . . . awesome. And d'you know what?'

The sharpness Len had sometimes directed at his own children when asked that question had been dulled decades ago. This Len, chatting on a wall in the pale sunshine with a grubby little black lad, would not have been recognised by his own.

'No, I don't know what, you tell me.'

The boy was thrilled, he had knowledge, and some-one who wanted it.

'Anyone can do it. I mean, like, anyone. You just phone up the telly programme and they let you go on.'

Len caught his enthusiasm across the chasm of decades.

'So why don't you?'

The boy deflated like his daughter's Yorkshire puddings. Len's had never deflated but now he wasn't trusted with the cooker, not since the incident with his economy sausages.

Maybe she should lock him out all day. He and the boy could go down the Graig, play in the river . . . no that was then. Trebanos in the Swansea Valley, when a stiff collar would stay white for three days. Before London. Before May died and took the key to the world with her.

The old man looked at the boy's face and saw the shuttered aggression the child called 'me gangsta face'. In five years it would have lost its charm; already it would be enough to intimidate the unprepared.

''Ow can I?' The boy lapsed into the street talk that was neither Jamaica nor London. 'Me got no robot.'

The conversation seemed over as the boy snaked off the wall. But he had nowhere to go and knew Len wasn't the enemy. The enemy was a world that couldn't see who he really was, inside his head.

He subsided back on to the wall, defeated by dreams he had no way of making come true.

Len knew it was easier not to have imagination; two world wars and a depression had taught him that. Keep your head down, do what you have to. But May, she'd always been dreaming. And that daft sister of hers, Bessie, quoting Shakespeare, and the two of them always laughing.

'What's your name?' Len asked.

'Linford. What's yours?'

That was hard. Mister. Mr Mac. His son-in-law insisted on Len, but it rankled. Even Mr and Mrs Poplett from church, and him a knight of Columba, called him Mr Mac. And they were never Bridie and

Philip, not even after fifty years and the children almost marrying.

'Len, my name's Len.'

The boy was unaware of the enormity of the old man's admission. The cloud lifted from the boy and he smiled.

'I got an Uncle Leonard.'

Len automatically made the speech he'd always made, but not for years now. Not since he was young, collecting dropped coal during the General Strike, trying to fill a single bucket in a day.

'No, it's not short for Leonard. My name's Leo. But Mam called me Len.'

'You got any brothers and sisters?'

The vivid sky blue of Len's old eyes got brighter as he thought of them, all but one half-brother, dead. All gone.

'Mam married three times, so I've got . . . I had three families.'

The oldest boy, Will Parker, he'd hardly known. His brother Eugene, sent to stay with 'The Aunts' in times of poverty. And Mr Wright's brood, Denis the rogue, Rene the precious girl, and Arthur, Len's favourite, the first to die.

'Yeah, same with us, we've all got different dads, but it don't make no difference, does it? Except I'm the only one left, the others are in care. I think it makes my mum a bit sad sometimes.'

Len had nodded to Linford's mum occasionally, a washed-out blonde with an ill-fitting body. The sort of woman he used to tut at. The sort of woman who was no better than she should be. Comparing his mam with a woman unable to keep her legs or her family together made him angry.

But anger wasn't what it was and, like smoke, he let it drift away.

The sun had been replaced by a chilly wind and horizontal rain driving the old man and the boy off their wall. The former on to tell the priest he was ready to die, the latter to find shelter.

Later Len walked slowly upstairs to his sitting room, sat in the red plastic armchair, part of the three-piece suite he'd surprised his eldest daughter with. She had been horrified by its intense and undiluted ugliness. But Len, a man for whom beauty lay in price, saw only a bargain and dismissed her aesthetic reservations. She spent hours making Regency brocade covers for the seats but nothing could redeem the sheer nastiness of its conception.

His youngest daughter, welcoming it into her house, suspected the elder had married just to get away from it.

On the arm of his chair lay the volume control for his ear piece. It meant he could turn up the television as loud as he needed without disturbing others watching with him.

But now he watched alone. Even when his daughter and son-in-law were in the house they stayed downstairs, popping in only to say goodnight.

Sometimes he cried with loneliness.

But he didn't know the way to be good company and they flinched at his implied criticism of their lifestyle, language and drinking habits.

He reached for his magnifying glass and, holding the television guide to the light, looked up and down the columns for *Robot Wars*.

*   *   *

The next day he set off for church again but this time hoping he'd see Linford. Sure enough, the boy was kicking a wheelie bin. When he saw Len he left it lying on its side in the middle of the road and came over.

'Yo, Len. How are you, ma man?'

The old man made that sound again, the one that meant neither yes nor no but this time implied he wasn't too impressed.

'Saw your *Robot* programme last night.'

Linford lit up, seeing nothing odd in Len watching it. Len's daughters would have been amazed; it was the sort of thing their father would have dismissed with three short tuts and a 'Rubbish' before flicking through the channels, whether or not they were watching the programme.

'Yeah . . . d'you see that Killer Dragon 2, oh, wow, it was like, wicked, yeah?'

Now he thought about it, he probably would have dismissed this boy with three short tuts and 'Rubbish' a few years back. Before he found what it was like being vulnerable, before he'd discovered the word Sorry.

'The Hammer was better. He beat the Killer, turned him over and put him on the fire.'

Linford considered this, frowning with the effort of debate.

'Yeah . . . I know the Hammer won, like, but, it's well, like, the Killer, right? It's awesome. Really beautiful. The way it was movin' round, and the speed, yeah? It was really beautiful. The Hammer, well, it just got lucky, that's all.'

It's not the winning, it's the taking part. The words came back to Len from his schooldays. A time before the Somme or Ypres were heard of, when people knew their place.

Linford went on, and if a tough kid from South London more used to guns and drugs than *Wind in the Willows* could be wistful, he was.

'I wish I could have something like that.'

'You can,' said Len, looking at his sad, pinched little face. 'And better.'

The little boy was immediately all resentment.

'Nah, man, don't you going sayin' them things –'

'Linford. We'll make you a killer robot. Better than any you've seen on the television.'

The little boy became a little boy again, all round eyes and wonder.

'How?'

Len remembered his youngest daughter's eyes when he'd put an orange down his shirt sleeve to show he had muscles like Popeye, her face when he'd carved a frog out of a block of salt, when he'd blown glass, brought home locusts, and taken her fishing in a sheep's stomach for tape worms. He had been magical then, but her eyes had been dead to him for years.

'Let's go nurgling.'

Linford was immediately on his guard.

'My dad says I'm not to do no burglin'.'

This advice from a convicted armed robber.

'No,' said Len smiling. 'Nurgling. Here, come over here.'

Linford followed the old man across the road and round the corner, narrowly avoiding a van that had appeared just as Len stepped off the kerb. The driver screamed and gesticulated. Len was just deaf and blind enough not to notice.

'Here.' They stopped beside a skip. 'Have a look in there.' Linford peered over the rusted yellow lip. 'Lovely bit of mahogany, that is, crime to throw it away.'

Len started to heave and pull at the length of wood half buried under builders' stour.

'You can' make a robot out of that,' said Linford.

'No . . .' Len succeeded in releasing it, a beautiful piece of polished mahogany five feet long by six inches wide. 'But it'll come in handy.'

He rummaged about in the skip some more and to Linford's astonishment produced a coil of copper wire and some castors.

'You see,' he said, breathless now with the effort, 'nurgling is taking what nobody wants. It's amazing what people throw away, so I do a bit of nurgling.'

'You gonna nurgle a robot.'

'We're going to nurgle the parts and put them all together.'

'How?'

The boy was sceptical again. To him milk came out of bottles, clothes out of shops and robots out of places he didn't even know the names of.

How? Len peered down at him. Yes, that was a good question. He'd learned his science at the Mond Nickel Company and, as a senior lab technician in teaching colleges, there was no piece of apparatus for physics, chemistry or biology he hadn't, in his time, rigged up. But his time was long gone. Could he still do it?

The face of his own son, sneering, made him pause. His son who told his own children of imagined abuse and neglect. Anything but take responsibility for a life dedicated to failure.

Len's eyes filled with the quick tears of the old thinking of the grandchildren he didn't know.

He turned to Linford and through the watery mist saw the trust in the small dark face with its enormous brown eyes. His son's eyes were blue, like his own. Distinctive, watchful, beautiful in a way. But not warm. Never warm.

'How, Linford? How? By magic, that's how.'

The boy sucked his cheeks in over his teeth. It was a black thing, and he was proud of it.

'Magic. That's for babies.'

His brittle sophistication made Len laugh. Linford laughed too.

For the rest of the day they toured the skips of South London. They soon had a system whereby Linford would climb into the skip and root through the contents bringing Len interesting odds and ends. One of the things they'd found was an old pram which they filled with their nurgles.

It was almost dark when they got back. Notwithstanding his youngest daughter's silent disapproval, Len took the boy into his kitchen, off the main one, and made them both doorsteps of cheese on toast and cups of tea, with saucers. It was the first time Linford had ever been given a cup and saucer, not a mug. He liked it. He liked it a lot.

Len pushed back the chenille table cover and the washed thin green check tablecloth then laid out their treasures. The deal table had been second-hand when Len bought it after the war. Linford's fingers ran over its smooth ridges, liking the texture but not knowing why.

'Right,' said Len, 'I'll make a start in the morning.'

The boy knelt up on his bentwood chair, excited. 'Len . . . when will it be ready?'

'When it's ready,' said Len, and saw the boy out before his daughter, aware of what could be said of old men courting the company of young boys, came hovering back to find toast crumbs all over the floor.

It had been years since excitement, not worry, kept Len awake but that night his mind was alive with thoughts of transmitters, reverse polarities and soldering irons.

He was up early, before the heating came on. He put on his long-johns and vest, his 'disreputable' trousers, as his daughters called them, a shirt and the zip-up cardigan his eldest had knitted him. He wasn't that keen on its dusky pinkish bobbles but it was warm, and it was February.

He went down into the cellar where all his tools had been put when he moved. They were laid out neatly, the planes, awls, ratchets, clamps and the last he'd used to sole the family shoes. Saws hanging on the wall and the green-painted set of drawers he'd made to house his nuts, bolts, screws, washers and nails on top of his youngest daughter's old toy box. He'd made that too.

He found all he was looking for, although it took him a while to remember where his lump of solder was, in the deal-table drawer with the string, a blue bead rosary and May's spare set of teeth.

He moved his Anglepoise lamp down from his sitting room into his kitchen and laid everything out. He balanced his magnifying glass on two half-bricks from the garden. His old oxy-acetylene torch, still fresh with grease smeared fifteen years before, cut the metal easily, his eyes protected by a pair of old sunglasses.

All day he cut and soldered, wired and tested. The hardest bit, he knew, would be the remote control.

After a week working on the robot, all day, every day, he thought he'd have to give up. His eyes were too dim, his hands too stiff. He couldn't do it.

Linford, who'd knocked on the door each morning saying, 'Is it ready yet, Len?' would have to be disappointed.

He was eighty-seven, he couldn't do it. It was the lowest moment of his life.

Then he heard May's voice. Saw her laughing, pulling her chin back into her neck, crinkling her eyes till they disappeared.

'Come on, Len,' she said. 'Your mam's here, you can do it.'

And there they both were, May in her floral dress and felt hat, ready for tea. His mother, Beatrice, dark hair in wisps around her always-laughing face, her wrapover pinny and capable forearms.

'Just this,' his mother was saying, her hand, younger than his, on his arm. 'Just do this for the lad, don't let him down . . .'

And he knew if he could just finish this, he could go. Slip away and be with them. He wouldn't have to miss them any more.

He looked again at the pile of wires, wheels and bits of metal and started again.

After almost three weeks he let Linford in. The boy was on his way to school, cured of his infestation.

On the deal table was a shape under a torn sheet.

The boy's eyes were flicking between Len and the table. In the old man's mind his son's face on Christmas morning and this one melted together. Linford wiped away the memories of resentful ingratitude.

Len carefully raised the sheet and the memories were replaced with shouts of joy and squeals of absolute delight.

On the table stood a sleek, ground-hugging, curved and cornered box armed with a fearsome tearing arm and hammer.

Linford was transfixed. It was state-of-the-art. It was Wicked. It was Bad. It was far, far beyond his vocabulary.

Len handed him the remote control, with its colour-coded buttons and miniature gear stick.

The boy stood in awed silence.

'Come on then, let's try her out,' said Len, leading the way on to the patio.

It wasn't until his daughter got home from work they realised they had played with the robot all day.

The following weeks saw Linford transform from being the boy nobody wanted to the school star. His robot, Stealth Destroyer, was photographed for the local paper and was to be seen demonstrating its fearsome abilities on the concrete playground at every break.

The head contacted *Robot Wars* and there was to be an audition for the next series. Linford was cool about it, he said he'd have to ask his mum.

The night he saw Len to ask him to be on the Destroyer's team, the old man was in bed. Linford thought he looked very small and a bit frightened.

His cheekbones were sharp under his skin and his

nose looked oddly hollow. Linford was aware there was something wrong but he didn't know what, even when Len's daughter brought him a Coke and told him Len might go soon, but not to worry.

'So, like, d'you wanna be the team captain when we do it on telly? I'd operate it cos I'm really fast, but you can talk about how you built it an' everything. What do you think?'

Len smiled and said, 'Maybe.' The word his daughters and now Linford understood as probably. Yes, but not now.

Linford was happy.

That night Len died.

After the funeral the cortège made its way to a rain-sodden field where Len's oak coffin was lowered into a flooded hole. Linford and his mum stood a little away from the well-dressed mourners. A woman, Len's middle daughter, dropped long-stemmed yellow roses into the grave.

A man, sharp-faced and angry, stepped up with a clod of fresh-dug clay and hurled it, his face contorted with hate, on to the coffin lid. It landed with a loud dead thud. This was the son whose name Len had all but forgotten.

Linford waited until they'd gone before he walked forward. It was raining hard now and the square-walled hole was filling with water. Linford wondered if the coffin might float. He looked down and saw the vivid yellow flowers bright against the polished oak. Nice bit of wood, he thought. Come in handy. But it was spoiled by the lump of clay, thrown by the spite-faced man, which had landed on the silver nameplate.

Linford didn't like that; he looked back at his mother but she was having trouble with her shoes in the mud.

From his pocket he pulled a baseball cap. Carefully he opened it up, took aim and dropped it, like a hoop over a fairground prize, on to the ugly lump of clay, covering it completely.

The rain stopped and the sun, unexpectedly warm and bright, lit up the grave.

It was perfect. The red Team Destroyer baseball cap sat in the centre of the coffin lid and visible from above were the glittering diamond words:

THE NURGLAR.

He watched the words sparkling for a few minutes then Linford didn't know what else to do so he said goodbye and went back to his mother.

They turned to walk home.

At the gates of the cemetery was a half-filled skip. It was then Linford realised he'd never see the Nurglar again.

His mum realised he was crying. She handed him a screwed-up tissue from her sleeve.

'Yeah, he was a lovely old man, Linford.'

He took the tissue and looked at it, lost.

'He was magic, Mum, magic.'

TOBY YOUNG

Office Politics

R AYMOND E. HARPER, the editor-in-chief of *Fan-fare: The In-Flight Magazine of the GulfStream Jet Set*, was the very picture of prosperity. His Anderson & Shepherd suit, his Hilditch & Key shirt, his Turnbull & Asser tie, his New & Lingwood shoes – all announced to the world that he was a Powerful & Important man. He was in Liz Smith only that morning, for Chrissakes. What was it she'd described him as? 'A high priest of the global parish'? Not bad for an eighty-five-year-old spinster. At least she'd spelt his name right. So why wasn't he happy?

By rights, he should have been luxuriating in the events of that afternoon. He'd just returned from the VH1 Magazine Awards, where *Fanfare* had picked up awards in three different categories: 'Airbrushing', 'Celebrity Wangling' and – the one he was proudest of – 'Least Hideous Cover Shot'.

More importantly, that idiot Bartholomew Hooper had won nothing. *Men: The Magazine for Man* had been nominated in five categories and Hooper, its editor-in-chief, had prepared five different acceptance speeches. Five! What a chump. Harper recalled with some satisfaction the little pile of screwed-up balls of paper that had grown beneath Hooper's chair as the afternoon wore on. Damn, if that wasn't a Kodak moment, he didn't know what was.

Better yet was the surprise Zach Goldman had prepared for Harper when he returned to the office. The billionaire owner of Global Media, which published both *Fanfare* and *Men*, had snuck out of the award ceremony early and arranged for the magazine rack in the lobby of the Global Media building to be covered with copies of *Fanfare*. What a fitting tribute. Oh! My! God! When Hooper first set eyes on that concession stand, Harper thought he was going to stroke out.

'What the hell's going on here?' Hooper had screamed at the little old lady behind the counter. Before she could reply he had started clawing at the copies of *Fanfare* like some demented lunatic, tossing them this way and that. A full-blown tantrum, right there in the lobby, at four o'clock in the afternoon! Another Kodak moment! Harper had already got his assistant to place that story on Page Six in tomorrow's edition of the *New York Post*.

Yet somehow it wasn't enough. At the back of his mind, something else still rankled, a blemish that the afternoon's events, satisfying though they were, couldn't quite erase.

'Muffy,' barked Harper, addressing his Radcliffe-educated assistant. 'Fix up an appointment for me with Office Services. Urgent.' He had an afterthought. 'And when you're through with that, go get me one of them Iced Venti Lattes from Starbuck's, would ya?' He paused for a second. 'And half a dozen of them Krispy Kreme Donuts.'

He leaned back in his Eames chair and stroked his

powerful, matinée-idol chin. He knitted his brow, as if contemplating the great affairs of state. He reached a decision.

'Muffy,' he announced. 'Better make it a dozen.'

'So, Ray, what can I do for you?'

Harper eyed the woman opposite him suspiciously. How could anyone let themselves get that fat? Marjorie Phipps, the head of Office Services at Global Media, must have weighed in at over 300 lbs. Where on earth did she get that red suit? Must have been at one of them special stores. What were they called? High and Mighty? Big and Tall? The Elephants on Parade, more like. He glanced at her right hand. Good God! She was married.

'It's my office, Marj,' said Harper, in what was supposed to be a world-weary tone, but came out as more of a whine. 'I can't deal with it. It's making me claustrophobic.'

Suddenly, Phipps shut her eyes and her whole body started wobbling violently. What the hell was going on? Then Harper figured it out: she was laughing.

'Forgive me,' she said, 'it's just that every editor at Global Media wants a larger office. Claustrophobia? It's the second-largest office in the building, if I recall. Can't you do better than that?' She started wobbling again.

'It's a goddamn closet, Marj,' protested Harper. 'How can I be expected to hold editorial meetings in there? By the time I've packed everyone in it's like Grand Central Station.'

Phipps adopted a patient expression as if explaining something to a child.

'The only way we could make your office bigger is if we allocated more office space to *Fanfare* overall and as soon as we do that you know as well as I do what'll happen – every other magazine in the building will start clamouring for more space. Sorry, Ray. No can do.'

Harper thought about this.

'It's got to be possible,' he said. 'Isn't there some way of making my office larger without allocating more space to *Fanfare* per se?'

This is too much, thought Phipps.

'Look, Ray, the only way this could be done is if you redesigned *Fanfare's* offices within their existing boundaries and then made your office bigger and everyone else's smaller.'

She leaned back and folded her arms. Surely that would put an end to it.

'OK,' said Harper. 'Let's do that.'

'What?'

'What you said. Make everyone else's offices smaller and mine bigger.'

She was shocked.

'You'd really be prepared to do that to your staff? Reduce the size of all their offices just so yours could be even larger?'

Harper paused. Just how much of his hand should he reveal? He decided to risk it.

'The thing is, Marj,' he said, leaning forward, 'I only want to expand my office by two square feet. The amount I'd need to take from everybody else's offices would be negligible. It wouldn't make any difference to them, but it would make a great deal of difference to me.' He gave her a meaningful look.

Suddenly, the truth dawned on her. Phipps was flabbergasted. The effrontery of the man!

'D'you realise how much it would cost to redesign *Fanfare's* offices? We're talking millions of dollars.'

Her words were lost on Harper. Apparently, he was under the impression he'd won the argument. He got up from his chair and prepared to leave.

'I'm going to take the matter up with Zach. He may well regard it as an appropriate reward for *Fanfare's* outstanding performance at the VH1 Magazine Awards.'

'Well, good luck,' said Phipps, trying to sound as sceptical as she possibly could. But in her gut she had a sinking feeling that Harper was going to get away with it.

Exactly a year later, Raymond E. Harper strode through the lobby of the Global Media building with the confident, purposeful gait of a young senator. The fact that the concession stand was festooned with copies of *Men: The Magazine for Man* didn't bother him. True, Hooper had only won two VH1 Magazine Awards that year, not three, but after last year it was only fitting that he should have his own little tribute. Harper wasn't about to tear into the magazine rack like some spoilt child. God, what a moron.

Harper also had his new train set to play with. He loved everything about *Fanfare's* new offices – its wooden surfaces, its tinted glass, its cigar-bar ambience. Above all, he adored his own office. It didn't look any bigger, of course, but then it was the size of an in-line skating rink to begin with. In one crucial respect, though, it was one thousand per cent better.

His office was now the largest in the building. More importantly, it was exactly one square foot bigger that Bartholomew Hooper's. It had cost Global Media $3.6 million, but, boy, had it been worth it.

Now then, he thought to himself. How exactly am I going to communicate this information to that chump Hooper?

CELIA BRAYFIELD

Listomania

'THE MORE you see of people,' said Mr Downs, 'the more you have to like cats, really.'

Have to what? Have to? Oh God, not something else I have to do. I can't do any more, I can't. Not one more thing. No, no, wait a minute. He didn't mean that. Joke, right? Joke. Smile, quickly. Look on top of it. You are on top of it. You are. Thirty seconds gone. Smile.

Jane smiled at Mr Downs. Mr Downs flashed his eyebrows and looked away through the venetian blinds at his companion, who was on the street outside. He had come to the surgery with another tall, well-built man. They wore the same jeans, with a motif embroidered on the back pocket. The other man was drooping against a wall and taking drags on his cigarette as if it had been lit on purpose to annoy him.

'And who've we got here?' she asked, turning to the pet carrier on the examination table. More than a minute gone already. Time allowed for consultation was twelve minutes. Dear God, a Burberry-printed pet carrier, with a matching label.

'His name's Rajah,' said Mr Downs.

A dark velvet paw crossed the plastic threshold, followed by black gossamer whiskers, a wet nose, a

141

sleek head, and then the rest of the cat. A superb cat, the colour of macchiato coffee, its tail tensile under her fingers.

'A Burmese.' Jane turned to her computer to enter the breed in the file. Owner, address, patient name, breed, age, distinguishing marks. Nearly three minutes gone.

'Absolutely,' said Mr Downs, with a glint of eye through his square spectacles.

It pleased Rajah to look graciously around the consulting room and sniff the air.

'Age?'

'Not sure. About two. I adopted him.'

Rajah permitted Jane to look at his teeth. Two years old seemed reasonable. She entered his age on his file. Four minutes.

'I never saw the point of cats until he came along,' said Mr Downs. 'I wasn't brought up with animals. One of my friends had him and couldn't keep him because she got a new boyfriend who was allergic. So I said I'd have him until she found him a proper home, and that was it, really. I just couldn't bear to let him go.'

Please, dear owner, don't talk to me, I haven't got time. No offence, but I really haven't. Vaccinations, operations, infections, allergies. 'Has he had his injections?' She felt below Rajah's silky ears for the lymph glands.

'Don't know, didn't ask,' said Mr Downs. 'What should he have had?'

'Feline enteritis and cat flu, we recommend. And a lot of people are going for leukaemia as well.'

'I didn't know cats got leukaemia.'

Rajah swished his tail. His heart sounded strong, his breathing was excellent, his abdomen was free of lumps, his eyes were bright, his teeth all present and exceptionally clean, his coat was glossy, his breath was sweet and his attitude to being examined was positive; positive for a Burmese, anyway. Just a wee bit of a growl when she felt his tummy. Six minutes left.

'The problem is,' said Mr Downs, 'he's jealous. Jealous of my partner. He goes for him. Teeth, claws, everything. Just without any provocation. Just bombs across the room and has a go. Yesterday we were watching *Antiques Roadshow* and Rajah just leaped on the sofa and fanged my partner's hand. He was bleeding.'

'Naughty boy,' said Jane, looking at Rajah's eyelids, which were a superb colour, loaded with haemoglobin.

The cat sighed. The ribcage heaved under the glossy pelt, the eyes rolled, he twisted his head out of her hand.

'Burmese can be very emotional,' Jane began, allowing Rajah to prowl the edge of the examination table so she could inspect his rear.

'Tell me about it,' said Mr Downs.

'And sometimes very insecure. Behaviour problems are usually linked to some kind of anxiety.'

Only four minutes left. Nestling under Rajah's tail was a fine pair of testicles, enrobed in ebony fur.

'He hasn't been neutered,' she said.

'Well, he might turn into a handsome prince one day,' said Mr Downs. 'And then I won't be pleased I sent him to the vet, will I? Is it a problem, leaving him his balls?'

'They're usually less aggressive once it's done,' said Jane. 'It makes them quieter generally. They don't stay out all night getting into fights, then come back and spray nasty smells on the furniture.'

'I just use Febreze,' confided Mr Downs. 'Is there anything I can do without giving him the snip? Because it's getting to the stage that my partner's saying either the cat goes or I do.'

Through the venetian blinds, the partner could now be seen standing in the middle of the pavement and glaring at the surgery door, his fists in the pockets of his grey hooded top.

'Try getting your partner to give Rajah his food,' Jane suggested. Two minutes, the clock was ticking.

'He's a vegetarian,' moaned Mr Downs.

'Pay Rajah extra attention when you and your partner are together. He needs to be reassured that your relationship doesn't threaten him.' One minute and ten.

Rajah stood at the corner of the table, swishing his tail again. 'But it does threaten him,' Mr Downs pointed out.

'Get some of those cat treats and when you sit down together to watch TV, give Rajah some of them. Or get your partner to do it.' Forty seconds.

'Won't he put on weight? I love him being so skinny. They say people's pets look like them, don't they. I keep hoping.' Mr Downs was not a slender man.

'They don't put on weight easily,' she reassured him. 'You can stroke him and talk to him as well. Just make him feel loved.' That's it, your time is up. We're over-running now.

Rajah mewed and shivered his tail. From the street

outside, the partner gave a petulant shrug and lit up another cigarette. 'Why is it down to me to make everyone else feel loved?' asked Mr Downs.

'I know,' Jane agreed. 'But cats do respond to a bit of extra TLC.'

'The more I see of cats,' said Mr Downs, 'the less I like people, really. You've got to agree. In your profession. I'll ask about the injections.'

'Bring him back if he hasn't had them,' she said. 'You don't need an appointment, we can do them any time.'

Jane entered her advice on Rajah's file. The consultation had over-run one minute and fifteen seconds. There was an automatic timetable checker installed in the computer system by the practice manager.

Mr Downs left, carrying Rajah, his partner falling resentfully into step behind him. Nobody else was waiting so she closed up the surgery and got into her car.

Jane's body drove her car. Jane's mind was a whirlwind of things she had to do, places she had to be, people she had to call, facts she had to remember, procedures she had to follow, things she had to buy or clean or find or put in Ella's school bag; Ella was her daughter. Her existence was represented by the list in the car: Marmite, cornflakes, Kleenex, Calpol, marking pen, swimming goggles, school shirts.

At that moment, Ella was just one more piece of life swept up in this great merciless twister of duties and carried away to oblivion in a cloud of dust and lies and broken promises.

She could have blamed her parents, who went through life in a frenzy of accomplishment, especially her father, who quoted Kipling on getting the hump to amuse his children.

> The Camel's hump is an ugly lump
> Which all may see at the zoo
> But uglier still is the hump that we get
> From having too little to do.

She could have blamed her teachers, because the more she did the more they praised her and gave her top marks, especially in biology. She could have blamed her profession, her parents' profession before her, competitive to enter and demanding to practise. She could have blamed the patients, or their owners, because, being deeply kind of heart, Jane could not see pain without wanting to make it better. However, Jane blamed nobody. To people like Jane, blame is just a waste of time. If she ever felt a twinge of resentment she stifled it and got on with the next thing.

People like Jane make wonderful mothers. Most days, she left the practice in time to pick up her daughter Ella from school. Today, with nothing in the diary except a tooth extraction on a German Shepherd and kidney stone in a crossbred shorthair, she was free by three and could treat herself to a trip to B&Q on the way.

It was a peerless luxury to spend an hour in the DIY store, taking a solitary stroll between the aisles of paint, wallpaper, tools, timber, tiles, nails, screws, bathroom fittings, curtain rails, patio slabs, cement, adhesives and grouting. It was luxurious because the things to do there were simple and finite. The list was

146

short: shelves, Polyfilla, Superglue. That was it. Three things.

Listomania had sneaked up on her. The original plan, as outlined by her husband, Richard, over many a happy bottle of wine at Rigoletto's café on the High Road, had been a classic happy-every-after scenario. They would get married and buy a flat, and he would do up the flat, and they would have some children and then they would sell the flat and go to live in the country somewhere with space and time and trees, and roses round the door.

In year one, they bought the flat, Richard lost his job and knocked down two walls, and Jane got pregnant. 'The place'll be a palace by the time the baby's born,' he promised her. But their marriage was already infected. To a doer like Jane, having a non-working spouse feels like running through life in concrete trainers.

In year two, the walls remained demolished, Richard brought home wine in five-litre boxes and Ella was born. 'When *are* you going to get this stuff out of here?' Jane asked, stepping over the rubble with the precious bundle in her arms.

'In my own time,' he answered, 'and when you stop nagging me.'

In year three, the walls remained demolished, Richard worked sporadically, and drank wine by the lake and Ella developed asthma, aggravated by the plaster dust. Jane hired a builder. Richard sacked him.

'We've got to get this place sorted,' she appealed. 'We can't bring up a family like this.'

'You're obsessed with the baby,' he accused her.

'She's your baby too,' Jane said.

147

'You do everything for her,' he said.

'Only because you don't do anything for her.'

'Only because you do everything and you shut me out so I can't do anything.'

Jane was not brave enough to say a baby's bottle could not be made in Richard's own time. Nor did she add that she didn't trust Ella with him because he was never sober after midday.

In year four, she started making lists. Listing what she had to do made her feel calmer. Richard left, to live with a waitress from Rigoletto's. 'I can't live with a woman who hasn't got any time for me,' he told her. 'You're obsessed with your career.'

'Last year you said I was obsessed with the baby,' she said.

'You've changed,' he had accused her. 'You've got so ambitious you haven't got time for anything else.'

'But you aren't earning anything,' she pointed out. 'You won't get a job and you won't work on the flat and we have to eat.'

'How can I get a job when you undermine me all the time? You and your bloody lists. You're always making lists. You've taken away my confidence.'

'But there's so much to do,' she protested. 'You don't realise. If I don't make lists I'll forget. You can't forget things when you've got a child to think about.'

'And my family,' he raged on. 'You're trying to take Ella away from me too. Well, now the court can decide about that.'

The court decided that Ella should spend every second weekend with Richard, plus a week of full-time holiday, and that Richard was owed a quarter of Jane's net income, in lieu of a share of the value of the flat, which was still a wreck with rubble on the floor, and now worth less than they had paid for it. Jane made lists of pros and cons. The only answer, said the lists, was to make the flat a habitable home, and therefore worth selling. Jane rehired the builder and gave him a list.

Without Ella, she got miserable at the weekends. One empty Sunday she found herself standing between four expectant walls of bare plaster, remembering one of her lecturers saying, 'If you can give a guinea-pig an enema, you can do pretty much anything else in life.' So she made a list and went to B&Q.

Painting the walls was her first job, and just as she was finishing, her neighbour looked in. Kath was probably fortysomething, as round as a bun and exactly unlike her husband Diarmuid, who was thin and twitchy with hollow cheeks and skin a peculiar greenish-grey colour. Diarmuid worked in the local tax office. In a family of large families, they were childless.

'My, that does look nice,' Kath said, venturing through the half-open door.

'You must be delighted,' she went on, looking around, 'after all what he left you to live with.'

'Yes,' said Jane. 'And it only took a couple of days.'

'A lovely colour. You chose it yourself, I bet. That's the thing about doing it yourself; you can have everything exactly the way you want it, isn't that so?'

'Yes,' said Jane. And so it began. Another Richard weekend, another list, another trip to B&Q, another frenzy of activity to heal her heart. Another room done.

'Isn't that superb?' said Kath. 'You've a real eye, Jane, you know that?'

And so it had gone on, for a couple of years now.

Two days after his first visit, Mr Downs returned, with his partner sulking behind him and Rajah in the designer pet carrier. Jane found she was pleased. It was an unfamiliar sensation. She didn't often have time to notice how she felt about anything.

'Vaccinations,' said Mr Downs. 'We do need some. He hasn't had them.'

'And how's the jealousy?' She set up the vaccines in their tiny glass vials.

'We-ell . . . we did what you said. He just ate the treats and fanged my partner anyway. But not quite so badly. He might be getting the idea. But we're going on holiday, so hopefully he'll miss us or something.' Part of what she liked about Mr Downs, Jane realised, was the affectionate contempt with which he viewed the petty insanities of those who shared his life, feline or human.

And then, of course, there was Rajah. Growling about being vaccinated, as a Burmese might. But one hell of a cat. Definitely a cut above the overfed suburban moggies that made up half the patient list. The thought of what Rajah might do to a home while the owners were on holiday was disturbing.

'I was going to ask you,' said Mr Downs, as if he could read her mind, 'about a kennel or something. We could get people to come in and feed him, but . . .'

'Burmese do not like being on their own,' Jane agreed. 'We recommend this place.' She gave him the brochure for the Purr & Bark Hotel for Animal

Companions, in Berkshire. 'They pick up from the surgery here by appointment. They're very good.'

'Perfect,' said Mr Downs. 'I'll get it set up for next Friday.'

When she got home that evening, Kath was hovering. 'I want to see your shelves,' she said, half giggling with excitement. 'Diarmuid said you must be putting up shelves – we could hear from the hammering.'

'I'm sorry . . .' Jane began.

'Don't you be sorry about a thing,' Kath commanded her. 'I think you're a marvel, all you do. You've made your place look really lovely. I was telling Diarmuid, the great lazy pudding, never does a thing in our place, you put him to shame.'

Jane was never good with admiration. 'It's just I get miserable when Ella's over with her father.'

'So you get up and you get going and you get things done instead of moping around,' said Kath. 'Good on you, I say. Oh, will you look at that. Aren't they the thing, those shelves? Like something you see on the telly.'

'I haven't painted them,' Jane explained. 'I'm going to paint them blue. Next weekend. She's going to her father for the whole week.'

'Never mind, love.' Kath patted her arm. 'You've got the right spirit and he hasn't. You'll be the winner, I'm sure you will. Diarmuid!' She called out into the corridor for her husband. 'He's lying on the damn sofa watching his football, what's the betting. Diarmuid! Will you come and look at this now?'

Diarmuid appeared in his own doorway, looking as healthy as a corpse risen recently from the grave. 'Come and see how nice Jane has made this flat of hers,' his wife ordered. 'Come and get some ideas for our place.'

'Nothing wrong with our place,' Diarmuid mumbled.

'Men have no imagination, have they?'

Later than evening, Ella complained, 'There's shouting in my wall, Mummy.'

When she listened at the head of her daughter's bed, Jane heard raised voices from the flat next door. Kath berated her husband loudly for several hours.

'I've made her jealous,' Jane said to herself.

'She shouldn't be jealous, she's still married,' Ella observed. Her daughter had suddenly developed an instinct for stabbing her in the soft underbelly of guilt with a killer remark.

'Yes, darling, but he doesn't look very well, does he?' It was all Jane could think of to say.

Next evening, Ella told her, 'There's banging in my wall now.'

Jane met Diarmuid shortly afterwards, gasping as he made for the stairwell, his arms around a plastic sack of rubble. Jane wanted to apologise for setting the example that had lost him his right to rest after a hard day at the tax office, but couldn't think of a way to do it without making the poor man feel worse.

The next Friday, Rajah arrived at the surgery as planned, on his way to the Purr & Bark Hotel for Animal Companions, whose van would call at midday to collect him. 'Be a good boy now,' Mr Downs admonished him. 'No savaging the room service. I don't want you getting barred for life.'

Behind the grille of the pet carrier, the cat sat like an

Egyptian statue, his eyes closed, his tail curled over its paws. He was more beautiful than Jane remembered. It seemed a shame to shut him in the back office while she saw the rest of the morning's patients.

By midday, the Purr & Bark van had not arrived. Omigod, the schedule was going to be derailed. Jane felt her chest start to shrink. It didn't take much, at that time, for her to get breathless with anxiety.

The telephone rang. The redoubtable tones of Purr & Bark's proprietor. 'We can't take your cat,' she announced, at maximum volume. 'I'm sorry, but we can't. We're having an outbreak. Feline idiopathic meningitis. Vet's quarantined us this morning – we're having to send the animals home.'

Rajah's eyes opened half a millimetre. It was not until some weeks later that Jane realised that she had never heard of feline idiopathic meningitis. At the time, she thought of Mr Downs and his partner, probably already at the airport, and of her afternoon list, which was long, and of how, with Ella spending the week with Richard and his mother in the country, the flat was going to be awfully empty.

The cat's eyes were open fully, two orbs of dark topaz, flickering as he watched her pace up and down the room. He shifted slightly on his paws. He seemed to expect something.

She called Mr Downs on his mobile. 'I could try another cattery, but it wouldn't be one we know.' Heavens, but she was plausible. 'Or I could take him home myself. We're not really supposed to . . .'

'But he's just irresistible!' Mr Downs sounded elated already. 'He's put a spell on you, hasn't he? So do it. I trust you. I'm sure he'll be fine. If he gets picky about his food, just try him with smoked salmon and I'll pay you back for it. See you in two weeks, eh? Bye, now.'

A great rush of guilt hit Jane so hard that she had to sit down. Rajah blinked at her. He nodded his head. No, he did not. Cats do not nod their heads, unless they are made of flocked plastic and placed on a car's rear windowsill. Jane ruffled her hair, hoping to get her brain back to normal. Because there was a strange lack of focus about her thoughts now. Nothing seemed clear any more. It made her feel quite dizzy.

Rajah decided to lie down. He settled himself in a watchful pose, with his front legs folded beneath his chest, neat as a duck on the water. There was nothing a cat could do that made Jane feel fonder. Her heart, her tough, scarred and well-protected professional heart, just melted when cats lay down on their paws like that.

'Come on,' she said, picking up the pet carrier. 'You're coming home with me.' Rajah shut his eyes again, as if he looked forward to eternal bliss.

At home that night, when she opened the carrier, he walked out calmly and set off around the flat, sniffing, his tail waving lazily.

Her task for the weekend was painting the shelves. After that, while Ella was still with Richard, she planned new tiles for the kitchen. In preparation, she assembled the stuff on the list: sandpaper, primer, brushes, paint, white spirit, jam pots, kitchen roll, old newspaper and a rag. Rajah jumped on the table to inspect these materials but promptly jumped off and headed for the sofa. Duty was buzzing in her head like a trapped bluebottle, but Jane ignored it and followed the cat. He rewarded her by purring.

Her fingers, used to being occupied, almost twitched

for something to do. Her mind was woozy with idleness. She got up and lit some candles, but it seemed to disturb Rajah, who raised his head and watched her. She sat down again and stroked him, which made him start to purr again and rub his head against her hand.

The space around her, a vast desert when Ella wasn't there, seemed smaller and warmer. Cosy, almost. Faintly, from the flat next door, came the sounds of Diarmuid hammering. Jane turned on the TV and found programmes about people painting up their homes, lashed into action by sneering presenters. I should be doing that, she told herself. But I will sit here with the cat for a while.

After a time she felt tired, a soft, luxurious kind of tiredness that snuggled around her like a lover's arms. 'Time for bed,' she said aloud, wondering why she was talking to herself. 'Goodnight, Rajah,' she said, and, having no Ella to kiss, leaned down and kissed the cat on the top of his head.

Immediately the room filled with smoke, dense, dark-brown smoke that billowed around her so violently that Jane leaped up, screamed and stumbled for the door. But the smoke was not choking, as she feared, and she could breathe it in and out easily. It was warm, and smelled of spices, cloves and cinnamon, and something fresh, like the seashore, but slightly burnt, like toast. And it was thick, although she thought she saw sparks in it. Her eyes were not stinging, but the smoke blotted out all the room.

Had Diarmuid hit a gas pipe? Had somebody burned their dinner? Had a firework been thrown through the window? She leaned against a wall, feeling panic give way to puzzlement. The smoke was clearing now, as fast as it had appeared.

There was a man on the sofa. A beautiful man with black hair and skin the colour of macchiato coffee, lounging at the end of the sofa. He crossed his legs, a rustle of silk. 'Well done,' he said. His teeth were fine and white, the incisors a little long. 'I thought you were never going to get it.'

'Where did you come from?'

'You know where I came from. You carried me in yourself.'

'I carried the cat in. Where's the cat?' There was still a smell of cinnamon in the room, but no sign of Rajah. Unless . . .

'I am the cat.'

'Don't be silly.'

'You knew the deal. Didn't you listen to our Mr Downs? You kiss me, I turn into a prince. Shazam. Just like that.'

Jane opened her mouth to say something instinctive and maternal, like, 'Rubbish,' then paused. The person on the sofa looked very much like a prince. He wore Asian clothes, in dark-brown silk, heavily embroidered in gold. A jewel glittered in one of his earlobes, possibly a diamond. There were gold rings on his fingers. Most persuasive of all, he had a languid air of inbred authority.

'There,' he said, as if he could read her thoughts. 'You see. It's true. Now, I'm starving. Whatever that was you put down earlier – don't ever give me that again. Have you got any real food in this place?'

'Nine out of ten cats . . .' Jane protested.

'Don't be pathetic,' he said, recoiling from the sofa

156

and prowling towards the kitchen. 'And I don't eat pasta, either.'

He was not tall, she noticed, but distinctly lithe. 'Well, you've got eggs, I suppose,' he said, shutting the fridge door with a disdainful hand. 'I'll order us something. It's not usually too bad.' From a pocket beneath the gold embroidery he produced a platinum credit card and a state-of-the-art mobile phone. 'Hello. Yes. Yes, it's me. Yes, the sea-bass. For two. And the prawns. And that cream dessert thing. Syllabub, that's right. Oh, and put in some smoked salmon as well. Yes, champagne as usual. As soon as possible.'

'Am I dreaming?' Jane asked him.

'No,' he said, strolling back to the sofa. 'And unfortunately you can't kiss me, or we go through all that smoke business and I turn back into the cat. But you'd have to catch me first, of course. And I'm pretty quick.'

'Do you like being a prince?'

'Well, wouldn't you? I like being a cat as well, really I do. But I wasn't about to go to that hotel place.'

When the food arrived, delivered by a uniformed chauffeur from, she noticed, an extremely smart restaurant, he ate his with ferocious speed, then finished what was left on her plate. She gave him all her syllabub anyway, since she was in the habit of denying herself cream. The smoked salmon he ordered to be put in the fridge for breakfast, and he handed her the champagne, saying, 'You people like this stuff, don't you?'

'That was excellent,' he said when the meal was over, wiping his mouth delicately at each side with his fingertips. 'I can sleep properly now. Didn't you say it was time for bed?'

157

Jane had a flash vision of the cat's furry testicles.

'*Please*,' he said, yawning to the full extent of his razor-sharp jaws, 'I hate to tell you this, my dear, but you aren't in season. I think there are a few females down the road somewhere who might be coming on, but it's a filthy wet night and I really can't be arsed.' He was making for her bedroom as he spoke. 'And in case you're wondering, I only mate with females. Not that I haven't been asked. Mmmn. *What* a comfortable bed. You can have the sofa, if you're worried.'

Jane sat on the sofa for quite a while. She pinched one hand with the other – yes, she felt pain. Yes, this was happening. Yes, that cat had turned into a prince, and he could read her mind and he was now sleeping in her bed. This is totally, one hundred per cent, guaranteed freaky. Why aren't I in shock? She ruffled her own hair, took a handful and pulled, but her thoughts refused to be helpful. The champagne didn't help.

She peeked into the bedroom. The man who was Rajah was deeply asleep, sprawled over three-quarters of the mattress, his silk clothes draped over the chair. She decided to play it safe and take the sofa.

Hours later, she felt something warm and heavy by her feet. There he was, sitting on her new velvet cushion and wearing, she was reassured to note, some kind of pyjamas in dark-brown linen. 'Isn't it breakfast time?' he asked.

She checked her watch. 'Do you usually have breakfast at 4.45 a.m.?'

'I don't know. I could murder some of that salmon.'

'You know where the fridge is,' she mumbled, and felt the warm weight of him leave the sofa. It seemed

158

like a good moment to reclaim the bed, but about half an hour later, when dawn was breaking behind the curtains, the man who was Rajah came into the bedroom and flung his gorgeous limbs over the foot of the duvet.

'Normally,' he said, shaking back his glossy hair and combing it with his fingers, 'I like to go out for a bit of a walk around now, but it's still pissing with bloody rain. So what's the point? Move over, please. I need more room.' And he curled himself around her feet and was instantly asleep.

Sleep, the way he did it, seemed like a wonderful thing. The way he turned his head was a poem in flesh. The curve of his arm was so utterly perfect that Herb Ritts should have risen from the grave to photograph it. The rise and fall of his chest as he breathed was as soothing as waves on a tropical beach. After a few minutes of watching him, Jane drifted blissfully into unconsciousness.

And so the day passed. Jane slept like a baby, she slept like a student, she slept like the Sleeping Beauty, and when she came close to waking up, sleeping seemed such a heavenly experience that she turned over and plunged in again, more deeply.

Some time in the afternoon she opened her eyes, to find the man sitting by the window, his arms folded over his chest, watching some birds in the tree outside, but sleep reclaimed her at once. Again, later, she sensed his weight on the bed and felt his body curl against the small of her back, and she shifted comfortably to give him room, and slept again.

In the early evening, the noise of the shower running finally woke her. She thought of the shelves she should have painted. They seemed very boring. After quite a long time, the bathroom door opened and the man who was Rajah appeared, a towel wrapped around his waist.

'I'm starving,' he said. 'Why don't we go out to eat? It's not raining any more. I know a place for steak that's not too bad. You do like steak, don't you? I just love it. Come on, get washed and let's go.' And he brushed his cheek against hers and ran his fingers through her hair.

So the weekend passed, most of it in sleeping, and most of the rest in eating sumptuous high-protein meals, the steak on Saturday, roast duck on Sunday, and turbot, and more and more prawns, all followed by opulent cream desserts. Occasionally, Jane wondered about cholesterol, or putting on weight, or indeed about painting her shelves, but the logic of these thoughts seemed so thin that they couldn't hold her attention for long.

'My God!' she said on Monday morning. 'Is that the time! I've overslept, I'll be late for work.'

'Oh *please*,' said the man, sitting up on his side of the bed with a grumpy expression. 'You can't be thinking of going to work.'

'But . . .'

'But nothing. You need to sleep. Chuck a sickie.'

'I can't do that.'

'You can give a guinea-pig an enema. You can do anything.'

'They need me at work.'

'So? You deserve a break, for heaven's sake. Call and say you're ill. I'm ordering you.'

And the strange thing was, she could not disobey him. It would have been easier to make water run up hill than cross the man who was Rajah. Besides, when she came back from making the call, he rubbed her back, and massaged her shoulders, and let her sleep with his smooth brown stomach for a pillow.

It was not all eating and sleeping. There was washing, as well. Jane had forgotten how pleasurable it could be to soak in the bath or stand in the shower and feel the water on her skin. When it did not rain, they went for walks, long unhurried strolls around the neighbourhood, observing the birds and the squirrels and the state of the dustbins.

There was a tricky moment one evening, as they passed the All Bar One on the high street, which Rajah became unnaturally determined to enter, even though he disdained alcohol, because there was a female in season at the far end of the bar.

'You don't understand,' he growled. 'She's calling.'

'She's just drunk,' Jane told him, trying to steer him away from the raucous doorway.

'Same thing. Let go of me.'

'I'll kiss you,' Jane threatened, realistically, since she had a firm grip on his arm. He hissed at her.

'Behave yourself!' she hissed back. 'If you start a fight they'll call the police.'

'You *people*,' he snarled. 'Now do you see why I don't mind being a cat?'

'You're so beautiful. How can you want to get all beaten up?'

'I do not get beaten up,' he said, his eyes flashing. 'But you should see the other guys.'

When she was sure he had stopped sulking, Jane opened the question that had been forming in the primordial soup that was now her mind.

'I will have to kiss you, won't I? If you're going back to Mr Downs.'

'No offence,' he said graciously. 'But he saw me first and he has got underfloor heating. Anyway, I'd have to share you with your daughter, wouldn't I? So yes, you will have to kiss me. Don't worry. It's instantaneous and I don't feel anything.'

'And his partner?'

'Oh, him. Well, we'll have to see about him, won't we?'

'Do you know things that people don't?'

'Of course I do. But you could know things too, if you just took time to watch what was going on.'

On Sunday night, Richard phoned to tell her when he would be dropping Ella off, just in time for them to wake up and pretend to be normal. When the doorbell rang, Rajah jumped to answer it in a flash.

'So,' he snarled, advancing on Richard while Ella ran past his legs looking for her mother. 'You miserable dick-head! You idle, fat-arsed waste of space! You lousy wanker! Get out of my face!'

'Uh . . .' Richard's mouth fell open in amazement, just before Rajah landed a punch on his nose.

'Fuck off!' Rajah yelled. His hair seemed to be standing on end. 'Just fuck off out of here while you can still walk, you arsehole!' The second punch split Richard's lip. 'Fuck off or I'll kill you!'

'Jane!' Richard squealed. The third punch caught him in the eye with a marvellous smack.

'Is that your boyfriend, Mummy?' Ella asked with vast admiration. 'I like his shoes.'

'I can't do anything, Richard,' Jane called out happily. 'You'd better do what he says.'

The neighbours' door opened and Diarmuid's terrified face appeared around it. 'Are you all right out here?'

'We're fine,' Jane assured him, trying not to laugh. 'Go on, Richard. You'll only get hurt.'

'What an idiot,' Rajah growled, leaning over the stairwell to watch Richard running away.

'He is that,' agreed Diarmuid, retreating behind his own door once more.

'You tore your clothes,' Ella said to Rajah, pointing at his sleeve, which had parted company with the rest of his shirt.

'It is not important, kitten,' he told her, and she giggled.

'It smells spicy in here,' said Ella. 'Have you been doing drugs, Mummy?'

'Be nice to your mother,' hissed Rajah, his hair still wild and threatening.

In the morning, after Jane's car-pool partner had picked Ella up for school, Rajah spent his usual half an hour in the bathroom then emerged and held out his arms.

'Time to go,' he said, smiling gently. 'It's been magic, hasn't it?' And he held Jane against his firm brown chest for not quite long enough, gazed darkly into her eyes, then tipped up her chin like a movie-star hero. She just had to kiss him.

Again, the room filled with smoke and the smell of sea and spices, and the warm arms around her disappeared, leaving Jane swaying where she stood. When the smoke cleared, the cat was sitting by the pet carrier in the middle of the hall, blinking at her, expectant.

Mr Downs was wonderfully tanned. 'I've had a great time,' he said, his eyes twinkling through his trendy glasses. 'All thanks to you. How about you? You're looking good, I have to say.'

'Er – yes. Yes, I had a nice break. Took some time off.' It seemed a ridiculous understatement, but already her memory of the past week was getting blurred.

'So you're feeling pretty fine?' Mr Downs enquired, taking possession of the pet carrier.

'I feel like a new woman,' she said, and it was true. She felt calm, for the first time in years. 'And your partner?' Nobody, she realised, was waiting on the street outside.

'Left him in Mykonos,' said Mr Downs happily. 'I realised I'd had enough. Nothing's worth that amount of hassle. Holidays help you sort your head out, don't they? You have to get away to realise what's important in life. And it's true, isn't it – the more you see of people, the more you like cats. You know that now, don't you?'

'Well, yes.' Am I blushing? I am blushing. For a displacement activity, Jane disabled the timetable checker on her work station.

'Well, I can't thank you enough,' Mr Downs said, heading for the door. Then he turned back and winked at her. 'Maybe we can all get together for a fish supper some time?'

'That'd be nice.'

'Wouldn't it just?' And the cat nodded its head. Jane

reached through the grille and let Rajah wipe his whiskers on her finger one last time.

When she got home that evening with Ella there was an ambulance in the car-park and paramedics were carrying a body on a stretcher towards it.

'Are they making a film, Mummy?' Ella asked.

'I don't think so,' said Jane, trying to look at the body in a caring, non-invasive and non-ghoulish manner. It was Diarmuid. His eyes were closed and his skin looked more ghastly than ever. And Kath came running out after the stretcher, struggling into her coat.

'It's his heart!' she announced. 'My poor Diarmuid, he's having a heart attack. Right in the middle of finishing our shelves! Keep an eye on the flat for me, Jane, there's a dear. God knows how it's all going to end. My poor man, I suppose it was just too much for him.'

'Why do people have shelves, Mummy?' Ella asked as Jane was opening their front door. There was still a tang of cinnamon in the air. It had really happened.

'I can't imagine,' she said, and that also was the truth. In vain she tried to retrace the steps of reasoning which had led her to spend all her free time in a frenzy of work for the sake of improving a home that was already perfectly adequate. A list had been involved. What was a list, exactly? She could not quite recall the concept of a list. 'Tell me, kitten,' she began, sitting down with her daughter, something for which it was always hard to find the time. 'Shall we sell this place and go and live somewhere in the country where there's less stress and stuff?'

'Can we have a cat in the country?'

'Definitely.'

'Yes,' said Ella. 'I think that's a very good idea.'

DAISY WAUGH

Pippa Positive

'. . . ᴀɴᴅ ɪғ ᴛʜᴇ doorbell rings, it'll only be the man delivering the bunk beds. So don't worry, OK? Don't go bonkers trying to get yourself downstairs. He'll *wait*. Anyway, they promised he wouldn't arrive before ten. So I'll be back – if the traffic's not terrible. Which it isn't on Wednesday, not usually. And I'm doing your creamed potatoes again for lunch. I hope you're going to eat it this time! OK? . . . Right then. Let's open the window, shall we? It's getting a bit niffy in here.'

Pippa Butterworth stood between the door and the window waiting for his response, feeling torn, as she always did, between impatience and pity. But David was a man of remarkably few words at the best of times. At the best of times, even in their courting days, he had barely registered a word she said. Now they had been together for fourteen years, and married for ten; a quiet, boring, efficient marriage mostly. Both parties, though they took care not to hurt or irritate each other more than necessary, had slipped into their solitary bubbles long ago.

On that cold Wednesday morning it was still dark outside, and Mrs Butterworth could hear the dreary patter of rain outside. She hovered, feeling perhaps she

166

had been a little harsh with the lunch comment and wondering whether she should kiss him or something, to remove the sting. None of this was his fault. She knew that. She knew she wasn't the only one who was suffering. But sometimes, recently, maybe in the last couple of weeks or so, as he had grown more inert, less like the David she could always rely on – she had caught herself wondering if he wasn't a bit lazy, lying there like that, showing no signs of even trying to recover. Sometimes she'd gaze across the room at his head on the pillow, so untroubled by all the trouble he was causing, and she wanted to shake him. She didn't allow herself to complain, ever, about anything. But sometimes, recently, she had wanted to scream, *I'm exhausted! I AM EXHAUSTED! I've got to get the children to school. I've got to get someone to look at the damp patch in the playroom, I've got to put the new climbing frame together, I've got to get to the supermarket; the carpets need shampooing, the window cleaner's gone AWOL, the iron's broken, Marcus won't eat anything except Hellmann's, the bills are piling up, your stupid office keeps calling, like we needed their help . . . and I can't – I can't – THIS was never part of the deal.*

So. She hesitated, forced herself to smile. She moved towards him – but the stale air, his sickly face in the grey dawning light – he looked and smelled like a stranger. She swung away again.

'All right, darling?' she said, wrinkling her nose, making her voice light. 'I'll see you later. You sleep well, now. And *get better*! OK?'

Pippa closed the door softly behind her and immediately broke into a trot.

'Daniel? Marcus?' she shouted down to the kitchen two floors below. 'Upstairs and brush your teeth. Quickly, please. And Marcus –' She caught him as he was dashing past. 'Come here – look at you! Your collar's all skew-whiff. How do you manage it? How do you manage to make yourself *so scruffy* before the day's even begun? Daniel – please don't take your toast into the hall. Hurry up. Come on. Brush your teeth and then – *quickly* – into the car.'

'Can we go and see Dad?'

'No.'

'Please.'

'No. He's sleeping. He doesn't want to be disturbed.'

'*Please* . . . Then can we see him tonight?'

'Yes. Maybe. We'll see how he feels. Now *hurry up*! We're going to be late.'

Pippa Butterworth lived with her husband and two sons, aged six and eight, in Ealing, in a villa with five bedrooms, a large garden, an open-plan kitchen/diner, three reception rooms and a brand-new conservatory. Mrs Butterworth worked hard at her life: at keeping in trim; at smiling a lot; at being a wife that Ealing could be proud of. David Butterworth worked hard, too. Or he used to, before he fell ill. He worked in the City, as an accountant for one of the banks, and he earned a great deal of money. All of which Mr and Mrs Butterworth managed to spend: Mrs Butterworth on the small things, like the bread-making machine, the miniature hoover you could attach to the wall, the autumn/winter cashmere range at Jigsaw; Mr Butterworth on the skiing trips, the household bills, the school fees, the fantastic loft conversion that Pippa

Butterworth jovially referred to as 'David's bachelor pad'.

David had a little shower room up there, too, and a plasma TV screen (for the sport), a state-of-the-art sound system, an exercise bicycle, a mini-bar and fridge. And there was a sofa-bed which he would sleep on from time to time; when he came home tipsy after a night out with the City boys, or on the rare occasions when he and Pippa Butterworth remembered each other long enough to start a fight.

Recently, of course, David had been in no position to fight or to drink with anyone, and yet he stayed up in his loft all the time. A thoughtful husband in some ways, at some point he had decided it was unfair on Pippa to have to lie next to him as he sweated and shivered and coughed his guts out. Pippa had always insisted that she wanted him in bed beside her, so she could help if he needed it, but the night he moved up to the bachelor pad (it was a trial night) was the first in a long time that Pippa Butterworth had managed to get any sleep. And David had never been invited back.

Conversations at the school gate follow a particular pattern, and have done for over a month, ever since David was discharged from hospital. Sometimes, depending on her mood, Pippa will vary her responses in the middle third, but she always takes care to finish on an up-note. She is a great believer in positive thinking.

'Hello, Pippa! How's David? Feeling a bit better now?'

'*Much* better, thank you. Thanks for asking! It's a slow old business, but yes. He's definitely on the mend.

Thank goodness! We'll have him up and about in no time!'

'I'm so pleased. And then you can all get back to normal. I expect you're looking forward to that.'

'Whatever "normal" is! *Hectic*, more like!'

Ha ha ha.

'Must be upsetting for the kids, though.'

'Not really, no. The kids are fine. We keep to the same routine and that's so important. Plus you know how it is – we mums have the men working so hard, the kids hardly see them anyway! Except at weekends. And even then . . .'

Pippa contemplates her children's weekend activities; starting with Saturday-morning judo classes, and progressing meticulously on, through swimming and football, alternating Saturday-night sleepovers, fencing for Marcus, chess for Daniel . . . to Sunday night homework, video and bed. She shrugs.

'And of course when he's well – you know what men are like. He's got the golf, or he's watching his *sport* –'

The ladies roll their eyes.

'Or he's fussing around on his blessed internet. Busy busy busy!'

'Mmm. Oh yes.'

'But he's a super dad. Super. I couldn't ask for more. I couldn't.'

'Isn't that lovely? Well – anything I can do. We must ask you both over as soon as he's strong enough. Will you let me know?'

Mrs Butterworth didn't want to linger at the school gate that morning. She needed to get back for the bunk beds. But Daniel's form teacher ran after her – *ran* (it

170

was that kind of a school) – to warn her that Daniel had started mucking around in maths.

'Maths?' said Pippa. 'But maths is Daniel's subject!'

'Yes, he's normally so good at maths.'

'Like his father. His father's the brainbox in the family. He certainly didn't get the brains from me!'

'He just doesn't seem to want to focus.'

'But Daniel *loves* maths.'

'Normally. That's why I mention it –'

'Hmm . . . Well, thank you, Miss Temple. Ever so much. I appreciate you taking the trouble. I'll have a word with him tonight.'

Miss Temple looked uncomfortable. 'Only I know your husband – I know Mr Butterworth's been a little under the weather recently . . . I was just thinking – is everything all right at home? Because it's so unlike Daniel . . . it's not just the maths, really. It's his whole attitude.'

'Goodness *no*. Everything's fine at home! He's quite the happy chappie at home! A bit of a handful, of course, like all eight-year-old little men. But that's how it should be.'

'I don't know, he seems a bit – How is Mr Butterworth now?'

'Much better, thank you. Thanks for asking! Yes, he's getting stronger every day.'

'I'm so pleased. I get the feeling maybe Daniel's been missing him a bit.'

'But we've got him upstairs 24/7!'

'Yes, but –'

'Which is so super, really. Isn't it? When you think about it. As I say to the boys, there isn't one cloud up there in that cloudy sky which doesn't have a silver

171

lining! Don't you agree? And if I know my husband, he'll be back at work in no time. So you tell Daniel to enjoy having his dad at home while he can. You tell him that!' Pippa smiled. 'And while you're at it, Miss Temple, tell him to pull his socks up. From me.' Pippa Butterworth hurried back to her car.

But the bunk-bed man didn't turn up that day. Someone from head office called to say the lorry wouldn't be coming until Friday after all. Which meant, among other things, that she had time to go to the gym as well as the supermarket before picking up the children again.

Pippa called in on David soon after they all returned. She tiptoed into the darkened room, and found the plate of creamed potato still untouched.

'Poor love,' she muttered, banging her shin against the coffee table, spilling a pile of GQ magazines on to the carpet and then fumbling to pick them all up again.

She took the plate downstairs and sat down with the boys to help them with their homework. Daniel was working on a fossil project which she didn't understand, but she showed Marcus how to sharpen a pencil with Daniel's pencil sharpener.

'After this,' said Marcus, 'can we go and see Dad?'

'We'll see,' she said. 'Now, come on, Marcus. *Concentrate*. You put the nib in here, *carefully*, that's right.'

'Just to say goodnight. Please, Mum.'

She didn't really want David disturbed. She wanted him to focus all his energies on *getting better*. Plus it was so cold up there, with the windows open, and all that bracing fresh air. She didn't want the children getting ill too. It was the last thing she needed. But on the other hand, the last thing she wanted was to be unkind.

'You can pop your heads round the door, OK? But I don't want you waking him up. Is that clear? Just blow him a little kiss. Whisper that you love him. He'll like that.'

'Yuk! He'll *hate* that.'

'Don't be silly, Daniel.'

And then Thomas Payne's mother, Ali, called, wanting to know if the boys could stay the night on Friday.

'On *Friday*?' Pippa laughed. 'Anyway, it's our turn to have Thomas over here.'

'Yes, but we were thinking of taking him off to EuroDisney at the weekend. To get his mind off Christmas.'

'How super! Well, I know Marcus and Daniel will be very sorry.'

'So I want Tommy *here* Friday night, rather than *there*, if you know what I mean. Because I don't want him getting overtired for Saturday.'

Pippa's instinct was to say no. Friday-night sleepovers weren't part of the routine. Plus there was judo to think about.

'Go *on*,' Ali laughed. 'Why not? You must be exhausted. It'll give you a break.'

Pippa hated it when her children went away. The house seemed so large and quiet and empty. She wandered from room to room, tidying things, never knowing quite what to do with herself. But the boys had to be allowed out on their own little adventures. It was an important part of growing up.

'Oh, pleeeeeeeeeeeeese,' yelled Marcus. 'PLEASE!'

'OK,' sighed Mrs Butterworth, smiling good-naturedly into the telephone, loneliness filling her up. 'Just this once, OK?'

She took the boys out for a pizza the following night, which was very much against Thursday's routine. But she had wanted them all to have fun on their last night together. And, if the truth be told, Pippa wanted to get out of the house. She was beginning to find David's perpetual, helpless presence oppressive. Which was why she had spent such a long time in the gym that morning, and why, at the hairdresser that afternoon, instead of the usual trim, she'd asked Nigel for a full head of highlights.

On Friday morning, after the usual school gate interlude, and a call on Pippa's mobile from David's doctor asking for an update on his health, she drew up at the house to discover the bunk-bed delivery man already waiting for her. She rushed to let him in, full of apologies.

'Hubby keeps the heating on short rations when he's not in then, Mrs Butterworth?' the man asked chirpily, following her in.

She stopped. 'Pardon?'

'I said does hubby keep the heating on short –' but she seemed flustered, and less dishy close-to. He lost interest. 'Oh, never mind.'

'He *is* in, actually,' she said coldly. 'He's upstairs. I leave the windows open because he likes to have plenty of fresh air.'

'Fair enough, Mrs Butterworth. Where do you want it then?'

'Want what? Oh! Ha! Sorry. Silly me! If you wait

there – would you mind? Just bring it into the hall. I'm going to nip upstairs a minute. Then perhaps you can help me get it up to Marcus' room and I'll make you a cup of tea.' She smiled. 'To apologise for keeping you waiting.'

She got past the first landing, halfway up the stairs towards the loft, and stopped, looked up at David's door. She felt sick. With every trip up here, these days, it was becoming more difficult to bring herself to open it; the lack of improvement on the other side; and then her struggle not to snap at him to *get a grip* . . . She hadn't been in yet this morning. The children had been running late for school. She hadn't been in – she hadn't been in properly, pulled open the curtains, sat down beside him and *talked*, since . . . She was distracted by the sound of movement in the hall. It had been stupid of her, she thought suddenly, to have left the delivery man on his own down there. What had she been thinking of? She glanced back up at David's door, shouted through to him that she would be back in a second, and trotted downstairs again.

Sure enough, Pippa discovered the delivery man examining silver-framed family photographs. She asked him sharply what he was doing.

'You've got some lovely things here, Mrs Butterworth,' he said, looking her up and down. 'Hubby a hard worker, is he?'

'Actually he's sick.' She could have kicked herself. There was a strange man in her house, and the front door was closed, and here she was telling him that the husband upstairs was no threat to him. 'Well – not really sick. Only food poisoning. He's just vomiting.

Or he was. Actually he feels a lot better now. Much stronger. He just said he was feeling very strong.'

The man smiled. *Slyly*, she thought. She was frightened. It occurred to her he might rape her. Or steal some of her belongings.

'Are you going to show me Marcus' room then?' he said.

'No. Actually I've changed my mind. The hall's fine. You can leave everything there.'

As soon as he had deposited the last of the flat-packs, and she had signed her name on the delivery slip, she told him him he couldn't have any tea after all. 'I've just remembered I've run out. So you'd better just leave,' she said. 'Sorry.'

'No tea for hubby, neither?' he leered. Or she thought he did.

'That's really none of your business . . . I mean. Well – *sorry*. But it isn't.'

He gave a disdainful laugh, one reserved especially for rich, rude, frightened women who lived off their hubbies' money. And he met a lot of them in his line of work.

The moment he left she made a tour around the ground floor to see if anything was missing. Nothing was missing.

The day loomed ahead, long and lonely, without even the prospect of the school gates for relief. But Pippa was not the sort of woman to give in to melancholy – far from it. She rolled up her sleeves and set to work on the beds. She would haul them up to Marcus' room herself and later, she thought, she would check in on David.

It was growing dark again by the time Pippa, exhausted and very hungry, finally stood back to admire her work. She only needed to attach the safety bars to the top bunk and the bed would be almost finished. She could sit down, make herself a cup of sweet tea, and take this opportunity to replace some of the name tags on Daniel's school uniform. Thoughts of David flitted through her mind; she ought to go and check on him. Later. Let him sleep. She would get some soup from the corner shop for his supper. And buy some washing powder, too. Washing powder, soup, kitchen roll, Cadbury's chocolate fingers. David loved chocolate fingers . . .

It was shortly after that, standing in the hall with her coat and bag, that Pippa finally noticed her door keys were gone.

She looked everywhere, in all her reception rooms, her kitchen, her conservatory. She was upstairs in Marcus's room, delving through the bunk-bed packaging, when she thought she heard the front gate squeak. She paused. Silence. She wasn't expecting anyone . . . More to the point, where were her wretched keys? She must have had them to get into the house when the delivery man –

The delivery man.

She felt sick.

Heavy footsteps on the front path, or so she thought. The blood was pumping so loud in her ears she couldn't be sure . . . And then . . . somebody clearing their throat? *Definitely*. There was somebody out there, clearing their throat . . . And a tinkling, jangling sound – *a key jangling*. Pippa was too frightened to move.

'David,' she said loudly, standing all alone in her big house, in the middle of Marcus's bedroom, 'shall we open that wine? Let's open that wine, shall we, David? Now that you're better. Let's have some wine.'

Outside, she heard a man laughing, the front door opening. Somebody walking into the hall.

'Hello?' he said. 'Anyone home?'

She grasped hold of the bunk bed.

'. . . Hello?'

She heard him walking slowly up the stairs, past Marcus' room, towards the fire door that led up to David's pad.

'. . . Mrs Butterworth? . . .'

She poked her head out on to the landing just in time to see his back disappearing – and like a fool, she screamed.

He spun round. 'Mrs Butterworth!' he said, smirking at her terrified expression. He held up the keys. 'You left them in the latch. I'm sorry. I didn't mean to scare you. And how is the patient this evening?'

Pippa was intensely confused, faint with confusion and fear. He was there in front of her, closer to David than she was. Popping in to see how hubby was . . .

'He's *fine*,' she said weakly. 'So kind of you –' She was leaning on the banister, and she thought her legs would give way. 'He's *fine*. Thank you. Thanks for asking . . . But I think he's asleep at the moment.'

'Well.' He smiled warmly at her. She was a brave woman, he thought. After all. Obviously very neurotic, but coping nicely under difficult circumstances. He admired her positive attitude. 'I've come this far, Mrs Butterworth. I'll just look in –'

178

'But he's asleep.'

'Not to worry. You sit down, Mrs Butterworth. You look like you need a rest. I'll make my own way up.'

David's doctor took the stairs two at a time.

'. . . He's getting so much better . . . We're having soup for dinner tonight . . .'

Gently, he pushed open the bachelor-pad door, switched on the overhead light, and a cloud of bluebottles rose up to greet him. David Butterworth's blanched-white body had swollen beneath its bedsheets, and his eyes were covered with maggots.

PENNY VINCENZI

The Mermaid

H E REALLY didn't like her. She was too – shiny. Everything about her shone: her lipstick, her nails, her jewellery – she had a lot of that – her shoes. She had perfect, shinily white teeth, and shiny swingy hair, and her skin was all golden, and gleamy too. He had a bit of trouble not liking her car, which was parked outside the house and which was very shiny indeed; it was silver and it had a top which let down, exactly the sort of car he would have loved if it had been his dad's. But it wasn't, it was hers. She offered to take him for a ride in it, with the top down, but he shook his head.

'Surely you'd like that?' his dad said. 'It'd be really good fun.' He winked at him. 'Martin'd see you, he's out on his bike.'

Martin lived in the same street, and went to the same school and was in the same class, and boasted about everything: his skate board, his computer, his bike, his mobile phone, his DVD player, his trainers. His dad didn't have a convertible car though. It'd be pretty cool to drive past in one. But not even that was enough to persuade him. It really hurt, but he shook his head.

He refused a meal at TGIs as well. He said he didn't like burgers any more.

'News to me,' said his father.

'I don't like them much either,' she said. 'How about a Chinese?'

He shook his head. 'I'm not hungry.'

'Jake,' said his dad, 'you're always hungry.'

'I'm not today.'

Julie went home alone, fairly early, feeling depressed. She couldn't have tried harder. Little beast. Sizing her up, deciding what to do about her. He always did that, Nick had said: 'You mustn't mind.'

She had said of course she didn't mind, but she did. She wasn't sure she liked the 'always' either. How many girlfriends had Nick taken home for God's sake. Anyway, it really rankled . . . being rejected by a nine-year-old. Thoroughly rejected. She'd been so sure she could impress him. Impressing was what she did; it was her job. Impressing clients, getting their business; she hadn't got to be head of New Business at Farquar and Fanshawe by being unimpressive, now had she? She'd realised of course this was quite a different game, but she had a nephew just about Jake's age and she knew the way to his heart. It was a pretty predictable path: new toys (not that what they played with these days could be dignified by the label of toy), rides in the car, trips to theme parks and lots of junk food. Only Jake's heart was clearly not to be found that way. Nick had warned her it might not be, of course: 'He's still grieving for Mary. And he's a funny little chap. Bit of an oddball.'

Mary, Jake's mother, had died two years earlier of ovarian cancer. She had been the perfect earth mother, it seemed: bread-baking, patchwork-making, sweetly content at home, caring for her little family. Jake's room still bore testimony to it: three walls and the entire ceiling covered with pictures that she had painted, forests and waterfalls and night skies and, Jake's favourite, a wonderful under-sea scene, with a mermaid sitting on a rock, combing her hair. He talked to the mermaid, when he felt really bad, told her how unhappy he was, and how terribly he missed his mother. He knew it was silly, but it seemed to help, and it meant he didn't have to say those sorts of things to his father and make him even more worried than he already was.

Mary had been a piano teacher, and Jake had been an immensely promising player himself; but since her death he had refused even to touch the piano, and had made his father keep it locked.

Julie had said (through slightly gritted teeth) that she would have expected Mary to have had more children. 'She couldn't,' Nick had said with a sigh.

She was secretly pleased; at least there was something Mary hadn't been good at.

Nick was not surprised by Jake's reaction to Julie. It was always the same. (He regretted that 'always'. It had just slipped out. Making it seem as if he had had dozens of girl friends. When there had only been a couple.) But he was very disappointed. He could see that he was only one step away from falling in love with this one. She was so – lovely. So pretty, and clever and funny, yet, underneath that, so really – well, nice. Gentle and concerned and that wonderful word Mary had used a lot, *simpatico*.

She had seemed to be really sorry when he told her about Mary; sorry and concerned.

'It must be so hard,' she said, 'coping with everything and being unhappy as well. It's exhausting, being unhappy.'

She had been married herself; married and divorced.

'It was – messy,' she said, twisting a strand of her shining brown hair round her finger. 'Messy and – well, just horrible. It still hurts.'

Initially, Nick had thought that never again would he so much as look at another woman, but somehow, as the worst of the grief eased and the loneliness intensified, he had wanted to have someone again. Not to marry, not even to be serious about, but just to talk to, be with, have fun with, and yes, all right, possibly a bit more than that. He knew Mary wouldn't have minded; quite the reverse. She had made him promise to at least consider marrying again. 'One day. You'll need someone. And so will Jake.'

Sure that he never would, he had promised. It seemed to calm her. She had been agitated, fretting over his loneliness, his inability to cope.

He had coped, of course. He'd had to. Coped with the grief, the anger, with Jake's grief and anger, and doing all the things Mary had done: learning to shop and cook, to wash and iron, to go to parents' evenings, to get the school uniform organised on Sunday nights, the lunch box every morning. It was a little easier for him than it might be for most men, because he was a teacher; the hours fitted around Jake's life. He had even, this year, managed a birthday party. He was pretty proud of that. His sister had offered to do it for him; he had refused, almost indignantly.

'I can do it myself. And Jake wants me to.'

Jake had been so good: so brave and good. And such a companion to him. They had done everything together – at first. Walked, cycled, listened to music, watched TV, gone to the cinema; and talked and talked and talked.

'I love you so much, Dad,' Jake had said one night. 'Not more than mum, I don't mean that. But however much I loved her, I've given you my love now as well.'

The first time Nick had invited a girl to the house, just for Sunday afternoon tea, Jake had been appalled. He had locked himself up in his room and refused to come down. Embarrassed, shocked at himself for causing Jake such distress, Nick had apologised and asked the girl to leave. Stupid of him, he had thought, stupid and insensitive. It was far too soon in time, it would become easier . . .

When he went to try and talk to Jake he was lying on the floor, gazing at the mural and the mermaid.

'Just leave me alone,' he said. 'Just go and talk to her if you want to.'

'I don't,' Nick said. 'She's gone.'

'Good.' But he went on staring at the mural. It was days before he so much as smiled.

'You'll have to be firm,' Trish, Nick's sister, said, when this had happened a couple more times. 'He can't stay joined at the hip with you for ever.'

'I don't think firmness is the answer,' said Nick with a sigh. 'God knows what it is.' Finding the right girl, he supposed. For both of them.

He had hoped so much that Julie was the right girl. He liked her too much to let her go. He continued to see her, lying to Jake about where he was, what he was doing, feeling like a guilty adolescent. Weeks went past; they met twice a week.

Their relationship moved on; he had stayed at her flat twice, had sent Jake to stay with Trish.

'I've got to go to a teachers' conference,' he said, blushing.

Trish laughed. 'Oh yes? Where is she holding it?'

'Don't tell Jake. It's too soon.'

'Of course I won't,' she said, 'but you can't go on like this.'

'I know,' he said, 'but he's so little. And so hurt.'

'He's not quite so little, Nick. He's nine years old.'

'I know. I know. But he is hurt.'

Jake knew his father was with Julie. He hated the idea so much it made him feel sick. Thinking of him doing the things they had always done together, with her. Like going to McDonald's and the cinema and walking in the park. As long as he wasn't mating with her . . . He knew about mating, they'd learnt about it at school. It sounded really weird; but he supposed once you got used to the idea it must be all right. His parents must have done it after all: to get him. It was the whole point, he knew that, of mating. It made babies. Supposing Julie had a baby; that would be really awful.

She'd come to the house once or twice since the first time. Trying to make him like her. She'd bought him something he'd wanted for ages, a Play Station Two complete with an advanced Star Wars game. He had thanked her for it with an icy politeness, because he knew he had to, but he never played with it, just put it at the bottom of his underwear drawer.

'She's horrible,' he said to the mermaid. 'Horrible and stupid. Thinking she can make me like her just by giving me things. Why can't my dad see that?'

The mermaid on the rock looked back at him sadly, as she combed her hair. He was sure she understood.

Julie was worried about Jake. She loved Nick; she really did. Enough to dream about marrying him. They got on so well: different as they were. Different as she was from Mary.

He was intrigued by the difference too.

'I can't believe it,' he said one night, 'that I can love someone like you.'

She had laughed.

'Am I so dreadful?'

'No. You're wonderful. But I thought high-powered people like you were tough and self-centred and out for all they could get.'

She laughed and kissed him.

'I am. I'm out to get you.'

'You've got me, Julie, you really have.'

But she knew she hadn't. Not really. Because of Jake.

He just wasn't going to let her win. She went on bringing him presents, offering treats, talking to him, teasing him, even ignoring him. It was quite hard actually; there were times when he could feel himself wanting to like her. Like when he didn't get in the swimming team and instead of telling him it didn't matter, she said it had happened to her once and she'd hidden one of the other girls' swimsuits so she couldn't swim either. He thought that was really cool, although of course he hadn't said so. And when they went to see *Lord of the Rings* and he was quite scared in some places and had shut his eyes and he knew she'd noticed and afterwards she said she'd been petrified and she couldn't understand why he wasn't too.

'She's just trying to get round me,' he said to the mermaid. 'Just trying to make me like her, so she can get round my dad. Well, she won't. I won't let her.'

The mermaid looked particularly sad that day.

Another time his father had bought him some poxy trainers from Marks and Spencer and she'd said how could he even think of such a thing, and made him take them back and buy him a Nike pair instead. That had been really difficult, not smiling and not thanking her then; but he'd managed. She'd left early the evening after that; he could tell he'd upset her and his father as well. He felt a bit bad, but he went up to his room and stared very hard at the murals and the mermaid and thought about his mother. How could his father forget her like this; how could he?

Nick was taking Julie away to Paris for the weekend, for her birthday; it was all planned. Jake was going to stay with Trish and they were being taken to Chessington World of Adventures for the whole of Saturday.

'He's just fine about it,' Nick said to Julie, giving her a kiss. 'He keeps saying how much he's looking forward to it.'

'Does he know where you're going?'

He looked awkward.

'Not exactly. I told him it was another conference.'

'Let's hope he doesn't find out, she said, and her voice was heavy.

On the Friday evening, just as she was leaving the office, Nick rang her.

'I'm so sorry,' he said, 'Jake's really unwell. He says his throat hurts and he's just been sick. I can't leave him yet. Maybe we can go in the morning. I'll check with Eurostar.'

'Nick –'

'Julie, he can't help being ill.'

'Want to bet?' she said and slammed the phone down after telling him there was no way she was going in the morning.

He rang her back and they had a huge row, but she wouldn't give in.

Jake had been listening to this conversation from the top of the stairs; he scurried back to bed and lay back on his pillows as he heard his father's footsteps on the stairs. He had always been able to make himself sick to order. It was a very useful accomplishment. They must think he was really stupid. Who went to conferences at the weekend?

He looked at the mermaid. Somehow she didn't look as sweetly sympathetic as usual. Her green eyes were quite hard. He stuck his head under the bed-clothes and pretended to be asleep.

Christmas was coming; Nick wanted more than anything to suggest to Julie that she spent it with them. He decided to talk to Jake first.

Jake didn't like the idea; not one bit.

'I don't know how you can even think of such a thing,' he said, and he meant it. 'Letting someone take

Mum's place. For something as special as Christmas.'

'Jake, she wouldn't be taking Mum's place. She'd be taking her own. With us.'

'And what's that?' said Jake. He could hear his own voice, hostile and rude. 'What is her own place? She doesn't have one with us.'

'Yes she does. She's our friend. Friends should be together at Christmas.'

'She might be your friend,' said Jake. 'She isn't mine. And I don't want her to be. Least of all at Christmas.'

'Jake! Do you know what her present to you is?'

'No,' said Jake.

'It's tickets for *The Lion King*. For the three of us. Really really good ones. You know how much you want to see that.'

'I don't want to see *The Lion King*. Not with her.'

His father looked at him very sadly for a while. Then he said, 'Jake, you're turning your back on a lot of happiness, you know. For me as well as for you. It isn't really very sensible.'

'I don't care,' said Jake. 'Anyway, I don't like her. So how can I be happy with her?'

'Very easily. If you'll allow yourself.'

'Well, I won't,' said Jake, and ran upstairs to his room. He flung himself on the bed and started punching the pillow. Mixed with being pleased about Christmas he felt cross with himself. He'd really wanted to see *The Lion King*.

He was careful not to look at the mermaid; he turned over and stared up at the night sky painting on the ceiling instead. It didn't look as brilliant and sparkly as usual.

*   *   *

189

Hearing Jake didn't want to see *The Lion King* was the last straw for Julie. She really couldn't fight him any longer. However much she loved Nick: and she did love him. It was hopeless. There was no chance of their making any sort of life together. She spent Christmas with her mother, and told her everything; her mother said she'd like to put Jake over her knee and give him a good spanking.

'Oh Mum. I don't know what good you think that would do.'

'Bring him to his senses. He's just a spoilt brat.'

'A very unhappy spoilt brat. He's still grieving for his mother.'

'Of course he is. But he's also having the time of his life, keeping his father all to himself. It's probably proving a very good distraction. Have you tried giving him a good talking to?'

'Mum! You don't understand. If I so much as breathe any criticism of Jake, Nick starts lecturing me.'

'Does he have to know?'

'Of course. He'd tell him.'

'And what about if you appealed to his better nature, explained how nice it would be for his father not to be alone all the time, that sort of thing?'

'He'd just say Nick wasn't alone, that he had him. And anyway, he doesn't have a better nature,' she added. She smiled at her mother; but it was a weak, watery smile.

Nick asked Trish if they could spend Christmas with her.

'Of course you can. But what about Julie, wouldn't you rather be with her?'

'I would. Jake wouldn't.'

'Nick! You know what I think about –'

'Trish, he's still missing his mother. I can't force someone else on him.'

She sighed. 'All right. But it seems to me you're still going to be saying that when Jake's twenty-five.'

'Oh don't be so ridiculous,' said Nick. But he looked very thoughtful as he put the phone down.

A job had come up at the New York office of Farquar and Fanshawe, and Julie had been told it was hers for the asking. She decided to ask for it.

She knew there was no point telling Nick the truth; he's stop her somehow, keep on saying that it would be all right with Jake, that he'd come round in time, that she had to be patient. She had had enough of being patient.

It didn't help that she wasn't feeling well. Sick and dizzy and desperately tired. Her mother guessed the reason; Susie looked at her in astonishment.

'Don't be ridiculous. It's – well, it's almost impossible.'

But she bought a pregnancy-testing kit and discovered it wasn't.

She got the job; as promised. Or nearly. Just a question, they said, of dotting i's and crossing t's. The New York office would like her to come over, meet the team and generally discuss terms. She said that would be fine. They booked her on to a flight, business class, and into the New York Plaza. They obviously were very serious.

'What are you going to do?' said her mother.

'Take the job.'

'But what about the baby?'

She shrugged.

'They're giving me enough to pay two nannies. I'll manage. I won't tell them for a long time. I'll be fine.'

'You ought to tell Nick. It's his baby too.'

'Yes, and he won't want it. Or Jake won't.'

'You don't know that.'

'Yes, I do.'

But she decided she should tell him anyway. She asked him to meet her after work.

'Come round to my flat, we can talk in peace there.'

Late that afternoon he phoned.

'I'm so sorry. Jake's not well. Really not well. Temperature, horrible throat, the lot. No, Julie, this time it's genuine. We've seen the doctor. It's tonsillitis. I can't leave him. Can we give it a day or two?'

'No,' she said. 'Sorry, we can't.'

'Why not?'

'Because – because I'm going to New York. In the morning. I've got a new job there – just going over to sign the contract.'

'Why didn't you tell me before?'

She was silent.

'Would you come round here then?' he said. 'Please.'

Jake really felt ill. His throat was agony, and he felt sick. And he was so hot. He thought longingly of his mother, and how she had looked after him when he'd had tonsillitis. The best thing of all had been putting those bendy cooler packs from the freezer on his forehead and kind of round his neck. It had really helped. His father had said he couldn't find the bendy packs and put ice cubes up in plastic bags which hadn't done the same job at all.

His mother had also read to him for as long as he'd wanted. His father wasn't that good at reading. He did it rather as if he was teaching his class. Still, it was better than nothing. He'd bought the latest Harry Potter, which Jake hadn't read yet.

Only now he'd announced that *she* was coming round.

'Sorry, old chap. Not for long, but it's important. I'll read to you till she gets here, promise.'

'No, it's all right,' said Jake. He felt near to tears. This of all nights, and she'd be here, all shiny and noisy and bringing him something she thought he'd like. 'I'd rather go to sleep, I think.'

His father went downstairs; Jake looked at the mermaid and felt like crying.

'I want Mum so much,' he said. 'Not her, not even Dad. You understand, don't you?'

The mermaid looked sorrowfully back.

He heard Julie arrive; he heard them talking in the hall, heard his father say, 'No, he's half asleep already,' heard her footsteps on the stairs. She came in, and looked at him: she didn't look so shiny, she was sort of huddled into a big thick coat he hadn't seen her wearing before, and she looked tired and had dark rings under her eyes and she was very pale.

'I've brought you something,' she said.

'I don't want anything.'

'You'll want this. It'll make you feel better.'

She suddenly sat down on the bed, closed her eyes.

'Are you all right?' he said. He was surprised that he cared.

'Yes. I'm fine. Just a bit – tired.'

'You've gone green,' he said.

'I'm all right. I feel a bit – sick.'

She pulled something out of her pocket, wrapped in newspaper.

'Here,' she said. 'One for your forehead, two for your throat. Let me put them on for you. I used to get sore throats and my mum said this would make me feel better. It really worked.'

She unwrapped three soft freezer packs.

Jake was too astonished to say thank you, and there was a sharp pricking feeling behind his eyes. He shut them. He didn't want her to see he was almost crying. He couldn't say thank you.

'Well,' she said, after a bit. 'I'm going downstairs to talk to your father. Don't worry, it won't take long. Then you can have him back all to yourself. For ever probably.'

For some reason, he didn't like that for ever. It sounded a bit – final. He looked at the mermaid: her expression seemed to be rather anxious, as she combed her hair.

He heard their voices downstairs in the sitting room, quiet at first, then getting noisier. He heard his father shouting that Julie was intolerant and insensitive and her shouting back that he was ridiculous and deluded. He heard his own name once or twice; after that he put his head under the pillow. He didn't want to hear any words. Finally he heard the door open, heard them in the hall, heard Julie shouting, half crying.

'I'm going anyway,' she said, 'and I won't be back. I hope you'll be very happy together.'

'But I love you,' he heard his father say suddenly. 'I love you very, very much.'

'Not enough,' she said. 'Not nearly enough. Sorry. And don't even think about trying to stop me. I've had enough. And I'll tell you who I feel sorriest for. Not you, not me. That poor little mixed-up kid upstairs. So he loved his mother. Of course he did. She was obviously the most wonderful person. Much more wonderful than me. But – she's gone. He has to move forward. You both do. And I don't think you ever will. Goodbye, Nick.'

The door slammed; he heard her shiny car roaring away down the street, and then his father coming upstairs rather heavily. He opened the door and looked at Jake.

'I just thought you'd like to know,' he said, 'that we won't be seeing Julie any more. She's going to live in New York. In the morning, actually.'

'New York! That's a long way.'

'Yes, well, I thought you'd like that.'

He looked awfully sad, Jake thought. Just for a moment he felt sad too.

Then he said, 'Yes, I would like it. Of course. Dad, I'm really tired, I want to go to sleep now.'

Only he couldn't sleep. He lay there, thinking about what she had said; about his mother being so wonderful, much more wonderful than her. It made her seem much nicer. And about how he and his dad had to move forward. He hadn't thought of it that way before. He looked at the mermaid.

'It wouldn't be forgetting Mum, would it?' he said.

'Not really. It would just be more – well, doing things a bit differently.'

The mermaid looked back at him. Her eyes weren't hard as they had been the other day.

He put the light on, and went over to his drawer to get out a clean hanky, and saw the Play Station tucked underneath his socks and T-shirts. He pulled it out and went back to bed. As he pulled his duvet up, he saw a scrumpled piece of paper lying there. It must have come out of her pocket with the ice packs. He straightened it out.

'Pregnancy-Testing Kit', it said. 'Instructions for Use'.

Jake felt quite dizzy himself. This must mean they had been mating. And she was having a baby. Obviously. She'd said she felt sick. People did feel sick when they were pregnant. He remembered his Aunt Trish being sick a lot before she'd had her baby. How horrible would that be! A baby in the house. He'd never get any time with his father at all. It was a very good thing she was going to New York. His father need never know.

'She's having a baby,' he said to the mermaid. 'But she's going to New York. So that's all right, isn't it?'

Only he felt a funny sort of lump in his throat, that wasn't just the tonsillitis. And his eyes felt a bit funny too. Sort of stingy. He looked at the Play Station and it was a bit blurred somehow. New York! That was a long way away. Well – it was really really good. He was glad. He tucked the Play Station under the bedclothes so his father wouldn't see it if he looked in on him, and turned the light out again. It took him a very long time to go to sleep.

*   *   *

In the morning he still felt terrible. He managed to wash and clean his teeth, but after that he felt really wobbly again. He went back to bed, and stared up at the ceiling. He realised he actually still felt funny about Julie going so far away. Well, she'd been around for ages. He'd kind of got used to her. Didn't mean he liked her. Didn't mean he wanted her moving in or anything like that. And certainly not with a baby. He kept trying to tell himself how wonderful it was that she'd gone, but he didn't feel as happy as he'd thought he would. Perhaps she was right. Maybe they should move forward, him and his dad. Well: he'd know next time. He'd be nicer to the next one. Only – she might not be so nice to him.

He kept thinking bout Julie, about how kind she'd been to him – or tried to be if he'd only let her – how she'd always known exactly which toys and books he'd like, how she talked to him as if he was a grown-up. He thought about refusing to go to *The Lion King* and how that hadn't really been very nice of him. And he thought about the other girls his father had brought home. They'd been awful, compared to Julie. They'd all talked to him as if he'd been about three.

'She was – nice,' he said suddenly. 'Nicer than I thought, anyway. I wish I'd been a bit nicer back.'

The mermaid stared sadly into her mirror.

Nick also woke up feeling terrible; as near to despairing as he could remember since Mary had died. And dreadfully alone again. He debated telephoning Julie, telling her he was sorry, asking her if they couldn't try just once more – and decided there was no point. Nothing had changed; and Jake had to remain his first priority. He couldn't force someone on him that he didn't like.

Julie had got used to waking up feeling terrible; but today it was worse than usual. Misery and remorse washed over her; had she been too harsh, too unforgiving with Jake? And was her mother right, should she have told Nick about the baby? Was it worth just one more try? She had actually lifted the phone to dial Nick's number; but then she saw Jake's hard little face, staring at her in dislike, and heard Nick saying he must come first and put it down again. Nothing was going to change. Whatever happened.

Jake was half asleep again when his dad came in; he looked very tired, Jake thought, and sort of grey. A bit like Julie had the night before.

'Sorry, old chap. I've got to go to school for a few hours. Inspectors are coming. Mrs Perkins is coming in to sit with you. I'll be back about twelve.'

'OK,' he said. And then, 'Dad –'

'Yes?'

'There's – I mean – are you sad about Julie going?'

'Yes, of course. But – well, I don't think she's right for us. That's what you think too, isn't it?'

Jake didn't say anything. Then all in a rush he managed it. 'Actually, I did quite like her. She wasn't too bad.'

'You didn't behave as if you quite liked her.'

'Well –'

'Jake, you didn't. Anyway, it's too late now. She's had enough of both of us. I can't get her back.'

It didn't seem like he knew about the baby. Maybe Jake should tell him. Just so he knew . . .

'Dad – Dad, there's something –'

Nick looked at his watch.

'Jake, I can't talk any more now. I'll be late. Mrs Perkins is downstairs. Hope you feel better soon.'

He looked at the mermaid when his father had gone. He felt terribly sad suddenly, and terribly guilty. He'd made both of them, his father and Julie, really miserable; and now he felt miserable too. He started to cry. Mrs Perkins came in and told him he mustn't upset himself and offered to read him a story. He shook his head. She left him, closing the door quietly behind her.

He couldn't stop crying.

'She was nice really,' he kept whispering to the mermaid. 'It'd be all right really. I don't want her to go. I don't even mind her having a baby, not really. As long as it's a boy anyway. I wish I could tell her.'

And he realised he couldn't and cried harder than ever.

Julie was sitting in the club-class lounge at the airport when her mobile rang. Funny, she'd been sure she turned it off. She checked it. She had. Must be the aircraft interfering with the system in some way. She put it back in her bag and went back to her gin and tonic and the presentation she was going to make to the New York office when she got there. The phone rang again. This was weird. She looked at the number. It wasn't one she recognised.

'Julie?' It was a terrible line, very faint.

'Who's that? I can hardly hear you. Mum, is that you?' No one else would be ringing her now.

'Julie, Nick wants to talk to you. He's got something important to tell you. And he's really happy about the baby.'

'The baby! How on earth did he – Mum, you shouldn't have told him. That was very wrong of you.'

'Just ring him. Oh and there's something else.'

The line went very crackly; Julie shook it.

'What?'

'Jake's been crying all morning. He doesn't want you to go. He really doesn't.'

'It's a bit late for that,' she said coolly. 'And anyway, how do you know?'

'I've been with him. Give him a call, Julie. Please.'

The line went dead. She looked at the flight board. Her flight had just been called She supposed she could just fit in a call . . . And found she suddenly felt rather happy.

Nick was sitting in his meeting; there was a dull leaden misery in his stomach. He kept hearing his sister's voice saying he couldn't go on like this and that Jake wasn't so little; and Julie's voice saying he had to move on. Were they right? Should he really stand up to Jake? Too late, though: she'd gone, she'd be on the plane by now.

His mobile shrilled; everyone frowned at him. Funny: he'd been sure he switched it off.

'Sorry,' he said hastily and checked it. It was off. But it rang again.

'Sorry,' he mumbled, 'must be a fault. I'll put it outside.'

Outside he looked at the number; he didn't recognise it. But there was a message: to ring Julie. On her mobile.

'Julie?'

'Yes?'

'I got a message to call you.'

'A message? Not yet. But I was just going to ring you. Nick, Mum says – Mum says you're really happy about the baby.'

'The baby!'

'Yes. You are, aren't you, Nick? Please, please say you are.'

'I –' He tried to stop the room swirling.

'The baby! Er – your baby?'

'Well, of course. Our baby.'

Nick had once done a belly flop and had all the air knocked out of his stomach; he felt like that now, dizzy, a bit sick, and absolutely confused.

'Our baby? Did you say our baby!'

'Yes. Our baby. You are happy about it, aren't you?'

'Of – of course I am,' he said carefully. 'Of course.' And discovered he was. Very happy. Terribly, terribly happy. Or would be. When he got used to the idea . . .

'And also, she said that Jake's been crying all morning. Because I'm going. And he wants me to stay.'

'I – don't know, I'm afraid. I haven't been there.'

'Oh I see. Well, she seemed quite sure. Anyway – listen – I don't have to go to New York. Well, I do now, but I can come right back again. If you want me to.'

'I want you to,' he said. 'So very much.'

'I will. I'm so happy. So terribly happy. I love you, Nick.'

'I love you too,' he said.

Julie phoned her mother.

'That was very naughty of you,' she said. 'Very naughty indeed. But I'm glad you did it.'

'Did what?' said her mother.

'Phoned Nick. Told him everything. I don't know what you're doing there, but –'

'Phoned Nick? Doing where? Julie, what is this? I'm at work, I haven't phoned anyone . . .'

'Oh Mum! You're a terrible liar. Never mind. Thank you. And – it's so wonderful about Jake.'

'Jake!'

'Yes. Look, I must go. Final call. I'll ring you from New York. But I'm not taking that job.'

Nick drove home very fast and walked rather unsteadily upstairs. He went into Jake's room and looked at him. He looked much better; he was fast asleep, and his temperature was obviously down.

'He's been ever so upset, bless him,' said Mrs Perkins. 'Wouldn't tell me why. But he's calmed down now. And the sleep should do him good.'

'Mrs Perkins – has – has anyone else been here this morning?'

'No, of course not. Just me and Jake.'

'Nobody at all? Are you sure?'

'Well, put it this way,' said Mrs Pekins, 'I think I'd have noticed if they had been.'

'And – you didn't make a phone call to me? At the school?'

'No. No, of course not. You said only if Jake was really much worse.' She looked anxious. 'Should I have done?'

'No, of course not,' said Nick.

He sat down on Jake's bed and looked at him. He

was holding the Play Station in his hand, and three ice packs were piled up neatly on the bedside table. Jake looked across at the mural. The mural that Mary had painted with such love. The one Jake liked best, the one with the mermaid.

He looked at the mermaid; she was sitting there, on the rock, combing her hair, her tail shimmering in the water. And just for a moment, he could have sworn that instead of a mirror she had a mobile phone in her hand.

Just a trick of the light. Of course.

CHRISTOPHER BROOKMYRE

Out of the Flesh

R ESTORATIVE JUSTICE, they cry it. That's what
happens when wee scrotes like you get sat doon
wi' their victims, *mano a mano*, kinda like you and me
are daein' the noo. It's a process of talking and understanding, as opposed tae a chance for the likes ay me
tae batter your melt in for tryin' tae tan my hoose. The
idea is that us victims can put a face tae the cheeky
midden that wheeched wur stereos, and yous can see
that the gear you're pochlin' actually belongs tae
somebody. Cause you think it's a gemme, don't
you? Just aboot no' gettin' caught, and anyway, the
hooses are insured, so it's naebody's loss, right? So the
aim is tae make you realise that it's folk you're stealin'
fae, and that it does a lot mair damage than the price
ay a glazier and a phone call tae Direct Line.

Aye. Restorative justice. Just a wee blether tae make
us baith feel better, that's the theory. Except it normally happens efter the courts and the polis are
through wi' their end, by mutual consent and under
official supervision. Cannae really cry this mutual
consent, no' wi' you tied tae that chair. But restorative
justice is whit you're gaunny get.

Aye. You're shitin' your breeks 'cause you think I'm
gaunny leather you afore the polis get here, then make

up whatever story I like. Tempting, I'll grant you, but ultimately futile. See, the point aboot restorative justice is that it helps the baith ay us. Me batterin your melt in isnae gaunny make you think you're a mug for tannin' hooses, is it? It's just gaunny make ye careful the next time, when ye come back wi' three chinas and a big chib.

Believe me, you're lucky a batterin's aw you're afraid of, ya wee nyaff. Whit I'm gaunny tell you is worth mair than anythin' you were hopin' tae get away wi' fae here, an' if you're smart, you'll realise what a big favour I'm daein' ye.

Are you sittin' uncomfortably? Then I'll begin.

See, I used tae be just like you. Surprised, are ye? Nearly as surprised as when you tried tae walk oot this living room and found yoursel wi' a rope roon ye. I've been around and about, son. I never came up the Clyde in a banana boat and I wasnae born sixty, either. Just like you, did I say? Naw. Much worse. By your age I'd done mair hooses than the census. This was in the days when they said you could leave your back door open, and tae be fair, you could, as long as you didnae mind me and ma brer Billy nippin' in and helpin' oursels tae whatever was on offer.

We werenae fae the village originally; we were fae the Soothside. Me and Billy hud tae move in wi' oor uncle when ma faither went inside. Two wee toerags, fifteen and fourteen, fae a tenement close tae rural gentility. It wasnae so much fish oot ay watter as piranhas in a paddlin' pool. Easy pickin's, ma boy, easy pickin's. Open doors, open windaes, open wallets. Course, the problem wi' bein' piranhas in a paddlin' pool is it's kinda obvious whodunnit. At the end of the feedin' frenzy, when the watter's aw red, naebody's pointin' any fingers at the nearest Koi carp, know what I'm sayin'? But you'll know yoursel', when you're that age, it's practically impossible for the polis or the courts tae get a binding result, between the letter ay the law and the fly moves ye can pull. Didnae mean ye were immune fae a good leatherin' aff the boys in blue, right enough, roon the back ay the station, but that's how I know applied retribution's nae use as a disincentive. Efter a good kickin', me and Billy were even mair determined tae get it up them; just meant we'd try harder no tae get caught.

But then wan night, aboot October time, the Sergeant fronts up while me and Billy are kickin' a baw aboot. Sergeant, no less. Royalty. Gold-plated boot in the baws comin' up, we think. But naw, instead he's aw nicey-nicey, handin' oot fags, but keepin' an eye over his shoulder, like he doesnae want seen.

And by God, he doesnae. Fly bastard's playin' an angle, bent as a nine-bob note.

'I ken the score, boys,' he says. 'What's bred in the bone, will not out of the flesh. Thievin's in your nature: I cannae change that, your uncle·cannae change that, and when yous are auld enough, the jail willnae change that. So we baith might as well accept the situation and make the best ay it.'

'Whit dae ye mean?' I asks.

'I've a wee job for yous. Or mair like a big job, something tae keep ye in sweeties for a wee while so's ye can leave folk's hooses alane. Eejits like you are liable tae spend forever daein' the same penny-ante shite, when there's bigger prizes on offer if you know where tae look.'

Then he lays it aw doon, bold as brass. There's a big hoose, a mansion really, a couple ay miles ootside the village. Me and Billy never knew it was there; well, we'd seen the gates, but we hadnae thought aboot what was behind them, 'cause you couldnae see anythin' for aw the trees. The owner's away in London, he says, so the housekeeper and her husband are bidin' in tae keep an eye on the place. But the Sergeant's got the inside gen that the pair ay them are goin' tae some big Hallowe'en party in the village. Hauf the toon's goin' in fact, includin' him, which is a handy wee alibi for while we're daein' his bidding.

There was ayeways a lot o' gatherings among the in-crowd in the village, ma uncle tell't us. Shady affairs, he said. Secretive, like. He reckoned they were up tae all sorts, ye know? Wife-swappin' or somethin'. Aw respectable on the ootside, but a different story behind closed doors. Course, he would say that, seein' as the crabbit auld bugger never got invited.

Anyway, the Sergeant basically tells us it's gaunny be carte blanche. This was the days before fancy burglar alarms an' aw that shite, remember, so we'd nothin' tae worry aboot regards security. But he did insist on somethin' a bit strange, which he said was for all of oor protection: we'd tae 'make it look professional, but no' too professional'. We understood what he meant by professional: don't wreck the joint or dae anythin' that makes it obvious whodunnit. But the 'too professional' part was mair tricky, it bein' aboot disguisin' the fact it was a sortay inside job.

'Whit ye oan aboot?' I asked him. 'Whit's too professional? Polishin' his flair and giein' the wood-work a dust afore we leave?'

'I'm talkin' aboot bein' canny whit you steal. The man's got things even an accomplished burglar would-nae know were worth a rat's fart – things only valu-able among collectors, so you couldnae fence them anyway. I don't want you eejits knockin' them by mistake, cause it'll point the finger back intae the village. If you take them, he'll know the thief had prior knowledge, as opposed tae just hittin' the place because it's a country mansion.'

'So whit are these things?'

'The man's a magician – on the stage, like. That's what he's daein' doon in London. He's in variety in wan o' thae big West End theatres. But that's just showbusi-ness, how he makes his money. The word is, he's intae some queer, queer stuff, tae dae wi' the occult.'

'Like black magic?'

'Aye. The man's got whit ye cry "artefacts". Noo I'm no' sayin' ye'd be naturally inclined tae lift them, and I'm no' sure you'll even come across them, 'cause I don't know where they're kept, but I'm just warnin' you tae ignore them if ye dae. Take cash, take gold, take jewels, just the usual stuff – and leave anythin' else well enough alone.'

'Got ye.'

'And wan last thing, boys: if you get caught, this conversation never took place. Naebody'd believe your word against mine anyway.'

So there we are. The inside nod on a serious score and a guarantee fae the polis that it's no' gaunny be efficiently investigated. Sounded mair like Christmas than Hallowe'en, but it pays tae stay a wee bit wary, especially wi' the filth involved – and bent filth at that, so we decided tae ca' canny.

Come the big night, we took the wise precaution of takin' a train oot the village, and mair importantly made sure we were *seen* takin' it by the station staff. The two piranha had tae be witnessed gettin' oot the paddlin' pool, for oor ain protection. We bought return tickets tae Glesca Central, but got aff at the first stop, by which time the inspector had got a good, alibi-corroboratin' look at us. We'd planked two stolen bikes behind a hedge aff the main road earlier in the day, and cycled our way back, lyin' oot flat at the side ay the road the odd time a motor passed us.

It took longer than we thought, mainly because it was awfy dark and you cannae cycle very fast when you cannae see where you're goin'. We liked the dark, me and Billy. It suited us, felt natural tae us, you know? But that night just seemed thon wee bit blacker than usual, maybe because we were oot in the country-side. It was thon wee bit quieter as well, mair still, which should have made us feel we were alone tae oor ain devices, but I couldnae say that was the case. Instead it made me feel kinda exposed, like I was a wee moose and some big owl was gaunny swoop doon wi' nae warnin' and huckle us away for its tea.

And that was *before* we got tae the hoose.

'Bigger prizes,' we kept sayin' tae each other. 'Easy money.' But it didnae feel like easy anythin' efter we'd climbed over the gates and started walkin' up that path, believe me. If we thought it was dark on the road, that was nothin' compared tae in among thae tall trees. Then we saw the hoose. Creepy as, I'm tellin' you. Looked twice the size it would have in daylight, I'm sure, high and craggy, towerin' above like it was leanin' over tae check us oot. Dark stone, black glass reflectin' fuck-all, and on the top floor a light on in wan wee windae.

'There's somebody in,' Billy says. 'The game's a bogey. Let's go hame.'

Which was a very tempting notion, I'll admit, but no' as tempting as playin' pick and mix in a mansion full o' goodies.

'Don't be a numpty,' I says. 'They've just left a light on by mistake. As if there wouldnae be lights on doonstairs if somebody was hame. C'mon.'

'Aye, aw right,' Billy says, and we press on.

We make oor way roon the back, lookin' for a likely wee windae. Force of habit, goin' roon the back, forgettin' there's naebody tae see us if we panned in wan o' the ten-footers at the front. I'm cuttin' aboot lookin' for a good-sized stane tae brek the glass, when Billy reverts tae the mair basic technique of just tryin' the back door, which swings open easy as you like. Efter that, it's through and intae the kitchen, where we find some candles and matches. Billy's aw for just stickin' the lights on as we go, but I'm still no' sure that sneaky bastard sergeant isnae gaunny come breengin' in wi' a dozen polis any minute, so I'm playin' it smart.

Oot intae the hallway and I'm soon thinkin', knackers tae smart, let there be light. The walls just disappear up intae blackness; I mean, there had tae be a ceiling up there somewhere, but Christ knows how high. Every footstep's echoin' roon the place, every breath's bein' amplified like I'm walkin' aboot inside ma ain heid. But maistly it was the shadows . . . Aw, man, the shadows. I think fae that night on, I'd rather be in the dark than in candle-light, that's whit the shadows were daein' tae me. And aw the time, of course, it's gaun through my mind, the Sergeant's words . . . 'queer, queer stuff . . . the occult'. Black magic. Doesnae help that it's Halloween, either, every bugger tellin' stories aboot ghosts and witches aw week.

But I tell myself: screw the nut, got a job tae dae here. Get on, get oot, and we'll be laughin' aboot this when we're sittin' on that last train hame fae Central. So we get busy, start tannin' rooms. First couple are nae use. I mean, quality gear, but nae use tae embdy withoot a furniture lorry. Big paintin's and statues and the like. Then third time lucky: intae this big room wi' aw these display cabinets. A lot ay it's crystal and china – again, nae use, but we can see the Sergeant wasnae haverin'. There's jewellery, ornaments: plenty of gold and silver and nae shortage of gemstones embedded either.

'If it sparkles, bag it,' I'm tellin' Billy, and we're laughin' away until we baith hear somethin'. It's wan o' thae noises you cannae quite place: cannae work oot exactly whit it sounded like or where it was comin' fae, but you know you heard it: deep, rumbling and low.

'Whit was that?'

'You heard it an' aw?'

'Aye. Ach, probably just the wind,' I says, no even kiddin' masel.

'Was it fuck the wind. It sounded like a whole load ay people singin' or somethin'.'

'Well, I cannae hear it noo, so never bother.'

'Whit aboot that light? Whit if somebody *is* up there?'

'It didnae sound like it came fae above. Maist likely the plumbing. The pipes in these big auld places can make some weird sounds.'

Billy doesnae look sure, but he gets on wi' his job aw the same.

We go back tae the big hallway, but stop and look at each other at the foot of the stairs. We baith know what the other's thinkin': there's mair gear tae be had up there, but neither ay us is in a hurry to go lookin' for it. That said, there's still room in the bags, and I'm about to suggest we grasp the thistle when we hear the rumblin' sound again. *Could* be the pipes, I'm thinkin', but I know what Billy meant when he said lots ay folk singin'.

'We're no' finished doon here,' I says, postponin' the issue a wee bit, and we go through another door aff the hall. It's a small room, compared to the others anyway, and the curtains are shut, so I reckon it's safe to stick the light on. The light seems dazzling at first, but that's just because we'd become accustomed tae the dark. It's actually quite low, cannae be mair than forty watt. The room's an office, like, a study. There's a big desk in the middle, a fireplace on wan wall and bookshelves aw the way tae the ceiling, apart fae where the windae is.

Billy pulls a book aff the shelf, big ancient-lookin' leather-bound effort.

'Have a swatch at this,' he says, pointin' tae the open page. 'Diddies! Look.'

He's right. There's a picture ay a wummin in the scud lyin' doon oan a table; no' a photie, like, a drawin', an' aw this queer writin' underneath, in letters I don't recognise. Queer, queer stuff, I remember. Occult. Black magic.

Billy turns the page.

'Euuh!'

There's a picture ay the same wummin, but there's a boay in a long robe plungin' her wi' a blade.

'Put it doon,' I says, and take the book aff him.

But it's no' just books that's on the shelves. There's aw sorts o' spooky-lookin' gear. Wee statues, carved oot ay wood. Wee women wi' big diddies, wee men wi' big boabbies. Normally we'd be pishin' oorsels at these, but there's somethin' giein' us the chills aboot this whole shebang. There's masks as well, some of wood, primitive efforts, but some others in porcelain or alabaster: perfect likenesses of faces, but solemn, grim even. I realise they're death masks, but don't say anythin' tae Billy.

'These must be thon arty hingmies the sergeant warned us aboot, Rab,' Billy says.

'Artefacts. Aye. I'm happy tae gie them a body-swerve. Let's check the desk and that'll dae us.'

'Sure.'

We try the drawers on one side. They're locked, and we've no' brought anythin' tae jemmy them open.

'Forget it,' I say, hardly able tae take my eyes aff thae death masks, but Billy gie's the rest ay the drawers a pull just for the sake ay it. The bottom yin rolls open, a big, deep, heavy thing.

'Aw, man,' Billy says.

The drawer contains a glass case, and inside ay it is a skull, restin' on a bed ay velvet.

'Dae ye think it's real?' Billy asks.

'Oh Christ aye,' I says. I've never seen a real skull, except in photies, so I wouldnae know, but I'd put money on it aw the same. I feel weird: it's giein' me the chills but I'm drawn tae it at the same time. I want tae touch it. I put my hands in and pull at the glass cover, which lifts aff nae bother.

'We cannae take it, Rab,' Billy says. 'Mind whit the Sergeant tell't us.'

'I just want tae haud it,' I tell him. I reach in and take haud ay it carefully with both hands, but it doesnae lift away. It's like it's connected tae somethin' underneath, but I can tell there's some give in it, so I try giein' it a wee twist. It turns aboot ninety degrees courtesy of a flick o' the wrist, at which point the pair ay us nearly hit the ceilin', 'cause there's a grindin' noise at oor backs and we turn roon tae see that the back ay the fireplace has rolled away.

'It's a secret passage,' Billy says. 'I read aboot these. Big auld hooses hud them fae back in the times when they might get invaded.'

I look into the passage, expecting darkness, but see a flickerin' light, dancin' aboot like it must be comin' fae a fire. Me and Billy looks at each other. We baith know we're shitin' oorsels, but we baith know there's no way we're no' checkin' oot whatever's doon this passage.

We leave the candles because there's just aboot enough light, and we don't want tae gie oorsels away too soon if it turns oot there's somebody doon there. I go first. I duck doon tae get under the mantelpiece, but the passage is big enough for us tae staun upright once I'm on the other side. It only goes three or four yards and then there's a staircase, a tight spiral number. I haud on tae the walls as I go doon, so's my footsteps are light and quiet. I stop haufway doon and put a hand oot tae stop Billy an' aw, because we can hear a voice. It's a man talkin', except it's almost like he's singin', like a priest giein' it that high-and-mighty patter. Then we hear that sound again, and Billy was right: it is loads ay people aw at once, chantin' a reply tae whatever the man's said.

Queer, queer stuff, I'm thinkin'. Occult. Black magic.

Still, I find masel creepin' doon the rest ay the stairs. I move slow as death as I get to the bottom, and crouch in close tae the wall tae stay oot ay sight. Naebody sees us, 'cause they're aw facin' forwards away fae us in this long underground hall, kinda like a chapel but wi' nae windaes. It's lit wi' burnin' torches alang baith walls, a stone table – I suppose you'd cry it an altar – at the far end, wi' wan o' yon pentagrams painted on the wall behind it. There's aboot two dozen folk, aw wearin' these big black hooded robes, except for two ay them at the altar: the bloke that's giein' it the priest patter, who's in red, and a lassie, no' much aulder than us, in white, wi' a gag roon her mooth. She looks dazed, totally oot ay it. Billy crouches doon next tae us. We don't look at each other 'cause we cannae take oor eyes aff what's happenin' at the front.

The boy in the red robe, who must be the magician that owns the joint, gie's a nod, and two of the congregation come forward and lift the lassie. It's only when they dae this that I can see her hands are tied behind her back and her feet are tied together at her ankles. They place her doon on the altar and then drape a big white sheet over her, coverin' her fae heid tae toe. Then the boy in red starts chantin' again, and pulls this huge dagger oot fae his robe. He hauds it above his heid, and everythin' goes totally still, totally quiet. Ye can hear the cracklin' ay the flames aw roon the hall. Then the congregation come oot wi' that rumblin' chant again, and he plunges the dagger doon intae the sheet.

There's mair silence, and I feel like time's staunin' still for a moment; like when it starts again this'll no' be true. Then I see the red startin' tae seep across the white sheet, and a second later it's drippin' aff the altar ontae the flair.

'Aw Jesus,' I says. I hears masel sayin' it afore I know whit I'm daein', an' by that time it's too late.

Me and Billy turns and scrambles back up the stair as fast as, but when we get tae the top, it's just blackness we can see. The fireplace has closed over again. We see the orange flickerin' ay torches and hear footsteps comin' up the stairs, the two ay us slumped doon against a wall, haudin' on tae each other. Two men approach, then stop a few feet away, which is when wan ay them pulls his hood back.

'Evening, boys. We've been expecting you,' he says. The fuckin' Sergeant.

'I assume you took steps to make sure nobody knew where you were going tonight,' he goes on. I remember the train, the guard, the bikes, the return ticket in my trooser pocket.

The Sergeant smiles. 'Knew you wouldn't let us down. What's bred in the bone will not out of the flesh.'

Four more blokes come up tae lend a hand. They tie oor hauns and feet, same as the lassie, and huckle us back doon the stair tae the hall.

'Two more sacrifices, Master,' the Sergeant shouts oot tae the boy in red. 'As promised.'

'Are they virgins?' the Master says.

216

'Come on. Would anybody shag this pair?'

The master laughs and says, 'Bring them forward.'

We get carried, lyin' on oor backs, by two guys each, and it's as we pass down the centre of the hall that we see the faces peerin' in. It's aw folk fae the village. Folk we know, folk we've stolen from. I think aboot ma uncle and his blethers aboot secret gatherings. Auld bastard never knew the hauf ay it.

'This one first,' the Master says, and they lie me doon on the altar, which is still damp wi' blood. I feel it soakin' intae ma troosers as the boy starts chantin' again and a fresh white sheet comes doon tae cover me.

I don't know whether there was ether on it, or chloroform, or maybe it was just fear, but that was the last thing I saw, 'cause I passed oot aboot two seconds later.

So.

Ye don't need many brains tae work oot what happened next, dae ye? Aye, a lesson was taught. A wise and skilled man, that magician, for he was the man in charge, the village in his thrall, willingly daein' what he told them.

Suffice it to say, that was two wee scrotes who never broke intae another hoose, and the same'll be true of you, pal.

I can see fae that look in your eye that you're sceptical aboot this. Maybe you don't believe you're no' gaunny reoffend. Nae changin' your nature, eh? What's bred in the bone will not out of the flesh. Or maybe you don't believe my story?

Aye, that's a fair shout. I didnae tell the whole truth. The story's nae lie, but I changed the perspective a wee bit, for dramatic effect. You see, if you werenae so blissfully oblivious of whose hoose you happen tae be screwin' on any given night, you might have noticed fae the doorplate that my name's no Rab. I wasnae wan ay the burglars.

I was the Sergeant.

I'm retired noo, obviously, but I still perform certain services in the village. We're a close-knit community, ye could say. So I ought to let you know, when you heard me on the phone earlier, sayin' I'd caught a burglar and tae come roon soon as, it wasnae 999 I dialled. Mair like 666, if you catch my drift. 'Cause, let's face it, naebody knows you're here, dae they?

Are you a virgin, by the way?

Aye, right.

Doesnae matter really. Either way, you're well fucked noo.

Aye, good evening, officer, thanks for coming. He's through there. Sorry aboot the whiff. I think you could call that the smell of restorative justice.

Go easy on him. I've a strong feelin' he's aboot tae change his ways. A magical transformation, you could cry it.

How do I know? Personal experience, officer. Personal experience.

SHYAMA PERERA

Singular Devotion

THINK ABOUT the human body as a book: if we recited out loud the sequences of DNA embodied in each of our 100 trillion cells, letter by letter, it would take a hundred years to get to those two precious words – *The End*. But DNA can never spell *The End*, because there are only four letters in its construction – A (adenine), G (guanine), C (cytosine) and T (thymine).

You'd think we'd need hieroglyphics; a Chinese alphabet; a whole bush fire of smoke signals to encapsulate human kind – this complex creature that can think, speak, act and invent at will. But no, we reduce to combinations of A & T and G & C. If it wasn't so miraculous, it would be funny.

My job is making humans out of nothing: or that's how it feels sometimes. I know all about the instructions encoded in each strand of DNA, but what it boils down to is an egg here, some sperm there, and presto – whiz it together in the blender of life and you've a dozen babies-in-waiting.

When I first started out as a fertility specialist, I felt like God, waving a wand and bringing plenty to those who had nothing: women who were barren; men who fired blanks.

The success rates aren't great but have improved enough to guarantee a hit every few days: 'Mrs Jones, you're pregnant – go home and enjoy your last months of uninterrupted sleep.'

Initially this is the biggest high you can get as a doctor, but inevitably we become bored: we get antsy; we want something more; a new way of pushing at the frontiers; of taking control.

Because, of course, we don't have total control: in amongst all that certainty, the hand of fate still has a call . . . You put together two sets of genes and they morph into one, switching on and off at random: straight hair, curly hair, wide nose, long nose; thick fingers, spatulate nails, hammer toes, dimpled bottoms, double crowns, knock-knees, dyslexia . . .

All of these and so much more activated by nature operating the controls and making decisions on our behalf. So: not so much playing God, as giving God the ingredients and letting him or her have final say. If you believe in God, that is.

My patients prefer to call it fate or chance. They find it exciting that after months of rational grind in hospital rooms, filling in temperature and ovulation charts, they can have a period of *not knowing*: of handing over the final product to karma. After all that unerring science, they want something unknowable.

I'm not like that. I think knowledge is the key to power, and the more we can uncover the more powerful we are. That's why, I think, I got this crazy idea into my head about cloning. Not my patients: I'd never take the risk. But what if I cloned myself? There would be no unknown factors: no tricks of fate. *No magic*.

Let's be frank: I'm a single woman of a certain age.

I've dedicated my life to furthering the boundaries of fertility and obstetrics. You don't get many shots at romance along the route. Anyway: having seen so many colleagues felled by the cosh of lust and reduced to the role of yoked guardian of an unknown future, the love thing isn't for me. It involves too much emotion, and the endorsement of duality through investment in property, rings, declarations and the other paraphernalia of commitment. What chaos!

As far as I can tell from patients, men undergo the fertility process to make their women happy – not because children make them happy. I had delivered enough babies to know I wanted a child for myself, not to compound a relationship. Why use a middleman when you own the keys to the warehouse?

At that point it was an interesting thought – nothing more . . .

It was New Year's Eve and I was on call. At midnight I brought a child into the world with the blackest hair, the bluest eyes and the reddest lips I had ever seen. The parents announced she would be called Joy, to represent their release from years of heartache.

'She looks like Snow White,' I said.

'Then perhaps she'll marry a handsome prince,' her mother replied, smiling for the camera. 'Thank you so much, Doctor.'

The father was taking photographs. Within twenty-four hours I had a print for the Fertility Unit's 'baby wall' – a massive montage of babies and growing children who owed their existence to our work. That afternoon I went through it snap by snap, identifying all those infants whose conception had been my doing.

It made me feel good: and broody. Perhaps it was time?

I had thought about artificial insemination but with governments more readily inclined to finger the poor saps who sit in hospital toilets masturbating with an eye on keeping the race alive, I didn't want a child who, in the thick of adolescence, would demand and receive the antecedents of an uninterested father to whom they then ran in a hormonal haze, demanding support, love and accreditation.

Cloning was the obvious answer. I would implant and generate the nuclei from my own cells in an unfertilised egg from which the nuclei had been removed.

I had plenty of eggs I could use: after all, it's my job to harvest fresh eggs from women and then, at a chosen moment, fertilise them in a dish with their husband's spermatozoa. There would be no hand of fate to change the odds, to play games with my expectations: what I would have at the end was another me – a perfect replica down to birthmarks, limb formation and iris patterns.

She would not, however, grow up exactly like me. My own mother had been on a different wavelength and wrongly second-guessed my inclinations right through childhood: my baby and I would be one. Nurture would supersede nature.

I would know everything there was to know about her, from her food preferences to her love of opera; from her hayfever allergy to her tendency to speed on motorways; from her competitiveness on the hockey pitch to her alcohol aversion.

Standing there by the baby wall, I worked it all

through. In unregulated parts of Europe, cloning was already under way. The proofs remained hidden, but the methodology appeared sound. As I packed up for the evening and made a last check on the labour ward, the pieces started to fall into place.

'Mark, I'd like a word.'

'Mon, I'm having a bad day. Is it urgent?'

'You've been having a bad few months: when does it stop?' He visibly paled, and I knew I'd got him. I nodded towards my room. 'It'll only take a minute.'

As I closed the door behind me, he was blustery and on the attack. 'What do you mean, I've been having a bad few months?'

'I see today you wrongly labelled a sample from the Macintoshes.'

'An error that was corrected immediately.'

'A good thing, or she'd have ended up with Mr Howell's sperm and Mr Howell's baby, and as he's black and she's white, that could have been difficult.' There was ice in the air. I went and stood at the window, looking out on to the wet London street. 'Another four eggs wasted. Mrs Macintosh is thirty-eight. She doesn't have many goodies left. She's been trying for two years.'

'I apologise for the mistake.'

'Then there were the three petri dishes of eggs you dropped in the lab last month. Three painful invasive procedures gone to waste; another large bill for the couples involved; and me lying through my teeth telling them that none of the embryos was healthy enough.'

'I'm grateful for that.'

223

'It pushes us down the league tables – the effort we put in doesn't correlate with the results.' He didn't respond, but he couldn't sink any lower at that moment and we both knew it. 'So what's the problem?' I felt him move uncomfortably behind me. I said, 'That cold has lasted months. You're still sniffing.'

'I can't shake it off.'

'Have you tried giving up the white powder?' Now I turned and looked him in the eye. 'You're making too many cock-ups and sooner or later we're going to have a major legal bill. The last thing we need is a drug-dependent consultant who's playing with his patients' lives, happiness and money.'

'I hear you.'

'Good. Because one more strike and officially you'd be out: struck off.' He nodded. I waited a beat and then said, 'But perhaps we can get past this? I want to ask you a private favour. Just between you and me.'

'Anything. I appreciate your discretion, Mon.'

He looked like he was going to be sick, but nothing I'd said was untrue and if it weren't for the fact that the implicit trust in our unit would have been shattered for ever, I would have unmasked him long before.

'I want a baby.'

'You want me to . . . ? You and me?'

'What? For goodness sake, Mark: how could you even think that?' I shook my head in wonder. 'No. I've had control for so long over other people's outcomes, I now want control over my own. I don't believe in magic: I don't want to take pot luck. I'll supply you with a fertilised egg. All you have to do is implant it.'

'Do you want me to harvest the eggs too?'

'No. Leave that to me.'

'But you'll need someone to take . . . Hang on, Mon: where's the egg coming from?' His eyes were on sticks: 'You can't be planning to take someone else's fertilised egg? No: surely not. It's unethical.'

'Isn't that your area of expertise?' I shook my head. 'No, Mark. I'm not taking someone else's fertilised egg but someone else's *un*fertilised egg.'

'Even if you used a lover's sperm it's still another woman's baby.'

'I'm not using sperm, Mark. I'll take an egg and strip it of its chemical memory, replacing it with my own.'

'You mean you're going to clone?' I smiled and said nothing. 'You're going to make a replicant? You can't do that, Mon! *I* can't do it.'

'You don't have a choice. Anyway: it'd be so exciting. You're a doctor – aren't you curious? We don't have to involve anyone from outside. Nobody need ever know.'

'But the baby? There may be side effects. Ask yourself why we're so rarely shown illegally cloned children. The animals with which we've succeeded are the result of hundreds and even thousands of previous, failed, attempts.'

'If it goes wrong, we abort. Pure and simple.'

'It's crazy. If anyone ever found out . . .'

'So you're unmasked either way?' I was lightheaded: on top of the world. 'Give me a couple of weeks to check the methodology and then we'll do it. After all, babies are our business.' I ran my hands over my flat stomach, imagining it swollen with bounty. 'I want to be a mother. I want to have a child entirely my own.'

I felt high at the thought of it: excited beyond

measure. And as he left my office in a state of shock, I was thrilled by the audacity of the idea and the excitement of the outcome.

We engineered it so Mark did the monitoring: the weekly scan to check all was well with my little girl.

'As far as I can tell, Mon, our little project is developing just as it should. The spine's straight, the brain's normal, the size is right.' He moved the ultra-sound control over my gelled belly. 'And a very sound heartbeat too.'

'Let me see.'

'There. The picture's a little bit fuzzy but good enough.'

From the start of the pregnancy, the nurses on our unit had been supportive but understood that, as their boss, I was shy about physical contact. It was Mark who, late one night, took the precious egg I had cultured into a 'blastocyst' – that is, the stage at which the fertilised egg has developed the nucleus that be-comes an embryo – and implanted it in me under local anaesthetic.

It was Mark who took the blood samples, Mark who did the Chorionic Villi testing, Mark who meas-ured the placenta.

Yet in the midst of this highly intimate and con-troversial exchange, relations between the two of us never rose above cordial. Indeed, he was often hostile, resenting the way he'd been cornered, and his bargain-ing power further diminished. Nonetheless, he calmed as the experiment started to take successfully and it was clear I wasn't carrying a three-headed monster.

Meanwhile, the most marvellous change had overcome my body. My hair had thickened and shone like burnished gold, my skin glowed with good health, I didn't have a single moment's sickness. At home I decorated a nursery and put in my favourite colours and shapes, knowing they would be hers too.

Like all mothers-to-be, I played music to my baby; I talked to her; I stroked her; I sang; I danced; I *loved*. And in amongst all that certainty – the knowledge that I was replicating myself within a new environment – there *was* magic. Not that of the dark arts – the handing of fortune to fate – but the happiness of expectation.

I called my parents in Spain and told them they were to have a grandchild. My handful of friends worried about the absence of a father, but were supportive in their views and advice. 'If you really know what you're doing, Monica, there's nothing to argue about.'

When, three weeks early, I went into labour, I did so with sanguine acceptance. Despite the crushing pain of the stomach cramps, there was no sense of panic: only of inevitability. The last scan had been carried out the previous week and I knew my daughter was a healthy weight. I called a cab and I called Mark:

'It's all happening. I'd guess I'm about four centimetres dilated. I'll see you there.'

Then I packed a bag and waited, bent double with the pain and excitement, by my front door.

Labour wasn't as I'd imagined it.

Many of our IVF mothers opted for elective Caesarean section as if fearing something would go wrong at the last minute if the baby came out naturally.

I didn't subscribe to this superstitious thinking. Far

worse was the thought of recovering from major surgery while trying to feed and care for a newborn infant. I preferred a few hours' pain to days of stitches, wound infections, bed rest and scars.

This confidence didn't, however, stop me crying out loud and demanding pain relief. Thankfully, as senior consultant, I got an immediate response. Mark called an anaesthetist out of the operating theatre and I was given a walking epidural – a shot in the back to numb the abdomen but leave the legs functioning.

It didn't quite work that way however and my knees gave way when I tried to stand, so I found myself on the bed, in stirrups, doing things in a more usual, and unrefined, manner.

'How long now?'

The midwife had a quick look:

'You're eight centimetres. Shall I put on the TV: you can take your mind off things.'

'I don't want to keep my mind off *this*.'

Mark said, 'Let her enjoy these final hours of peace; the last thing she needs is to watch Jerry Springer and send her BP soaring.'

The midwife left and Mark turned to face me. He was smiling for the first time in months.

'How are you feeling?' he said. 'Are you memorising every moment for afterwards?'

'It's amazing. I don't feel anything after that injection. Yes: I'm memorising everything. Are you writing it all down?'

'I will be.' He came and peered between my legs. Curiously, at that moment, I felt no awkwardness; no shame: having a baby is what we're put on this earth for – it carries nothing with it but a badge of victory and achievement. 'You've still a little time. I'll grab a sandwich and be back.'

Left alone, I mused about the future. I had decided to call my daughter Dora. It was a firm and upright name but still with a touch of romance, unlike Monica which is functional and tinged with filing-cabinet grey. She would grow like me, but she would have the option of exploring other facets of her personality.

It was here I saw scope for research: would she make the same choices if given a larger set of options? My daughter's voyage through life would be a tool for my own self-examination.

I was so excited by the thought of all this that I barely noticed Mark and the midwife had returned until she spoke.

'You'll be ready to push soon. Is the epidural wearing off?' When I nodded she said, 'Good. Do you want a boy or a girl?'

'It's a girl. I have a feeling in my water.'

In the corner, Mark was scrubbing his arms and pulling on surgical gloves. 'I'm sure you'd still love it if it was a boy, Monica.'

Aware that we had to maintain the pretence in front of an outsider, I smiled. 'I'll love it even if it emerges with half a brain and two tails.'

The midwife laughed. 'No danger of that.'

And then suddenly the pain was overwhelming. I let out a loud groan – it was as if my insides had been put into a cement mixer and were about to explode out of my body like the creature from *Alien*.

Push, push, push: I had said it so many times myself, and suddenly it was me doing the pushing; my baby who was stuck in the bend; my body that was being forced to extremes; my fears that were being exploited. Push, push, push.

'If we don't get this baby out in the next ten minutes, Mon, I'm using forceps. Get your breath back and just go for it.'

So I took a few large breaths and went for it: with all my heart and with all my soul because I could not bear the pain any longer and I just wanted it to end. And suddenly they had the head in their hands and were pulling her out: *pulling me out of me*.

'Doc, stop for a second. The cord's around the neck.'

I forced myself to slow, knowing they needed a few seconds to release the child before it asphyxiated.

'OK. Got it. I'll need to check the baby before handing over to you. Push now. And again. And again. And here we are.'

Both Mark and the midwife were now poring over my baby, clearing the meconium from her nose, checking her pulse, rubbing her body which I could see was blanched from the momentary loss of oxygen.

The midwife wrapped the baby in a piece of cloth.

'Congratulations, Doc, you're a mother. But you called wrong – it's not a little girl, you've a lovely baby boy.'

'No. It's a girl.' I took the baby and kissed her head.

Mark cleared his throat.

'I think you'll find it's a boy.'

'That can't be.'

But when he didn't respond I became confused and pulled open the white sheet. There was, unmistakably, a penis between the baby's legs. I felt dizzy and tired

230

from the strain of giving birth. I wanted to scream. For several seconds I questioned my own sanity.

I said, 'Something's gone wrong.'

'I'll get you a cup of tea,' the midwife said.

'How can this be, Mark? You can't clone a boy from female cells.'

He grinned. 'Two can play at that game, Mon. I too have access to unfertilised eggs. I too know how to cultivate my own nuclei . . .'

I stared at him uncomprehendingly.

'This is *your* baby?'

'This is *me*.' He grinned as I felt the walls starting to close. 'You shouldn't play with fire, Mon: it's too easy to get burned. If you'd asked nicely, I'd have helped you. But you tried to blackmail and now I have the last laugh. Are you going to tell on me?'

I shook my head, frightened by what he was saying.

'I can't believe you did that. Why? What was the point?'

'What's your favourite saying about genes: *in amongst all that certainty the hand of fate still has a call*? The same is true of gene science. You can never trust a human being to do what's right when we all have individual agendas. There's no such thing as certainty. You told me it was stupid to rely on magic, but we do that because it allows for what's unknown.'

I looked down at the baby and all I could see was the infant features of my real-life torturer.

Mark came and stood by the bed.

'So, my love, our little experiment has not had the expected result. And it remains, of course, our secret. I assume I'll have visiting rights?'

The midwife came back with the tea.

'I've made it hot and sweet,' she said. 'I'm used to all this, but I guess it's still a shock when you're the one at the receiving end.'

JILLY COOPER

My Measly Excuses

A S I BEGAN my career by writing short stories, I feel deeply ashamed that I am the only author in this lovely anthology who has not contributed a story. Having just spent several months trekking round the country, however, promoting my last novel, I am desperately trying to get stuck into the next book. Terrified of losing the threads if I embarked on a short story, which always takes me weeks to produce, I am selfishly offering instead a piece I wrote in the early seventies for the *Sunday Times* on the trials of being a writer and a mother. I was obviously as bad at managing my time then as I am now, but I hope it will ring a few bells with young mothers today.

*   *   *

Nothing, I wrote, tears me apart more than the conflicting loyalties of work and family. Take last week, for example. The school holidays were drawing to a close, my daughter was due back at nursery school on Monday, my son was going to a new school on Tuesday. We had had four non-stop weeks of visitors – great fun, but not conducive to work. Next week, I thought longingly, I'll get back to the typewriter and catch up.

Then two days before she was due back, in the

233

middle of Sainsbury's at that point of no return, with a long queue behind and a pyramid of impulse buys on the cash desk in front, my daughter announced she felt sick, and engagingly spat Trebor Refreshers all over me. Next day she'd developed high fever, and the doctor diagnosed measles.

'Oh poor little duck,' I thought – then, in the next second: 'Oh God, bang goes another week's work!'

I raced as always for Mrs Beeton.

'Complications,' I read out, 'include bronchitis, pneumonia. An attack of mumps occasionally follows. Convulsions at the end can be fatal.'

'Oh, poor darling,' I said, 'she'll need her mother. But when the hell am I going to get all that work done?'

'Rubbish,' said my husband. 'The Nanny can look after her perfectly well. Measles is no worse than a bad cold these days.' And he promptly escaped to his office. But there are times even when you know someone else can look after your child perfectly well, that you feel bound to look after her yourself.

The first day my daughter was really ill. And, at the risk of sounding soppy, nothing is more heartrending than a flushed haggard little face on the pillow, a hot hand clutching yours. Never do you feel more indispensable – for the first day at least.

Day two was another matter.

My daughter abandoned her Dame-aux-Camélias act, and emerged a scarlet-faced mini-Hitler, querulously screeching out orders like an Eartha Kitt played at 78.

'Read,' she kept howling, 'read NOW.' Then two minutes later: 'WANT a drINK!' and the incessant

'Turn OVER,' as every twenty seconds she got bored with the programme on television. After an hour or two, my Florence Nightingale act was slipping badly.

I retired downstairs for a break. Ten seconds later she shrieked as though she'd been murdered. Racing up two flights, I discovered she'd lain on a cold flannel. I went downstairs again – another shriek. She wanted a biscuit. Finally she dropped off to sleep, and I grabbed an opportunity to work. But five minutes later there were more yells – she wanted to go to a birthday party. Deciding she must be delirious, and needed humouring, I let her put on her red party dress, which matched her face. She lay in bed raging with temperature like a stricken masquerader.

The doctor arrived with a pretty Scottish nurse.

'I'm terribly worried about her,' I said.

But upstairs, my daughter had made a dramatic recovery and, back in her nightie, all smiles, cheeks bulging with toast and jam, was watching a war film on television. The senior dog rose and goosed the Scottish nurse, who said he was a tremendous 'pairsonality'. A religious programme followed the war film. The camera panned in on Christ on the cross. 'That's Jesus,' I said. 'He takes care of you.'

'No, he don't,' said my daughter. 'My Nanny do.'

She was plainly better. I shut myself away to work, but to no avail, for my worries had promptly shifted to my son and his first day at school the next day. His new-niform (as he called it) was already laid out – all unworn like a bride's.

I had also been worrying all the holidays about the fact that he couldn't tie his laces. We'd got round it until now by buying slip-on shoes, but the school's list specified lace-up gym shoes. I decided to give him a crash course, and bent over him, instructing, cajoling.

'Oy can't do it,' he said crossly, 'while Oy can hear you breathing.' Two minutes later I was presented with a perfectly tied bow. I felt as though I'd conquered Everest.

Euphoria evaporated with the arrival of my husband, who pointed out quite kindly that the char had dusted all the wires out of the hi-fi, that I'd forgotten yet again to collect his Grand National winnings from the betting shop, and that I was making too much fuss about my son's first day.

'How's Emily?' he said.

'Fine,' I replied sulkily.

'I told you measles was no worse than a bad cold.'

I slept badly that night, waking up every five minutes panicking that I wouldn't wake up in time to take my son to school. At 6.15, however, he wandered in bug-eyed but completely dressed in new uniform, collar askew, garters inside his socks.

'Did you sleep?' said my husband, when he woke up.

'Yes,' I lied, trying to be brave.

'I didn't – at all,' he said.

Later I took my son, wild with excitement, to school. His watchword, like Huckleberry Finn's, has always been 'trust in the unexpected'. He looked so vulnerable, disappearing into a sea of other blue-blazered boys. I drove home with a lump in my throat.

At least with him at school, and my daughter recovering fast, I felt I should get some work done. Total disaster. I couldn't settle to anything, fretting all day whether he'd be all right, would he like them, more important – would they like him?

Hours early, I tarted myself up and set out to collect him. I sat in the sunshine outside the school, biting my nails, watching elegant mothers drive up in their dark glasses and smart cars. Eventually, small boys appeared blowing down rolled-up pictures, duelling with cricket stumps. I'll be good for ever, I prayed, if he comes out happy. The forecourt was now full of grinning pupils with pudding-basin haircuts. Suddenly I recognised one of them as my son, not a tearstain in sight.

Information about his day filtered through on the way home – sporadically, like the first results on election night.

'We had fish fingers for lunch . . . and tadpoles, we did them in class. Oy asked a boy if he could do laces, he said No. Oy said Oy could . . . mostly. Oy've got a friend, but he was told to be because Oy'm a new boy. Moy friend doesn't wear gutters on his socks.'

Relief and joy flooded me. What on earth was the point of worrying about anything? Trust in the unexpected. Then, inevitably, came the sunset touch. My son eyed me beadily.

'Oy think,' he said, 'you ought to wear smarter trousers when you pick me up.'

KATHY LETTE

Recipe For Disaster

LOVE! THAT's the magic ingredient, cupcake. That's what makes a balanced and well-organised and above all, beautifully arranged family life and happy home . . . What? Don't look at me like that! We *are* happy! . . . Even without your father . . . Scared him away?! I did *no such thing*. I *adore* male company . . . especially if he owns it, ha ha ha . . .

Oh well, shoot me for having a sense of humour! It's just, now that my darling little daughter is sweet sixteen, I feel I can talk to you as an equal . . . Put the cat out, will you? And pick up some basil while you're out there. Oh! And could you quickly do that bit of washing up there that needs doing? You are *such* a treasure!

I *am* listening, sausage, I am. It's just that I have seventy-five home-made fondue fancies to make before dawn. I know it's important to you, dumpling, I do. Pour me a little nip of my home-made sloe gin and I'll tell you everything, OK?

Well, it's just that when I became such a huge success – the 'Doyen of Domesticity', *Vogue* calls me. The 'new Martha Stewart' – or was that *Newsweek*? . . . Well, the TV shows, the appearances on other prime-time shows to *promote* the TV shows, the radio slots and book signings and newspaper columns and hypermarket tie-ins, the magazines – mass market retail brand no less – the speciality home products, the cooking of fondue fancies for the President's lunch, for Chrissake, here, at home, tomorrow – make it a double shot, will you, sweetie? Well, your father just couldn't stand the competition. The man is weak, that's the problem. He may be your father, but he's a weak, weak man. I mean, imagine it! Reporting me to the police! It was only a stun gun. I didn't really *wound* him! Your pathetic old man just couldn't stand the heat in the kitchen . . . ha ha ha.

What! What on earth do you mean, *neither could I*? That's not fair! I didn't hire my enablers to . . . There's no need to swear, missy. What? Why *can't* I call them that? Because that's what they are – my staff *enable* me to bring my message of domesticity and simplicity to the rest of America . . . OK then, have it your own way. My *nannies* and *gardeners* and *cooks* and *house-keepers* and *ironing ladies* and *personal seasonal closet reorganisers* as you insist on mundanely calling them – free me from the chores of . . .

No! Not of being 'the person I claim to be'! That's cruel and you know it! I have always been a very 'hands on' mum. Didn't we design Hallowe'en-themed paper lanterns together just last week? . . . Well, yes, it *was* for a magazine shoot . . . but it was also quality mother and daughter bonding time. And didn't we marbleise our own Thanksgiving ornaments? . . . Oh no, that was for the American Housewife Society, wasn't it? And what about all those home-made soaps? . . . OK, I admit that I did forget you were allergic, but it was only one night in hospital . . . The *last* thing we did together? Um . . . well, let me think. Um . . . Yes! We reorganised the condiments cupboard together. Just last week. Well, all right, *you* did most of it, but you got your pocket money, didn't you? And just look at us now! Chopping the Japanese noodle salad together. You can't say we don't have fun, my little felafel. Can't you chop any faster? A break!? Absolutely not. You've got twenty cabbages to go.

Yes, all in all, I think I haven't done too badly as a mother – seeing as I have become one of the Busiest and Most Successful Women In America . . . No! Not by advising other women to stay at home! That's *not* what I've . . .

Hypocritical?! . . . Misogynistic?! . . . Selfish?! . . . *Me*!!!!! How can you say that when I have dedicated my life to helping other women? Not all women are as well off as you, young lady! Oh no. But that doesn't mean that they can't create a happy, inspirational home. Most women don't have 'enablers'. Most women need to know for *them*selves how to keep a peeled banana fresh! How to decorate a Christmas tree with bottle tops! How to prune the topiary in the shape of their husband's name! And *I* am the one to tell them.

I have taught the wives of this country to tap into their initiative, their ingenuity, their practicality! And all by just using things that are lying around the home! The Christmas cards out of potato shavings! The pine-cone centrepieces! I have taught the women of the world how to bring a pot-pourri of magic into their families' lives by baking, sewing, doing, sampling, kneading, inventing, making . . . They're out there *now*, wandering through the woods collecting filberts and pine needles, washing then painting path gravel. *I have taught an insecure nation of moms how to come up with fresh and exciting picnic ideas each season*!!! How to find that magic ingredient called 'love' . . . You are *not* chopping that cabbage finely enough. Japanese noodle salad needs to be very fine. If I've told you once I've told you a million times . . . Don't point that knife at me like that! Puddin' pie! Put that knife down! I don't know *what's* got into you . . .

What's got into *me*? *Your boyfriend*? What on earth do you mean? Your boyfriend has *not* got into me! That's a scurrilous lie. To even think such a thing – oh God, I feel sick. What do you mean by 'It must be someone I ate'?! I'll wash your mouth out with the soap we made together. Who ever told you such a thing! I'll sue . . . Oh. *He* did . . . Well, I don't know why you even bothered putting him on your menu. That boy's *coq au vin* is *so* undercooked.

Look, it was only once. It was a rare mistake. I mean have you any idea how lonely it is being an Icon? Pass me those tissues, will you? No not *those*! The recycled, organic floral ones. Having to live up to the image of the happy, smiling parent with *Kinder* frolicking by the family hearth and sleigh bells in the lane? Selling perfection is very, very stressful.

But lamb chop, I did it for *you* . . . To protect you from making a terrible mistake. The sort of mistake *I* made at your age by losing my cherry parfait to your ungrateful father. I always told you that boy wasn't Michelin standard. And now I've got him to *prove* that he's just not good enough for you . . .

What did you say? Did I hear correctly? Did you say that *I'm* the one who is not good enough for you???!!!

Good enough! I'll have you know, young lady, that I am now a superlative! Oh yes. As the *New York Times* has pointed out, I am getting so famous, I no longer need a last name. Like Hilary, Jackie, Madonna, Cher – I have become simply a one-word icon. No more than that. A human adjective. Just decorate a holiday centrepiece with gold-leaf pine cones and every woman at the table will be counted on to gaze admiringly at the display and declare, 'Oh, that's so very . . .'

What did you call me!? How *dare* you call me that! You little bitch! Get out! Go on. I can't help it if you insist on making yourself so unattractive! I keep *telling* you that pastels and linens are all a woman should wear. I keep suggesting that you dress more like me. A crisp pink button-down is the most desirable look for a . . . Don't you dare call me that name again . . . And under my own imported, terracotta-tiled roof! Get your bags and get out, you ungrateful little cow. And after all I've done for you! *I* taught you how to make dinner-table ornamental wreaths with beeswax candles!

No, wait. Do you think you could leave tomorrow instead, pumpkin? I've got to hand-embroider the napkins, stencil the table-cloth, make a cassoulet for fifty and show the handyman how to blow-dry the chickens' plumes for the farmyard photo shoot – and all before dawn . . . Oh typical! Just like your father! Timing your running out on me for its maximum disruption in my life . . . I've got the President coming tomorrow for a family get-together – and I have no fucking family! All I ever do is give! Like rays of the sun, I just radiate out my recipe of simplicity and domesticity and magic. My simple message of just – *using things that are lying around the home.*

PAULINE McLYNN

Mr Smith's Return

FIVE YEARS into their childless marriage Mr Smith's wife choked on a fish bone, fell face first into her home-made bouillabaisse and expired. This momentous tragedy took less than fifteen minutes and left Mr Smith a widower with full custody of a runty cat called Tyke and a dormer bungalow in a small estate of no great importance to anyone but the Conservative politician who found himself constantly fighting a marginal seat. For a week the house was full of family (Mr Smith's only brother, a dour bachelor who smoked too much) and sundry neighbours. They cooked casseroles, filled sandwiches, drank cheap wine and beer, then disappeared to leave Mr Smith and Tyke to get on with the rest of their lives. Initially Mr Smith spent his time ignoring personal hygiene, wetting the cat's fur and replenishing the liquor stock as he drank, then realised that he looked like a hippy, his liver hurt and the cat was saturated. It was time to get back to running his business, a small, independent newsagent's ten minutes from home. Coincidentally, this was also about the time taken by the late Mrs Smith to die and the journey's irony was never quite lost on her husband.

As the cat was little inclined to housework and Mr

Smith had a fear of the vacuum cleaner a charwoman was engaged to come once a week to do for them, and from then on they led their quiet bachelorhoods amidst relative order. If the cleaning lady had a fault, it was to try to introduce new women to Mr Smith. He managed to shun most advances and, at any rate, Tyke never seemed to take to any of the potential dates. His reaction to any questioning of this was a shrug followed by a faraway look, a handy technique that Mr Smith began to copy. Mr Smith reasoned that his romantic life was at an end and little could, or should, be done about that. Accordingly, when he took on an assistant at the newsagent's he chose an unfeasibly plain girl called Dora, who wore her name like a badge. Tyke's romancing had ended at three months of age when he was dispatched to the local vet to be castrated; an event which caused his and Mr Smith's eyes to water, even in memory.

The late Mrs Smith had been a houseproud woman with a talent for sewing. Hence the dormer was festooned with all manner of ruche and pleat, pelmet and cushion. Pink was the theme of the season before her death and so it remained after it, the brightness fading gently with each passing year. She had also been something of a plantswoman and her attic workroom was a veritable botanic garden. Some months after her untimely death Mr Smith realised that his aching heart would never heal if he continued to enter her sanctum each day to water her plants (most of whose names he could not pronounce), confronting daily her absence and his loss. And so he covered her beloved sewing machine with a dustsheet, turned his back on the greenery and bolted the door shut with a heavy lock. Tears masked his vision as he hammered the metal into place, and as they cleared he found himself pounding his own left hand into a pulp. His body tightened, receptors waiting to receive pain as nerves collated the damage and prepared to send the hurt coursing along his arm. But to his amazement, and fascination, nothing came. He was inured to outside forces. Life was a blanket of slow-motioned misery, each day passing numbly into the next. After a time he grew accustomed to the absence of real delight and reached an accommodation with himself. He might almost have said he was content again.

With his princess locked in her tower, Mr Smith felt spent and couldn't muster the resolve or energy to redecorate the bungalow. He learned to ignore its feminine accessories, while studiously dumping cushions and antimacassars as soon as Tyke had shredded them. It was a system and it seemed to work.

Left to his own devices, albeit reluctantly, Mr Smith was free to indulge in his other great passion: golf. He was a man who did not mind playing a round alone, and he frequently did, relishing the wasted walk and a solitude that felt pertinent to his lonely circumstance. At the same time he was more than able to hold his own in two- and more-somes when the club required it, and all who accompanied him shook their heads in private at the terrible fate of such a lovely man.

With no wife to tell him otherwise, Mr Smith turned his back garden into a putting green, practising all the hours that nature gave (he was disinclined to invoke God in any such equation since his widowerhood, annoyed by the arrogance of an Almighty who could be so cruel). His game improved and he began to win prizes. As the cushions steadily made their exits, crystal goblets appeared on the sideboards, alongside ugly lamps with fringed shades and dodgy trophies in wood and pewter engraved with his name. Once, at Christmas, he won a sixteen-pound turkey and a ham, which he donated to charity as he and Tyke could never hope to make significant inroads into that amount of food by themselves.

One balmy summer's evening, a Tuesday, Mr Smith was breaking in a putter on his self-made green. Tyke lounged indolently on a clump of catnip, wearing an inscrutable grin. In the distance a lawnmower growled and from time to time faraway shouts of playing children wafted in on a non-existent breeze. Amidst the comfort of the familiar was a strange motor's roar. Eventually it identified itself, as a removals van pulled into next door's driveway followed by a beaten-up station wagon full of duvets, a woman and a sulky teenager with a bad hairdo. Mr Smith could not tell if the youngster was male or female; perhaps a little of both, he decided. The woman chatted to the air as she removed the 'Sold' sign from her front garden and surveyed her new empire. The cul-de-sac was alive with talk of paint, and grass-cutting, and don't-take-this-out-on-me. Eager to remain invisible, Mr Smith and Tyke fled indoors, the former to a glass of brandy, the latter to the press under the stairs. The fractured silence echoed for another hour before calm and the old equilibrium was restored. They slept fitfully that night.

Mr Smith took care to leave early for work and return late in order to avoid his new neighbours. Something in the woman's voice, though pleasant, warned of friendliness, and he didn't feel available for anything that might entail. However, he was at the coal-face in his shop and the public could not be banned from this place of commerce. Actually, the public could, but it would have made poor financial sense. And so it was that, on Dora's break one day, Mr Smith found himself face to face with his neighbour. She was a petite ball of energy, with dark bobbing curls and a jaunty walk. She bought a *Cosmopolitan* and a bar of hazelnut chocolate and confessed that she should have neither. Mr Smith, in turn, neglected to confess his address and so alert her of their mutual domestic proximity. He rang in her money and sweated until she left. And for ten minutes afterwards. Why, he could not exactly say.

All was well for our Mr Smith until the evening he was putting the finishing touches to his very own sand bunker. A stand-off had occurred between him and Tyke, both feeling it was for his exclusive use. Tyke regarded the patch as the most wonderful litter tray this side of Dudley, and he greatly enjoyed its outdoor aspect. Mr Smith resented shovelling out the cat turds each day and was trying to hit upon a clever way of covering the sand. Suddenly, a head bobbed above the wooden fencing dividing his property from next door.

'We meet at last,' sang the woman's voice.

Mr Smith backed up to the bank of rudbeckia behind him. He managed a sound like 'ngya' and fell silent again, eyes wide with social uncertainty. He was well able to talk to women at his shop and on the golf course; what had got into him here and now?

'I wondered if you and your other half would like to

come over for a drink some evening?' the woman continued.

'Kate?' Mr Smith exclaimed, surprised to have said his late wife's name aloud for the first time in an aeon. Tyke threw him a quizzical look. 'No,' Mr Smith blurted.

'Oh, right,' the woman said, disappointed and not a little stung by his curt rejection.

Time to act and quickly, thought Mr Smith. 'No,' he reiterated, kicking himself mentally as he did.

'I understand, believe me,' the woman said, and began to disappear behind the fencing.

'NO!' Mr Smith called. At least it halted her descent. 'What I mean is, thank you very much, but we can't accept your offer. Or, that is, I can, but . . . Kate . . . cannot. Kate . . . is . . . dead.' The statement hung there, smacking of the unfinished yet standing alone as a complete fact of Mr Smith's life. He didn't know what to add to take the baldness off it and, tempted as he was by a long 'er . . .', he left it.

The woman's hand raced to her mouth in horror. 'Oh Lord, no, it's me who should apologise. I had no idea. I'm so sorry. You must think me a total idiot. Please take some time to forgive me and, if you ever do, perhaps you would like to come visit sometime?'

And then a strange thing happened. Well, two strange things to be precise. Tyke climbed up on to the fence and presented his tummy for the woman to rub, and Mr Smith found he had gripped the trowel so hard it hurt.

'My name is Helen, by the way.'

'John,' Mr Smith managed, through gritted teeth, then went to find the first-aid box.

It was Dora who first commented on the after-shave lotion.

'Boss,' she said.

'Yes?' Mr Smith replied.

'No,' she continued patiently, understanding that he was an ardent golfer and therefore not of this world. 'Your after-shave, it's called Boss, isn't it?'

Dora felt on solid factual ground, as this was the same as the scent worn by The Digger Foley, an Irish builder she was attempting to stalk at Hilites Night Club. The Digger's was usually intermingled with the smells of Guinness and whisky chasers and Dora shivered to remember him. Mr Smith took this to be a bad sign.

'Don't you like it?' he asked in a worried voice, aware of the fact that he'd found a dusty bottle of the stuff at the back of the bathroom cupboard and there was every chance that it had turned rancid since its last outing.

'No, no,' Dora said. 'Someone just walked over my grave, that's all.'

In the tortured silence that followed, Dora desperately tried to pinpoint what she had said wrong. Mr Smith bolted for the door and home, where he showered thoroughly before throwing away the new shirt he'd been wearing, along with the offending bottle of Boss. As he was sinking into a lather of self-loathing at his despicable behaviour, and the betrayal of his dead wife's memory, back at the shop Dora finally copped to her mistake.

'Shit,' she muttered, reaching for a packet of Yorkshire Toffees.

It was only when Tyke stopped eating that Mr Smith rallied himself to deal with the outside world again.

Not that the cat seemed under the weather, no, his spirits were as high as his normal indolence, he just wasn't interested in his food. Mr Smith took to rustling up treats: free-range chicken, liver, even once a half of silver teal duckling. And though Tyke made an effort, he did little more than lick the meal all over (thus ensuring that it was his and could not be shared), and nibble daintily at a few morsels. Mr Smith took the cat to Mr Apples, the unlikely-named veterinarian of the region, who pronounced Tyke fit as a fiddle and perhaps a little overweight. Mr Smith suspected a cancer, swelling his beloved feline, and ordered a round of expensive tests, all of which were returned negative.

'Is there any chance he's being fed elsewhere?' Mr Apples asked, not unreasonably.

The very thought struck horror into Mr Smith. After all, he and Tyke were in this together and did not need anyone else.

'I shouldn't think so,' he pronounced loftily, and made a note to change vets.

Imagine, then, our hero's surprise to hear his neighbour's musical voice chatting to Tyke one evening and asking if he'd like some tuna. Mr Smith peeked over the fence to see *his* cat wind himself, purring, around the woman's legs then tuck into a mound of fish. Mr Smith cleared his throat nervously.

'Eh, Helen,' he squeaked, astonished to be addressing her by name. 'Have you been feeding Tyke much over the last while?'

His neighbour laughed. 'That little villain has practically moved in,' she told him. 'You'd think he never saw a bite at all the way he wolfs down his grub.'

Mr Smith caught Tyke's happy and mischievous eye and promptly fell back into his own garden. He lay winded and groaning in the sandpit, uncomfortably aware of the odour of disturbed cat turd. Helen climbed up her side of the fence and, seeing his predicament, immediately scaled the wooden barrier and ran to his aid. She knelt by him cooing and checking his arms and legs for breaks and bruises. Mr Smith's face boiled as his treacherous body stirred and, inappropriately, his penis began to swell beneath the pleats of his brown corduroy pants.

'Christ,' he mumbled, trying to rise and flee the scene. In so doing he inadvertently grabbed his neighbour and toppled them both on to the ground. His face was an inch from hers, her breath warm and rhythmic upon his lips. And then, to his dismay, he kissed her, hard and long and hungrily, leaving them both quite breathless and aroused. Mr Smith pulled away, distraught. He stumbled to his feet, shaking.

'I shouldn't have. I'm so, so sorry. I'm the lowest crawling thing on earth,' he revealed.

Helen smiled. 'I really rather enjoyed it, John, and I wish you wouldn't apologise. It can't have been that bad.'

'It was,' Mr Smith roared.

He hulked away towards his house, leaving a bewildered neighbour to nurse her hurt. 'Kate,' he whispered to himself, over and over.

'You've got cat shit on your jumper,' his neighbour's daughter called to him over the fence. She shot her mother a disgusted look, then disappeared in a funk of teenage attitude.

The next time Helen encountered John Smith she cut straight to the chase.

'How long has your wife been dead?' she asked, in a tone that precluded lies, or escape.

'Two years, three months, five days and seven hours.' He paused. 'Pretty much to the minute,' he added.

She nodded; proof of some point he didn't get, let alone understand. 'And what age are you?'

'Thirty-four,' he answered, now totally at a loss.

She left him to stew. Mr Smith considered joining a monastery.

An uneasy calm settled over numbers seven and eight of the cul-de-sac. This was largely due to the residents' avoidance of each other. But, as with all alleged good things, it came to an end. The evening in question was a close and muggy one: 'murder weather', according to Dora. Mr Smith was clearing out the sand bunker for the umpteenth time and wondering why he had ever doubted Tyke's appetite. He heard a muffled sound from the adjacent garden and prepared to run away. Then the muffle became a sob, and that sob borrowed another, and another, as it built to an aching paean of sorrow. He dared to look over the fence. Helen was sitting on a step, crying. He was torn between embarrassment at discovering her in this private moment and the notion that he should somehow comfort her.

'Is anything the matter?' he asked, gently.

Her lovely face was awash with tears as she brought her gaze to his. His heart filliped and skipped along its strings.

'Nothing you can help with,' she answered.

The conversation was clearly at an end, but Mr Smith could not leave matters between them as they were.

'Are you sure?' he persisted. 'Try me and see.'

She gave a long sigh, by way of gearing up. 'It's Rachel,' she explained. 'She's never forgiven me for her father leaving us.' It was a big admission and John Smith held his breath until she was ready to continue. 'To be honest, I don't want to break her heart and tell her that he was never likely to stay.' She paused again, searching for words to adequately explain their situation. 'I just don't think he ever really liked us, me and her. That's why he took off.' She gulped in air, too late to staunch those last thoughts from speech. 'Now, of course, nothing I do is right or good enough.' She wiped her eyes with her sleeve. 'But that's all normal, all in a day's battle for the two of us. The real problem is that I promised to make her a dress she's designed for the start of term . . .' Again the tears rolled down her cheeks. 'And my wretched sewing machine has just packed up on me. I have to finish it tonight and I don't see how I can, now.' The sobs came freely and Mr Smith longed to hold and comfort her. In horror, he realised that only one thing could truly do that and, although it was within his gift, he was not quite sure that it was actually within his abilities to grant it.

An eternity seemed to pass. Tyke rolled up to his neighbour's house and promptly went to the crying woman, to help as best he could. Mr Smith was stung by his own cowardice. It was then that he made his momentous decision.

'Helen,' he said. 'Give me ten minutes, then follow me into my house.'

John Smith's head rang with the white noise of anguish as he scaled each step of the stairs to the attic room. His legs were weighted steel straining against this unnatural act. His hands shook and each breath taken ached. His splintered heart darted jagged pains through his chest. He stopped at the door, its hefty lock rusting into eternity. As he fumbled with the key, he began to cry.

'Kate,' he whispered. 'My love. Give me a sign. If this is not what you want, tell me. If I am betraying you, let me know.'

Hot scalding tears fell from his eyes, burning along his cheeks and down on to his uncertain hands. The key turned. Helen climbed the steps and stood by his side. As he pushed the door she took his trembling hands in hers. They stood to marvel and gasp. John Smith had his sign. There, in the neglected attic, every plant and bush was alive with flowers and buds. The last of the evening light bathed the room in a vibrant glow of orange and red and the hope of a new beginning. The dust-sheet lay folded by Kate's sewing machine as it waited, patient and ready, for the next Mrs Smith.

MARIKA COBBOLD

Laterna Magica

A MIRROR IN three parts. I am reflected in each; full
frontal, left side, right side; bloody awful in all of
them; tired, washed-out as if I had been left in the rain
for a week not just run through it for a couple of
hundred yards. Lank pale hair, blotchy skin, unremarkable lips, Botox-smooth forehead. 'You don't look a
day over forty,' the woman in the dress shop had told
me. 'That's just great,' I said, 'seeing I'm thirty-nine.'

She had muttered that she was only trying to be nice.
People shouldn't *try* to be nice, they should just *be* nice
. . . or not if that was the deal.

Shortly I would have to be nice myself; amusing, in
fact dazzling wouldn't go amiss. The show must go on,
that's what everyone has always told me. Lately I have
asked myself why. Why does it have to? Because if we
allow ourselves to stop we might never get started
again, like travellers lost in a snowstorm whatever
we do we must carry on because the alternative is
too soft, too tempting, too easy and . . . The End. I
pick up the bottle of foundation and squeeze some on to
a tiny sponge, dabbing. Slowly the pale-honey liquid
erases the map of Sin City that had become my face:
spider veins and freckles, tiny spots and dry patches, all
pointing to Too Much Sun, Too Little Water, Too

Much Alcohol, Too Many Sleepless Nights. I look at my face in the three-way mirror. My hair is scraped back and now I am paler than ever with the foundation masking even the faint pink of my lips. I should let them see me like this. But no, that would be self-indulgent. 'A problem shared is a problem doubled,' my grandmother used to say; my grandmother who had donned top hat and tails and performed magic tricks for a roomful of frightened and bewildered evacuees twenty minutes after receiving news that her husband of five months was missing in action. She had known him for twelve years and loved him about the same amount of time but she lost him in less than a minute.

The children from the East End had watched her, their faces pinched closed with worry and suspicion relaxing little by little until all (bar a small red-haired girl in the front row) were laughing, or smiling at the very least with two jumping up and down with excitement. My grandmother had walked back into the makeshift dressing room at the back of the village hall and washed away her sooty moustache and her blackened eyebrows. Then at last she could weep. But the held-back tears were packed so tightly at the back of her eyes that when they fell they dropped as two tiny pearls. The pearls that my grandmother wept are set into the lid of her silver powder compact. She had left it to me and I keep it on my dressing table, always.

Cheeks or eyebrows first? *Cheeks first*; that's what the new beauty editor had said. *And none of that shading with a bronzer either. Instead, brush a peachy pink on to the apples of the cheeks. You get the apples of your cheeks like this* – grinning like a death mask.

*   *   *

The bowl of dark-red apples had stood on the counter, a splash of colour among the beiges and creams of the hotel lobby. I put my hand out for one and I don't even like apples. 'I just can't resist a freebie,' I had explained. 'I don't call that greed. No, it's about that slightly guilt-edged thrill of having something given to you and nothing asked in return.'

He smiled at me, the delighted grin that seemed reserved for me, as if I had just leapt out from a giant cake wearing a bunny costume.

'What?' I asked, encouraged, coquettish.

He kissed me on the top of the head as he filled in the hotel check-in form. 'I just love your enthusiasm; even for a bloody apple.'

I bit into the fruit and grimaced; it was the usual story; the prettier, the more perfect-looking the apple the less taste it had.

It was two in the morning and we had run off, left the party and our old loves to drive off together into the night. In our defence we were very young. Then again, men younger than we were then had given their lives for their country, written immortal symphonies and plays that made people laugh and weep in recognition hundreds of years later. So all right then, we were in love, and temporary insanity is at least a defence in the eyes of the law.

In the tall mirror of the dreary hotel bedroom, my make-up removed, I looked beautiful. He said so and I knew he was right. But as I told him, I never was until I met him.

We suited each other, I thought, as we lay in each other's arms, damp with sweat and breathless; both of us tall, slim, nervy, clever, vain.

257

'This is real, isn't it?' he asked. 'It's not just sex, not just infatuation?'

I raised myself on one elbow and gazed down into his slanted green eyes, the eyes of some wild animal my sister had said earlier that evening. 'Don't be so middle-class. So what if it is just sex?' I was enjoying my recklessness, too full of love, of him and of myself, to worry about anything at all.

He laughed, pulling me down on top of him. 'You're right; let's get rid of the grown-ups.'

'Go out and face the world,' he said the next morning when all my bravado had vanished on the back of the night sky. 'That's right, put that red lipstick on and go out there and stand up for yourself. He was a bully. You know that you have every right to end it.'

'And Julie?'

'It's in the past.' He shrugged his shoulders, palms turned skywards, the corners of his wide mouth pulling downwards. 'It's all in the past. There's no point looking back. People just have to get on with their lives.'

I looked at his charming face and the concern that did not quite reach the eyes and shivered.

'What?' he asked.

'I think someone just walked over my grave.'

I plucked my eyebrows, perfecting the arch, flinching as I removed a particularly stubborn hair.

'Does that hurt?' he had asked. In the mirror I smiled at him. 'No. And if it does it's a satisfying pain.'

'Like sex?'

Now I had turned round, still smiling. 'Better,' I lied.

*   *   *

Now I fill in my eyebrows with a brown pencil. Light-brown and absolutely no hint of a red tone. I am a woman who asks questions; as a journalist it's my job, but I never question the beauty editor. I glance at my watch; half an hour to go and I look longingly at my bed. Coming in wet from the rain, I had paused by the bed and stroked his pillow, picking it up and sniffing the pillowcase that smelt of lemon and of him. I wanted to creep in under the duvet and lie there, where it felt safe and it seemed, quite wrongly of course, that no one could find me. But they were on their way, too late to stop them now.

He used to love watching me make-up, sitting cross-legged on our bed, our eyes meeting in the mirror. 'Natural is overrated,' he said. 'I like a woman who understands artifice.' When he introduced me to his friends he said, 'I know she's blonde but she's the nearest thing to a French woman I could find at a Hunt Ball.' I loved the way he was interested in girly things. It didn't seem likely, judging by how he looked, six foot three, broad and muscular. 'He's like a gay best friend who isn't gay,' I had told my girlfriend Charlotte. 'We go shopping together, wandering round markets picking out just the right cheeses and fruit and cuts of meat. Clothes too, he loves coming with me when I buy clothes.' And Charlotte had agreed that he sounded pretty much ideal.

It is dark now; gone six. I can hear their steps in my mind, like distant hooves, approaching, stage-style. I have a friend, James, who is an analyst. Once, a long time ago, I had confided in him how I worried that I'd lose it all, that my happiness might turn sour because it

259

had been born out of the pain of others. I had not known it back then, the night I ran off into the December night with my new love, but Julie had already looked out a wedding dress. It was a previous thing to do when she was not even engaged but it showed the dreams she had invested in the man I was busy kissing under the just-so (not too many or too gaudy) Home Counties stars.

He is such a calm, comforting person, my friend James, with his big hands and warm brown eyes. I had felt sure he would say the right thing, banish those silly thoughts from my head.

Instead he had nodded. 'It's possible,' he said, and the smile prepared and waiting on my lips vanished leaving me to stare at him, wide-eyed and hurt.

'I know I'm being silly,' I said, trying to steer him back to my script.

'No.' He searched for his pipe in the pocket of his tweed jacket. 'Not at all.' Men who wore tweed and smoked pipes were *always* comforting; so what was *wrong* with James? 'You're not being silly. It's my belief that things do even out, eventually. It's the law of the universe.'

I looked sullen. 'They weren't even engaged, him and Julie. Bill and I were, but it never would have worked.'

James had smiled the serene smile of he whose arse is not on the line. 'Well, you asked me.'

Mascara is essential on the ageing eye, not eye-liner, nor shadow, but mascara, three coats.

Don't be afraid of mascara, the beauty editor says. *It's a fallacy that more than one coat is too much.*

Flies' legs. What about furry flies' legs?

That kind of thinking is, like, so old-fashioned.
Flies' legs, spider's legs, whatever. Just pile it on:
smoky.

He said I was sweet. For a while I was sweet. I cut my
hair in a sweet bob and kept my fringe in place with a
cute clip. 'You have the softest little hands,' he said,
and he took my hand lifting it to his lips, kissing it
tenderly while gazing into my eyes. I looked back into
his eyes, smiling dreamily, trying not to think of my
mother saying that no gentleman actually kissed your
hands but just bowed down low and brushed the air
above.

My father had been a hand-kisser of the elegant
variety; no slobbering of lips on skin there. My
mother seemed to find it hard to remember what
good could be said about him. He had left her when
their first child was nine months old. The child was
me. The day he left, my mother took to her bed and
stayed there until the next morning, having first called
Mrs Brown next door asking her to mind me. (Grieving was such a controlled thing for the women that
came before me; with none of my abandoned screaming and throwing of wedding gifts and precious
articles of special importance.) The next day she
had emerged from her room, puffy-eyed but with
immaculately powdered cheeks and her lips set in a
determined cyclamen line.

She had gathered me up from Mrs Brown and gone
to see a man she knew who took the photographs for
the front of the knitting patterns she and her friends
favoured, offering me up as a child model. I got the
job; I was a beautiful baby – even those who were not

my mother said so. She later told me that she knew we would have to earn our own keep as my father was the kind of man who forgot his obligations. I remember her, my mother, standing before some mirror or another; in the hall, in her bedroom, in a restaurant, chattering, darting between subjects, leaning in towards her reflection, stretching her upper lip taut as, gilt powder compact in hand, she freshens her make-up. 'That good-for-nothing man has not sent us any money this month either, dear. Goodness, where have all those lines come from, I look a perfect fright. Oh your Aunt Gill will be pleased when she arrives next week, she's always been jealous of my complexion but there's nothing to be jealous about *now* really, you've grown out of your blazer *and* your mac.' And the lid would snap shut and she would turn away from her reflection and I would meet her wide blue gaze straight on.

These days to powder or not was the question. Shine was unbecoming, however fashionable it might be, yet natural was best once you got to a certain age; you did not want to stand there smiling in the harsh light from a south-facing window or beneath an energy-saving bulb with the stuff gathering in the creases around your eyes and mouth. The answer I had found was to use just a tiny bit of the lightest light-reflecting variety, loose of course and applied with a puff and any surplus removed with a large soft brush.

Unlike my father, my husband prided himself on shouldering his responsibility. 'Look at me,' he demanded, standing there naked in our bedroom after I had told him I was pregnant. And I had looked; gazing adoringly at his slim, long-legged body.

He patted himself on the back. 'These shoulders are wide enough to carry all of us.' At that I put my hand to my lips and burst out laughing.

'Why do you always have to spoil the moment.' His eyes were childlike in their hurt as he covered up.

I hurried over to him and put my arms round him. 'I'm sorry. I don't know why I laughed. I love your shoulders, they are so . . . They're so touching, my darling.'

'Great, touching are they?' But I could see that he was placated and by the time I had undressed it was all forgotten.

The only known cure for cellulite is a dimmer switch. But when making up you had to have the harshest of lighting, however dispiriting, or you could find yourself walking out like Coco the Clown or an ageing soap star. As I pout at my reflection I am tempted to draw a generous outline with a lip pencil. *Never*! the beauty editor said. *And don't use those so-called long-lasting lipsticks either. They never stay on half as well as their PR professes, creeping off well before the eight hours, leaving behind a dry shrunken feel.*

'It doesn't look good, all that muck on your face.'

'I thought you liked me wearing make-up.'

'You use too much . . . It looks ridiculous. No, don't look so stricken. I'm sorry, but I'm only telling you how it is. It seems I'm the only one who does since you became successful.'

I had been sitting, like now, at my dressing table, my

hair piled on top of my head in an artful mess, my pale neck exposed, ready to be kissed. Instead I see his reflection behind me; his boyish face turned into that of a sour old woman, his mother. Someone should warn you about the possibility of your husband turning into his mother.

Of course it hadn't been easy for him, the pregnancy that had turned his wife from a fun-loving girl to a plump partridge nesting. 'You go. I'll just have a nice quiet evening in.' I said it more times than not. And then the baby arrived and she was beautiful and greedy and wanted to feed most of every evening so that he was greeted, coming back from work, by a milk-soaked, wild-haired woman and a screaming clawing infant. To our friends he joked that he had never seen his daughter with her mouth shut. Apparently he told his mistress, a woman, I later found out, who wore no make-up and did not shave her legs or armpits, that he felt displaced, surplus to requirements. A little boy lost. Little boy, get lost, I had said at the time, but then I forgave him, although when we kissed and made up the kisses had lost much of their sweetness. But you keep going when you have a child, don't you? You have to carry on.

Three of me in the mirror in front of me. Three of me in our world: the competent, together, successful woman my friends and family saw; the mummy, meek and mild, that my children knew; and the pinched-dull woman in men's jogging bottoms and her hair all lank, who he said I reserved for him. He had a special, rather stagy little laugh to accompany such bitter comments, as if he was performing to his own private audience.

'You don't understand what this chaos does to me.' He was back from work, arms flayed about indicating the disorder of the room: a toy cooker, its door wide open, a saucepan of toy beans spilt on the floor. Three novels, a dictionary, two folders of papers, an odd sock, a dog chew, a cushion with its innards spilling out.

'I know. Awful, isn't it,' I agreed.

'You think it's funny? Driving me insane with your sluttishness, your lazy bloody idleness.'

I stared at him. 'Wow! Where did that come from?'

You might have had a bad day, my mother taught me, *your heart might be broken, the tax man might have taken your last pennies, but there is never an excuse for shabby nails.* I have removed the shell-pink varnish and oiled my cuticles, pushing them down into the bed of the nail with the tip of an orange stick dipped in cotton wool, and now I apply the clear undercoat. Then I inspect the row of coloured bottles on the silver tray on my dressing table: dragon-blood red, cherry, raspberry, strawberry, coral, rose, silver. I pick dragon-blood red. Some people leave each coat to dry before applying the next one but I do it the manicurist way, coat upon coat and then do nothing, sit like a dog begging for a good ten minutes. After that you can move and even turn the page of a book or a newspaper but nothing more strenuous for another fifteen minutes. I usually choose to lean back in my chair and close my eyes. Wasting time, he used to say. Thinking creatively, I would reply. You have to have moments of stillness in each day to give birth to thoughts and watch them grow and fly and you might as well allow your nails to dry at the same time.

Sulking in the car. Sleeping in the aeroplane. Making love in front of an open balcony door on white linen sheets with the Mediterranean breeze caressing our bare bodies and the Umbrian hills looking on. I lay in his arms and thought how good he always smelt and how soft his skin was, baby soft, and how like our daughter he was with his eyes closed and the thick black lashes sweeping down towards high cheekbones. It was his beauty that made me fall in love and his love-making that made me stay. That and the fact that he whimpered in his sleep whilst our loved and shielded child smiled in hers.

I hear the tyres of a car on the rain-washed street and my heart beats faster. Was it time already? I listen out for the car door closing and for voices but the car had driven on by and I sigh with relief.

The week in Umbria had been as lovely and as fleeting as a remembered dream. I pick up the cut-glass scent bottle and direct the fine spray of thyme, sage and orange blossom on to both wrists. *Every woman should have a signature scent*, the beauty editor says. I knew that. I had looked for one since I was thirteen. Then I thought I had found it; Dior-issimo, lilac and lily-of-the-valley, a touch of Eden for £4.00, a small fortune back then for a mere child. I needed that scent. I embezzled to get it, I, a good girl always, honest to a fault, fell from grace for a bottle of heaven scent. The funds I embezzled were for a leaving present for our English teacher. It was no comfort that no one liked her. I felt bad. The scent still smelt divine but behind it came a whiff of sulphur. In the end I made a deal with my conscience; as penance I would never wear that beautiful scent again. I looked for another to love as much, buying expensive bottle after expensive bottle, twirling around in the expensive cloud, before growing sick of that latest perfume within months. During the first part of a relationship that kind of behaviour is known as Endearing. Later it changes its name to Wanton Waste.

'You said you'd try.' His green eyes were narrowed in hurt and dislike. I was too tired, too worn to ask why it was that when he believed himself in love with another woman, *I* became the villain of the piece. 'You said you would be more considerate of my needs, of my feelings, but you just couldn't care less, could you?'

I looked around the room. The children were in bed, on time for once, their toys put away in a large wicker basket. The puppy sat on his bean-bag, still, eyes like glass buttons fixed on us, the tip of his tail wagging slowly like the head of a snake. His toys too were cleared away. I was standing by the ironing board ironing the last of a pile of his shirts. Dinner was in the oven, all the ingredients, beef, onion, carrots, sweet potato, leeks, turnip, all put into the casserole, everything cleared away. My work, the work I had not had time to finish, sat in a folder on the kitchen table that I would lay the moment I had finished the ironing. I began to laugh. You're being ridiculous. Look at this lovely kitchen, nearly tidy, think of your children, good mostly, and pretending to be asleep in their little beds. And there's your puppy in his basket watching

267

you with adoring eyes. You really are being quite ridiculous.

'God, you're smug, you're so damned pleased with yourself, living in your little North London bubble, writing your mediocre pieces for your ridiculous magazine. Why are you grinning? Why are you grinning, you bloody bitch.' The egg timer, fashionable stainless steel, Italian, hit me just above the ear.

He was sorry, oh so sorry. But I had to understand, he said, how I provoked him, pressed all the buttons to make him lose control. And he wasn't looking for excuses, just telling it how it was.

The hairbrush is part of a silver-and-enamel-backed set that had once belonged to his mother. The mother he professes to have adored, his glamorous, amusing, adventurous mother. He has one of those child's cardboard suitcases filled with postcards sent by her. The mother who he could not make love him enough to stop her flittering across the world in search of a love he was too young to understand. The mother who made him decide he was unworthy of love and therefore that those professing to love him were either liars or fools. Poor boy. Go away and never come back. Pack your bags with your Boss suits and your Gucci loafers and your Tiffany cufflinks and leave and never come back because the price of loving you is way too high. By the time he closed the front door behind him we were both crying because in spite of everything, so he said, he loved me.

I brush the hair behind one ear and pull it in front of the other, hiding the violet bruise with the angry red centre, faint now through the foundation and concealer, then touch up my lipstick. There, I was done.

'Darling, you look fabulous.'

I look around my drawing room filled with chatting, laughing people. Everyone has a drink. Everyone is talking to someone. It is a good party.

I turn to the beauty editor with a smile. 'Thank you.'

GIL McNEIL

Battenberg Cake

EVERY THURSDAY Lily went round to Mary's for tea. And every Thursday she ate two slices of Battenberg cake, even though she didn't really like it any more. She'd really loved it when she first started going: the pink and yellow checks of sponge and the layer of marzipan seemed the height of sophistication to her then. She'd liked peeling off the marzipan and dividing the cake into four little coloured sponge squares, although she hadn't done that for quite a while now. But Mary bought it for her specially and it seemed mean to suddenly announce that she'd gone off it. So they sat and drank tea by the gas fire and talked about the war. And ate cake.

'So what have you been up to this week then. Still working hard at school?'

'We've got our exams soon, so they're giving us loads of homework.'

'Well, you keep at it. I was terrible at school, never paid attention. But you're a clever girl, you'll do well. And is your mum all right?'

'Yes.'

'No more arguments?'

'No.'

This wasn't strictly true. They argued most of the

time, Lily and her mum, about the smallest of things. But there was no point telling Mary. She always took her mother's side, and said annoying things like, Oh you'll miss her when she's gone, which always made Lily feel a bit uncomfortable and slightly guilty. But honestly sometimes she thought her mum did it on purpose. Really embarrassing things like asking her if there were any boys she liked at school, as if she'd tell her, even if there were. And she sang in the car, really loud. And whenever they went clothes shopping she deliberately chose the most disgusting thing in the whole shop for her to try on, on purpose.

'I used to have terrible rows with my mother when I was your age. I wanted to be out at the dances in the village, and she was dead against it. I could manage Dad fine, but she was a different story. The times I cried myself to sleep, but she was right. I was too young. You can't see it at the time, but your mother knows best, you know.'

Lily seriously doubted this, but nodded. It didn't do to argue with Mary. She could get quite adamant if you tried to contradict her. A bit like her nana, who could be pretty determined about things too. She'd gone a bit loopy now, and thought that there were miners tunnelling up from the old mines through her living-room floor. Lily's granddad had been a miner years ago, and somehow she seemed to have rewound herself to the years when she'd lived in a miner's cottage by the pits. She'd sit in her chair banging on the floor with the coal shovel, shouting at them to lay off, and you had to go along with it, because it was the only way to get her to calm down. You felt a bit silly, especially as her room was on the second floor. But she

271

still had her lucid moments, and the matron said she was harmless enough apart from the banging.

They didn't make the pilgrimage north to see her very often, but Aunty Vi went in every week, and then spent most of the evening on the phone updating the rest of the family. Mum often got a bit upset after she'd called, and said she wanted Lily to give her tablets if she ever got like that. Which Lily thought was typical attention-seeking behaviour, and not the kind of thing a good mother should say at all. And anyway, what kind of tablets did she mean, and where was she supposed to get them? You couldn't just walk into a chemist and ask for enough tablets to kill your mother because she'd gone loopy and thought miners were tunnelling up through her floor. Otherwise Aunty Vi would definitely have got some by now. Last week she'd had to spend nearly an hour getting the budgie back in his cage because Nana had let him out for a fly-round and the window had been open. He'd flown straight out, and then sat shivering on the window sill, like he couldn't make up his mind if he wanted to fly off or come back in. Poor Vi had to balance on a chair and lean out with a box of seed and talk him back in.

Mary poured the tea.

'They found Mrs Thomas out wandering again. In her nightie. They should do something about her, they really should. It's not fair on the rest of us. Having her wandering about singing at all hours.'

Mary wasn't too keen on the other residents in her block. The warden kept an eye on them all, but he wasn't meant to do much more than help out with moving anything heavy, and wash the bins out every week.

'And Mr Granger died, last week sometime. Went into hospital with his foot, and that was it. That hospital's a terrible place. Always has been. Killed more people than Hitler during the war. You won't get me in there, that's for certain. And he wasn't even that old.'

Lily thought he'd looked absolutely ancient to her, the last time she saw him. And completely mad. He was wearing all his medals, on what looked like his pyjamas, and shuffling along the landing with a small carrier bag of rubbish to put in the bin. Mary didn't like her talking to the other people in the flats. She said Lily was her friend, not anybody else's, and anyway most of them were common, and not the sort of people a nice girl like her should be wasting her time on. Lily thought this was a bit snobby, but secretly was rather pleased that Mary guarded her time so jealously. It was nice to feel special.

Mary had made her feel a bit special ever since they met really. Lily had been getting off the bus after school, and Mary had been getting off too, and the handle on her shopping bag, one of those old-fashioned string things, had suddenly given way, sending her potatoes rolling into the gutter. Lily picked them up, and helped her fit them back into her bag. But it was hard to carry it with only one handle, so Lily offered to help. She'd walked across the road towards the flats with her, and been invited in for tea. When she was leaving Mary had asked to come again, next week if she liked, almost shyly. But with a look in her eyes that betrayed how lonely she was.

Lily recognised it. She was a bit lonely herself, sometimes. She wasn't exactly popular at school. Not unpopular, but not one of the crowd. She read too much, and was a bit too serious. So she said she'd come back next Thursday. Her mum was pleased, and said it was a nice thing to do, visiting an old lady to keep her company, and her dad had said he thought it was a good idea too. He said there were too many lonely old people just longing for someone to talk to, and old people could be fascinating if you had time to listen.

And as it turned out Lily enjoyed her visits almost as much as Mary. She loved hearing about the war, and Mary seemed to take her opinions about things seriously. Which was a bit of a novelty at thirteen, when nobody takes your opinions seriously about anything.

'Have you got time for another cup of tea?'

'Oh yes, please.'

She liked the way Mary always asked her if she had time, like she was a busy person with lots of things to do. Not just going home to do her homework. And the second cup of tea was usually the signal for one of Mary's stories.

'Light the fire then, dear, while I put the kettle on.'

That was another thing she liked. Mary trusted her to light the gas fire. Her mum or dad always did it at home, like she would blow the house up if they let her use a box of matches. It was ridiculous.

Mary came back in with a fresh pot of tea. She always made a pot, and used a tea strainer. She thought tea bags were common.

'I got that mirror down to give it a clean today. But I couldn't get it back up again. It's terrible, you know,

274

getting old. You do something a hundred times, and then you go to do it again and you just can't manage it. You feel just the same inside, you know, but you just don't have the strength any more. I mean they're the same arms I always had. They look the same, well almost. So how come they've gone all weak on me? It's terrible, you know. I wouldn't wish it on my worst enemy, watching yourself fall to bits. I sometimes wish that bomb had finished me off, I really do.'

Lily knew it was no good trying to calm her down with some platitude about how she was still young, or something stupid like that. It was best to just stay quiet, and try to look sympathetic.

'I'll put it back for you, if you like.'

'Oh would you, dear, thank you.'

The mirror was a rather ornate gilt thing, but it wasn't that heavy. She hung the chain over the screw in the wall, and then stood back to see if it was straight.

'Perfect. Clever girl.'

Winter afternoons were best. It got dark and they sat by the fire and Mary told her stories about the war, and they both got so engrossed they didn't even put the lights on and sat in the gathering darkness. She told her about the day her house was bombed, and she lay buried in the rubble for nearly twelve hours until the ARP Wardens dug her out. Her husband was home from leave. He was killed. She heard him crying, and then everything went black. She'd spent a long time in hospital after that, and the doctor told her to take up smoking to steady her nerves, which just goes to show they can't make their minds up, doctors. And little beads of pink glass emerged every now and again, like little raised bumps under her skin, glass which had been travelling round her system from the bomb when the windows had all blown in. And they were perfectly smooth. She'd kept them, for ages, but somehow they'd got lost when she moved, otherwise she'd have shown them to Lily. Lily was rather pleased they'd disappeared: she wasn't sure she really wanted to see glass beads stained pink with somebody's actual blood.

Mary talked about working in a munitions factory in Wales in the Great War, when she was just sixteen. Travelling across the sand dunes on the special little railway they built, to the factory, which was just a collection of wooden huts really, built by the sea as far away from the village as they could get. And every so often you'd hear a loud thudding noise like thunder in the distance and you'd know one of the huts had gone up. And wonder if it was any of the girls you knew. Common lot, most of them, Mary said. They wore lipstick and bobbed their hair and flirted with the men.

Mary was brought up on a farm, and after the war she'd gone back to work in the dairy with her mother. But she couldn't settle; it seemed so quiet after she'd been in lodgings with the other girls, so she'd gone into service, and worked her way up to housekeeper. Nice little room of her own and all the best food. Which is how she'd met her husband. They'd married late and though they'd tried for a baby they weren't lucky. Which was a good thing really given how things turned out. The child would probably have been at home when the bomb fell. She still dreamt of him, fifty years later, her Robert. In his naval uniform, smiling.

*   *   *

Mary loved talking about the beautiful clothes she used to have – costumes, she called them. She'd had a blue-and-white flowery costume for a nephew's wedding, and a very smart tweed suit that Mrs Willett who lived next door used to say made her look like a film star. And she bought a beautiful black crêpe dress and jacket for her uncle's funeral, and a smart hat with a tiny black veil, and she'd had her hair cut short and permed. And when she went home to Wales everyone said how smart she looked, and treated her like she was a special guest, and she realised that it wasn't home any more, and she'd be better off staying in London.

And she talked about food a lot. Meals she'd cooked, grand dinners and lunches when she was in service. She knew how to do things properly. Doing things properly seemed very important to her. Pheasants and partridge, whole salmon in aspic, and grand puddings that took hours to make. Things people didn't know how to make any more. And cakes, and pastry. She had cool hands, which she said were good for pastry. The old cook at one of the houses where she'd worked had shown her some of her favourite recipes, even though housekeepers didn't usually get involved in the cooking. But she liked to be busy, and anyway it came in handy after the war, when she'd worked as a cook in the City, and then finally for an old gentleman who loved her steak and kidney puddings and would have eaten them every day if she'd let him. He'd left her that lovely painting of the sea when he died.

They talked about Mary's childhood, and her life on the farm, when she would crack ice in the water bowls and carry big jugs of cream in from the dairy.

And she asked Lily about when she was little, as if her stories were interesting too. Lily told her about Northumberland where they always went for their holidays, she and her sister and her mum and dad. When her nana was younger, and her grandad was still alive. It was a great place to be a child, with trips to Seahouses when they went out on the fishing boats to see the seals. She and her sister would pretend to be Grace Darling. They'd both longed for some sort of calamity that would mean it was up to them to rescue the entire family in a small rowing boat. They'd row out into the storm, and then they'd get presents from everyone for their bravery, including the Queen. Lily had thought they might get little crowns with jewels in. Actually the only time they were allowed in a rowing boat, on a lake in a park, one of them managed to fall out and get covered in green slime. But this didn't really put them off.

Lily remembered her nana combing her hair, gently, not like her mum who sometimes pulled. And her nana knitted doll's clothes for them, little woollen suits and bonnets with satin ribbon, and she read their comics to them. And one Christmas she and her sister stripped half the pine needles off the Christmas tree and mixed them up with flour and water in a big china mixing bowl to make a Christmas cake, while their mother sat in the front room aghast and seething with resentment, because if she'd tried anything similar when she was little she'd have been given a slap.

And Mary remembered her brother David setting fire to a haystack while he was practising smoking his pipe. And how her dad had chased him across two fields before giving up and saying he would never speak to him again. But he forgave him in the end, and they worked the farm together for years. Although David never really did get the hang of a pipe.

When Lily went to university her mother promised she'd keep an eye on Mary, and went in every week and took her in a bit of shopping. They had a cup of tea, and talked about the weather, and how Lily was doing, and how you couldn't buy a decent chicken any more, that tasted of proper chicken.

Mary wrote to Lily at university, and said she hoped she was keeping warm and working hard, and sent her little bits of money squirrelled away from her pension, a few pounds which Lily never felt she could spend on booze or anything frivolous, which was a bit annoying really.

In the midst of her first real love affair she was consumed with new-found passions, but still found time to write back and give Mary a few snippets about campus life, parties, and staying up till all hours talking about books, and going on marches against apartheid, and Nazis, which amused the old lady no end, although she pretended to be shocked. She reckoned she'd done enough against the Nazis for the both of them, but was glad Lily seemed to be enjoying herself.

And then Mary died. Very suddenly, of a cold that turned to pneumonia before anyone really knew what was happening. She died in her sleep, in her own bed. Which was just how she'd always wanted it.

There were only two people at the funeral. Lily and her mum. Distant relations sent wreaths. One with chrysanthemums in. Which made Lily cry. She'd been fine during the service, which was pretty short. Mary had left very precise instructions about her funeral. She wanted to be buried with her husband, in the freezing municipal cemetery that seemed to go on for miles. It was raining, and bitterly cold. Mary had chosen the hymns she wanted. 'There is a Green Hill Far Away'. And 'All Things Bright and Beautiful', because she'd liked it at school. And the Vicar obviously had no idea who she was, though he did his best.

But when Lily saw the chrysanthemums she began to cry.

'Oh Lily, don't, you'll start me off too. She was very old you know.'

'I know. But she hated chrysanthemums. They reminded her of when she was bombed in the war. There was a vase on the table, yellow ones. And she hid under the table, and watched the house fall round her, and in the dust she saw the flowers. She told me. She hated them ever since.'

'Let's go home.'

'All right. Thanks for coming, Mum. It would have been horrible on my own.'

'Oh I wouldn't have let you come on your own. She was very proud of you, you know. She told me it was just like having a granddaughter. Just like being a nana. She loved you very much, you know.'

'I know. I loved her too. Both of them. I mean Nana, but Mary too. Because she sort of chose me.'

'I know.'

'It just seems so sad, that nobody else was here.'

'Well, it's a long way, Wales, isn't it, and anyway we're here.'

'Yes, I suppose so.'

'I was listening to something on the radio the other day, while I was driving home from work. Some daft thing about freezing people and then defrosting them in a hundred years or something. Like turkeys, only slower. So they could be immortal. And it made me think, about Mary, and Mum, and actually, you know, it's much easier than that. You don't have to get defrosted.'

'What?'

'To be immortal. All you need is someone to remember. To know that you hated chrysanthemums.'

'Or loved Battenberg cake.'

'I know, she told me. I didn't have the heart to tell her that you'd gone off it years ago. Your nana had a brown teapot, you know, for as long as I can remember. And every time I see one I think of her. So I've bought myself one. I saw it in that china shop in the high street, and I just had to buy it. It's the small things. You take care of the small things and they last for ever. Like magic. You can't see it, but it's there.'

'Magic?'

'Yes. Battenberg and brown teapots. Silly, really.'

'No it's not, Mum. It's lovely.'

'Come on, let's go home. I've made a shepherd's pie.'

Years later, when Lily had her own daughters, and was busy with work and trying to fit everything in, she still found the time to make shepherd's pie, the way her mum made it. With carrots and peas, and a dash of tabasco in the gravy, just to liven it up a bit. And sometimes she'd buy a Battenberg cake, and sit by the fire. And think about Mary. And the small things. That last for ever.

ARABELLA WEIR

Through Thick and Thin

THE APTLY named Mademoiselle Sévère brought down her ruler with a resounding thwack on to Ally's desk, deliberately missing Ally's hand by only a few inches – little enough space to instil terror but a wide enough gap to bypass accusations of brutality. Mademoiselle Sévère conducted every class, every day, with the same ruler gripped tightly in her left hand. She never used it to measure anything. She never hit anyone with it. It served only as a nominal weapon, a flat wooden threatening object. School legend did not tell of any occasion on which she'd actually struck someone with it but by design each pupil, past and present, had felt sure that injury was a real, and ever imminent, possibility.

Ally was drawing on the piece of paper the ruler landed on and, naturally enough, Ally's drawing was brought to an abrupt halt. She looked up adopting as meek and innocent an expression as she could muster. This wasn't that easy given that meek and innocent were not the first two words one might use to describe seven-year-old Ally.

'What on earth do you think you are doing, Alison Mackie?!' Mademoiselle Sévère boomed.

'Drawing some grass, Mademoiselle,' Ally replied,

genuinely bemused. She couldn't think what she'd done wrong but she was sure that Mademoiselle Sévère, with her exacting and idiosyncratic rules, had found something to displease her – she usually did.

'You changed the direction of your colouring-in.'

From the expression on Mademoiselle Sévère's face it was clear to Ally that a reply was neither expected nor desired. Which was just as well because Ally had no idea what her teacher was talking about.

'You were drawing across the page and I saw you move the paper around so as to draw up and down the page.'

Ally hadn't known paper movement and realignment of crayons wasn't allowed. She did now. 'My hand was getting tired.'

'Sloppy and inexcusable. Here at Le Sacré Coeur we always draw in the same direction. If you begin drawing up and down that is the manner in which you will finish the drawing. Do you understand?'

Ally slowly nodded her head. She didn't really understand at all and although she was not far off eight she couldn't see how changing direction colouring-in could made any difference to anything. But she'd been at the strict school for long enough by now to know that resistance to Mademoiselle Sévère was fruitless.

A few moments later the teacher changed her beady focus of attention and Ally was, at last, able to sneak a look at Kat. Since her first day, nearly a year ago now, Kat had always sat next to Ally. They were best friends. Kat had witnessed the whole scene firsthand and reacted accordingly, rolling her eyes and flopping her tongue out like a cow's. She allowed herself a few seconds of undetected tongue-lolling to drive her point home. It expressed perfectly Ally and Kat's secret shared view of Mademoiselle Sévère – horrid, bossy, and French.

Ally and Kat had been best friends since Ally's first day of school. Ally had joined halfway through the first term of the school year. She had been moved from yet another school in yet another country that her father had been working in. She'd hated moving and hated, even more, having to join an already established class. Starting this new school, Ally had been convinced that she'd be an outsider, as she usually was. Her father's stays in each country were often so short that she never got time to settle in. However, much to her delight, Kat had taken an instant liking to her. It might have been because they were the only two pupils in their class who couldn't muster up a French relation between them. It created an immediate bond.

The London-based school had initially been built to provide a French education for French nationals working in London. Over the years entry had been extended to the children of other nations but only if they could provide a blood link to a French person. Ally was English and Kat was American and both had only ever been to France on holiday. So neither of them really knew why they were at this school. They did once wonder if the school's proximity to Kat's swanky penthouse flat had anything to do with it. Ally lived miles away, though, so that couldn't have been the reason in her case. Being young they didn't subject the matter to a lengthy analysis and were simply glad to have found each other. They couldn't have guessed that the only thing in common between their respective parents was a shared desire for their child to speak impeccable French.

Kat's home was invariably the after-school destination for the two inseparable girls. Kat's father, Bob, was a film director and they lived in a palatial flat opposite a museum that looked, to Ally, like a castle. Ally had never heard of any of the films her friend's dad had made but she guessed they must have been successful because they lived so grandly. Ally's family lived in a very ordinary house in an ordinary street in an ordinary way. Kat's family lived extraordinarily. Ally had never met anyone who lived in a big flat before – not a family. Her granny lived in a flat but it was little, so little she could hear her granny's wee hitting the water in the pan when she went round for a visit and she didn't much like that. Ally reckoned you could fit two, maybe even three, of her own house into Kat's flat. They'd have to be lying down but they'd easily fit.

And so it was that Ally and Kat spent all their time in Kat's luxurious home. One day Kat's mother, Betty, announced that she had a big treat in store for the girls. They were to attend the world premiere of *Mary Poppins*, a new film about a magical nanny. The girls were very excited. They weren't absolutely clear what a premiere was but they did understand that it was a big deal and no one in the whole world would have seen the film before they did.

The much awaited day finally came and Ally and Kat, dressed in all their velvet finery, accompanied by Kat's mother, went to see *Mary Poppins*. Ally had never seen so big a crowd as the one outside the cinema. Maybe a world premiere meant everybody in the whole world went to see the film on one day, she wondered, as they pressed their way through the throng.

Ally and Kat held hands throughout the duration of the film. Neither had ever seen anything so wonderfully affecting before in their lives. They memorised all the words to 'Supercalafragalistic . . .' and sang the song night and day. They could even sing it backwards, like Mary does in the film. They both agreed that Mary Poppins was indeed, as she said of herself, 'practically perfect in every way'. On the way home they decided that when they grew up and had children of their own they'd each get their very own Mary Poppins. Being of a more pragmatic nature than her friend Ally sort of knew secretly that this wasn't very likely but she loved sharing a fantastical dream with Kat.

At the end of the school year as summer was in full swing Ally's father shattered her world. He announced that they were 'off again'.

'But you said that was it! You promised we'd moved back to England for ever!' Ally wailed.

'I know, darling, but things have changed, I'm sorry.'

'I'm not coming! I hate you! I'm not leaving Kat, I'll die without her!' Ally protested dramatically.

And so it was that Ally moved again to yet another school in yet another country. This time she didn't find a friend – no one could replace Kat in her eyes and she'd never let anyone. As the years passed the promised exchange of letters and photographs dwindled and by the time Ally graduated from school and went to university she had no idea where Kat lived or what she was doing.

Fifteen years later found Ally back in London working as a GP and married with two young children, Peggy and Toby. One Christmas in her customary desperate search for something not designed to simulate gun death or something not Barbie-emblazoned Ally bought a video of *Mary Poppins* for her children. She hadn't thought about Kat for a long while, in fact she couldn't remember the last time she had consciously given her any thought. A few years previously she'd sent a card announcing Peggy's birth to the last address she'd had for Kat, the same palatial flat of their childhood, but the card had come back with 'addressee unknown' scrawled across it. In a way, Ally realised, she'd found herself oddly relieved not to have reconnected with her old friend. Bonds like the one they'd had rarely stay intact, she'd reasoned; it was best to leave the memory as a fond but distant one.

To Ally's relief Peggy and Toby adored the video and watched *Mary Poppins* on a loop for the entire Christmas period. Once the extensive holidays were over and she had some time to herself again Ally found herself thinking about Kat more and more, wondering where she was, what she was doing, if she had children she watched *Mary Poppins* with. She developed a near obsession. She found herself searching the web for Kat's name – a complete waste of time as it turned out. Ally had got very excited when, at one point, the search seemed to be proving fruitful. But it turned out to be something to do with Kat's father who had long since died – having once been involved with

288

movies it appeared that his passing merited a mention on some obscure where-are-they-now Hollywood website. At one stage, late at night, in a fit of wine-fuelled madness, Ally had entered the words 'Mary Poppins' into the search engine. She'd suddenly had a fantasy that she might find Kat that way. But all she'd got back was yard upon yard of information from the myriad of grown-up demented *Mary Poppins* fans. Try as she might, and she did try, Ally was unable to find anything.

A few months later when Ally's burgeoning obsession had been taken over by the events of daily family life, she had a blow. Chrysoula, her crotchety Turkish *au pair*, decided to leave. Straight out of the blue, just like that, no warning, no discussion, no permission asked. She just upped and left. Ally didn't mind losing her as a person since she was always bad-tempered, always sulky, and never emerged from her room unless she absolutely had to. But she did mind losing the help and had no idea how she was going to manage on her own. Ally spent the next three days, following Chrysoula's departure, searching for a replacement. She'd taken emergency leave from her practice for a week but time was running out and she was getting nowhere.

On the eve of her last day off from work, run ragged with worry and exhaustion, Patrick, Ally's husband, announced that he too was leaving. He was, he gaily told her, off to join Chrysoula in Antalya where they planned to open a bar together. Apparently they loved each other, had done for some time and he was happier than he'd ever been before in his life. Ally found this last fascinating detail not only supplementary to requirements but also pretty difficult to picture given the recently departed *au pair's* unceasing bad humour. But off Patrick went leaving Ally not missing him as a person, she was forced to admit, but more as the last pair of hands she could count on to help out with the kids.

So there she was completely alone at midnight the night before she was, in theory, returning to work, with lunches boxes to be filled, sports bags to be equipped, a rowdy breakfast looming and all alone in the world. Ally did what any sensible woman would do in the same situation, she downed a bottle of wine and crashed out on her bed fully dressed.

By some miracle, using some hitherto ineffective threats delivered at full voice, some very efficient and speedy bread-buttering, refusing to worry about un-matching socks and skilfully dodging queries about Dad's whereabouts, Ally achieved the impossible. She arrived at work on time having dropped the kids off at nursery – it has to be said their arrival didn't usually coincide with that of the cleaning lady's but she didn't seem to mind taking care of them until the school opened.

As she settled down at her desk to take a breather before the onslaught of patients started to shuffle into her office Ally realised that although she'd done well this morning she wouldn't be able to repeat the success too often, if at all. The fear loomed at the back of her mind all day long and by the end of the day Ally could feel panic building up inside her. What was she going to do? Where was she going to find her Mary Poppins? Why was this happening to her? With a heavy heart Ally realised there was nothing for it – she would have to get an agency nanny, at least in the short term, there was no alternative. Ally knew it was risky, she couldn't afford it, she might get a horror and, worst of all, the kids might hate her. But it was the only solution for now.

Three days later Ally had, with some difficulty, bad feeling and risk to her job security, taken the morning off work. She prepared herself to meet the applicants the agency had rustled up for her. Not one of them sounded a bit like anything even approximating Mary Poppins. Knowing my luck, Ally mused as she waited, they'll be more like the nanny out of *The Omen*, the one who ties a rope around her neck and jumps out of the window at the boy's birthday party. She dismissed the image, quickly deciding one of the devil's disciples was more likely to apply for a job in a posh person's grand house rather than one being offered by an NHS doctor living in a grotty old Kentish Town semi.

Ally stood at the door giving the last applicant as sincere a pleasant farewell as she could manage and then collapsed wearily into the only decent armchair the living room offered. She hadn't thought it possible but reviewing her evening it seemed to be the case – each one of the women applying for the job of taking care of her precious children had been more fierce and unfriendly than the last. Ally tried to be grown-up and consider her options. But she didn't have any and she knew it. She burst into tears of desperation. Her world had fallen apart and she didn't seem to be able to have any skill at putting it back together again. Suddenly she felt a huge gust of wind blast through the window and under the door. Ally was puzzled as it hadn't been windy outside when she'd come in. Then she heard a little rap at the door. She briefly toyed with the idea of not answering it. It couldn't be anybody except a Godbotherer, she reckoned. She sat still, hoping they'd go away. They knocked again, though no louder than the first time, Ally mused admiringly as she heaved herself towards the door.

Ally's jaw dropped open in amazement. There on the doorstep stood the grown-up Kat. She looked exactly the same as when Ally had last seen her almost thirty years previously, only taller.

'Close your mouth, Ally, we are not a codfish,' Kat said, walking briskly past her and into the hall.

'How . . . where . . . who?' Ally stumbled as she closed the door.

'All in good time. Now, you're in trouble and need my help. I'll stay as long as it takes.'

'Stay?'

'I'm going to be your practically perfect person in every way until you get back on your feet.'

'You'll be my nanny? But how did you know? Where have you been? I've tried to get in touch with you so many times. How did you know where I lived? What have you been doing all these years? How did you know I needed help? I don't understand any of this.' Ally was reeling. She was torn between mindbending confusion and delight.

'Now, I assume you've got a spare bedroom. I'm pooped and I'll need to be up bright and early if I've got your two to deal with all day.'

Not surprisingly Ally lay in bed that night completely unable to fall asleep. Suddenly it came to her. Kicking herself for being so childish in this most urgent hour of need, she realised the truth – she'd had some sort of an accident and had dreamt the whole fantasy up. Gently tiptoeing over the creaky hall floor she opened the spare-room door just to reassure herself that everything was as always. Kat had not returned. But, no, there she was fast asleep wearing a crisp white nightie and a beatific smile. Ally closed the door behind her gently. She wasn't hallucinating – Kat was really there. Somehow, someway, from somewhere her old friend had reappeared in her life just when she needed her most.

Two months later life for Ally and her children had not, as she'd hoped, returned to normal. It was much, much better than the normal they'd been accustomed to – rushed meals eaten individually, frantic morning rows as Ally and Patrick tried to get the kids together and themselves out of the house ready for work wearing some semblance of clothing, late nights, TV and sweets used as persuaders. Now they ate healthily and moreover as a family; the kids were happy and adored Kat, Ally went off to work feeling secure and relaxed about the kids' welfare, the house was neat and cosy. As she made her way home from work after her last day before the summer holidays Ally allowed herself to say aloud, 'Our life is now practically perfect in every way.' She laughed out loud as she heard the words and had to stop herself skipping down the street.

Ally, Toby and Peggy spent the happiest summer of their lives – visits to the local paddling pool, picnics, kite flying – they indulged in every activity ever thought of to amuse kids. Ally found that she was really enjoying her children for the first time she could remember. Now this is what I *thought* having children would be like, she mused one evening as she lay in bed.

As the summer drew to a close Ally had an epiphany – she decided to give up work to spend as much time as she could with her offspring before they got too big. Ally had never been more sure of a decision. The next morning she sprang down the stairs two at a time to make her big announcement. She found Peggy and Toby sitting at the kitchen table happily munching their way through their cereal.

'Where's Kat?' Ally asked, popping on the kettle to make a cup of tea.

'Oh she's gone,' Toby said, his mouth stuffed with Shreddies.

'Gone?' Ally could feel a sense of foreboding welling up inside her.

'Don't worry, she said she'd come back if we ever needed her again.'

'What?!'

Neither of the children responded, they were evidently taking Kat's mysterious departure in their stride. Ally was very mindful of raising hysterical questions, thereby upsetting the kids, but she was desperate to know what had happened.

'What did she say?' she said, trying to sound as relaxed as possible.

'She said you were giving up work so she wouldn't be needed,' Toby reported between quick appraisals of the toys on offer on the back of the cereal pack. 'Oh yeah, she also said that we know she loves us, which is true.'

'That is truth,' Peggy chipped in.

Ally didn't respond – her mind was spinning. How did Kat know that she'd decided to give up work? How *could* she have known when Ally had only just decided herself last night? Where had Kat gone? When was she coming back? She was about to put some of these questions to Toby but he spoke first.

'Mum, if we get fifteen more packs we can get a surfboard for Magic Mouse. So can we? I'll definitely, definitely eat them all up, promise.'

Ally took in her son's earnest expression and decided against further enquiry – it wouldn't be fair on him. She'd have to find out the answers by herself.

That evening, after the children were tucked up happily in bed – having spent a day showing absolutely no signs of trauma at Kat's absence, Ally had noted – she set about trying to find out what had happened to her friend. As she sat there mentally sorting through the normal means of contacting a person it slowly began to dawn on her – she had absolutely no contact number, address, next-of-kin information for Kat. Unlike the last time Ally had sat in the kitchen wondering how she was going to manage, she wasn't worried this time, just racked with curiosity and loss. She'd enjoyed having Kat and, although the intimacy of their youth had never sprung up again, Kat's benign presence had helped Ally find her feet, her life, herself again and she was very reluctant to let go.

A few weeks passed and Toby started big school and Peggy went full-time to nursery. Ally, with more time on her hands, decided to do some real detective work. Using her privileged position as a doctor she accessed a missing persons' website. To her relief, she found no match there. Next she entered a nationwide hospital private-information website reasoning that if Kat had ever had an operation or an accident then the relevant hospital would have an address for her. Ally knew that it might not be where she lived now but at least it would be a starting point. The information that came back was not what Ally had been expecting. 1.) Catherine Healey born at Middlesborough General 16.3.2002.2.) Catherine J. Healey treated for fractured femur at Dundee Infirmary 23.6.1996. 3.) Catherine Healey born 11.3.1961 deceased 18.7.1988 at the London Clinic – cause of death, congenital heart failure.

Ally stared at the screen. There was obviously a mistake. The date of birth corresponded with Kat's but the rest didn't make any sense. Just a funny coincidence, Ally decided with a shudder, getting up to go and make a cup of tea. As she trudged back up to her office she decided to do another search but this time using a US search engine instead – in case Kat had gone back to America. This proved unfruitful. There were no matches found except a car dealership in Houston called Catherine's Crazy Cars apparently owned, bizarrely, by someone called Ted Koch, and an sub-aqua training centre in the Cayman Islands owned by a Catherine Healey who, judging by the picture posted on her website, was the world's first pre-pubescent professional diver.

Somewhat relieved that she could now concentrate exclusively on home ground, Ally went back to her cosy British search engine. After a tedious search through various regional phone books, Ally found herself drawn back to the dead Catherine Healey match. This time she went into the records to check the address of this girl. She knew it couldn't be Kat but she was curious. In the box for patient's address it read unknown but in next of kin it read Betsy and Bob Healey. Ally felt as if she'd been knocked on the head – these were Kat's parents' names. She then moved her eyes slowly across the screen to the box where the parents' address should appear. It read 'The Penthouse, Parkview Mansions, Kensington Gore, London, SW7'. As a child Ally had known that address as well as her own.

She couldn't begin to make sense of it. If Kat was dead, had been dead for nearly fifteen years, then who had come to her house, who had she let look after her children, how had that person known all about her? She sat there for a while trying to take the whole thing in. She couldn't fathom whether she felt angry, conned, grateful, sad or blessed. She had no idea. Kat, or a form of Kat, had come back into her life and brought with her a harmony Ally hadn't known since the idyllic innocence of their youthful friendship. Really, Ally thought, as she drifted off to sleep, Kat came back as my very own Mary Poppins – a practically perfect person in every way.

MARY LOUDON

Babymagic

Because you are mostly below, I see you from
    above,
As if from space, one planet in awe of another;
My daughter, the map of my new world unfurling
In my arms, in my lap, at my feet.
In your cot, sleeping,
Oblivious and absolutely complete,
Arms flung north and east,
You are a whole landscape, stretching and
    expanding,
I must bend to reach.
You are you
And I am, impossibly,
Loving you from a distance already.

In this world of you I find much:
The mundane thrills; the pedestrian delights.
At the heart of your moderate developments
Lies my immoderate pleasure.
It works the other way as well.
Fears are rehearsed when children die who are not
    you;
When people suffer, or are cruel.
My sister dies alone and for a time

My fantasies are manifold.
I concentrate instead on the better views you have
   to offer:
Eric Clapton sings the blues
And you squeal with pleasure.

But when I lose some video film
(Ingrained upon it,
Your first solo traverse of the kitchen floor)
I grieve out of all proportion to the loss.
I remember shooting the film.
You were new, my sister was dead, I recall
How dearly I wished you permanent then.
Knowing you not to be so,
I feel you partially absent already –
Absurdly so, for here you are, my present,
The baby I loved,
Obscured and illuminated
By the child you are now.

I want you to outlive me.
Actually, I want you to live for ever.
I can conceive of no universe without you
Which could possibly make sense.
But I am no guarantor:
The day you were born I understood that
The harbour I offer is impermanent;
That my desires for you, so fierce,
Lack essential substance when opposed.
I would dive under that metaphorical bus for you,
The real bus, too.
I would keep you from all peril,
Suffer any disease,

Put my heart in your way
For others to pull apart.
But I am only your mother,
And you deserve a braver love than that.
My job is to deliver you to the world,
Entire, intact,
And breakable.

www.piggybankkids.org

PIGGYBANKKIDS was established in 2002 by Sarah Brown to support charitable projects that create opportunities for children and young people. The charity, and its subsidiary company, PiggyBankKids Projects Limited, work on a number of specific initiatives chosen by the Trustees to benefit relevant charities.

Contact:
Hugo Tagholm
Programme Director
PiggyBank Kids Projects Limited
16 Lincoln's Inn Fields
London WC2A 3ED
Tel: 020 7936 1294
Fax: 020 7936 1299

PiggyBankKids registered charity number: 1092312

PiggyBankKids Projects Limited registered company number: 4326134

One parent families

making change happen

ONE PARENT FAMILIES and One Parent Families Scotland provide an independent, confidential, free helpline and advice service for people bringing up children on their own called Lone Parent Helpline (0800 018 5026). They put lone parents in touch with local sources of help, offer free booklets and factsheets on a wide range of subjects, including jobs, housing, benefits, child support, and education. As well as providing services, the charities carry out research, represent lone parents' interests to government and the media, run training courses, and set up local projects to test new ways of working.

For more information:

One Parent Families
Tel: 020 7428 5400
Email: *info@oneparentfamilies.org.uk*
Web: *www.oneparentfamilies.org.uk*

255 Kentish Town Road
London NW5 2LX
One Parent Families registered charity number 230750

One Parent Families Scotland
Tel: 0131 556 3899
Email: *info@opfs.org.uk*
Web: *www.opfs.org.uk*

13 Gayfield Square
Edinburgh EH1 3NX
One Parent Families Scotland registered charity
number SCO 11688

Kate Green, Director, One Parent Families

Author Biographies

CELIA BRAYFIELD is the author of eight novels, the latest of which is *Mr Fabulous & Friends*. She is a single parent with one daughter and lives in London. A trustee of the National Council for One Parent Families and a director of the National Academy of Writing, Celia is now working on a novel about the English countryside and Deep France, an account of her year in the village of Bearn.

CHRISTOPHER BROOKMYRE'S books include *Quite Ugly One Morning*, which won the 1996 Critics' Award for the best debut crime novel, *Boiling a Frog*, which won the 200 Sherlock Award for the Best Comic Detective, *One Fine Day In the Middle of the Night*, and most recently *The Sacred Art of Stealing*. His new novel, *Be My Enemy*, will be published in October 2003.

SARAH BROWN is a consultant at Brunswick Arts, a public relations company specialising in the arts and cultural projects within the Brunswick Group. She also runs a non-profit venture, PiggyBankKids, which supports charitable projects that create opportunities for children and young people. Last year she edited the anthology *Magic* with Gil McNeil, and this year she has also edited *Moving On Up: Inspirational Advice to Change Your Life*, a PiggyBankKids project to raise funds for Big Brothers and Sisters, the child mentoring charity. She is married to Gordon Brown, Labour Member of Parliament for Dunfermline East and Chancellor of the Exchequer. They live in Fife and London.

CLAIRE CALMAN is the author of three novels, *Love is a Four Letter Word*, *Lessons for a Sunday Father* and *I Like it Like That*, and her short stories have appeared in a number of anthologies and magazines. She is also a broadcaster and poet and has performed her distinctive brand of pithy verse live on Radio Four. She lives with her husband and the world's largest private collection of unfiled paperwork.

RUSSELL CELYN JONES is the author of five novels: *Soldiers and Innocents*, which won the David Higham Prize, *Small Times*, *An Interference of Light*, *The Eros Hunter* and *Surface Tension*. He is a staff reviewer for *The Times*, a lecturer at Warwick University and lives in London.

MAVIS CHEEK has a daughter and lives in London. In 1988 her novel *Pause Between Acts* won the *Shel* John Menzies First Novel Prize. She is the author of eleven novels, the most recent of which is *The Sex Life of My Aunt*.

MARIKA COBBOLD was born in Gothenburg, Sweden. Educated in Gothenburg and Lausanne, Marika now lives in London. She found popularity with her first novel, *Guppies For Tea*, reissued this year. Her critically acclaimed latest novel is *Shooting Butterflies*.

JILLY COOPER is a well-known journalist, and author of many bestselling novels, including *Riders*, *Rivals*, *Polo*, *The Man Who Made Husbands Jealous*, *Appassionata* and *Score!*. She and her husband live in Gloucestershire with several dogs and cats.

SUSAN CROSLAND was born and bred in Baltimore, Maryland. As Susan Barnes, she talked her way into her first job as *Sunday Express* features writer for the great John Junor. Her *Sunday Times* interviews with famous politicians and the rich have been republished in book form. With two dauthers by her first husband, she married Anthony Crosland, who was British Foreign Secretary at the time of his sudden death. Her acclaimed biography *Tony Crosland* was followed by four bestselling novels. Her non-fiction book, *Great Sexual Scandals*, was published in 2002.

CAITLIN DAVIES was born in London and spent twelve years in Botswana, working as a teacher and journalist. She is the author of a novel, *Jamestown Blues*, and a non-fiction book, *The Return of El Negro*. Caitlin is a lone (but definitely not alone) single parent.

PHIL HOGAN lives in Hertfordshire with his wife and four children. He is the author of a novel, *Hitting the Grove*, and *Parenting Made Difficult*, a collection of his columns for the *Observer* magazine. His second novel, *The Freedom Thing*, will be published in 2003.

HOWARD JACOBSON is the author of seven novels including *Coming From Behind*, *The Mighty Walzer*, and *Who's Sorry Now?*, and four works of non-fiction. Of the latter, *Roots Schmoots* and *Seriously Funny: an Argument for Comedy* were made into television series for Channel 4. He writes a weekly column for the *Independent*.

KATHY LETTE has been a singer in a rock band, a newspaper columnist in Sydney and New York and a television sitcom writer for Columbia Pictures in Los Angeles. She is the author of the bestselling novels *Puberty Blues* (now a major motion picture), *Girls' Night Out*, *The Llama Parlour*, *Foetal Attraction*, *Mad Cows* (made into a movie starring Joanna Lumley and Anna Friel), *Altar Ego* and *Nip 'n' Tuck*.

MARY LOUDON is the author of *Secrets & Lives*, *Middle England Revealed*, *Revelations*, *The Clergy Questioned*, and *Unveiled, Nuns Talking*. She has won four writing prizes, appeared frequently on radio and TV, reviewed for *The Times*, and been a Whitbread Prize judge. She is married and has two young daughters.

NICHOLA McAULIFFE is an actress who has won awards for work as diverse as Ibsen's *Wild Duck* and Cole Porter's *Kiss Me Kate*. She is the voice of James Bond's Aston Martin and also his BMW. 'The Nurglar' is her first published work. Her first novel, *The Crime Tsar*, together with a children's book, *Attila Loolagaz and the Eagle*, will be published in 2003.

PAULINE McLYNN is the author of three novels,

Something for the Weekend, Better Than a Rest, and *Right on Time.* She has contributed to the serial novel *Yeats Is Dead* and the charity collection *Girls' Night Out.*

GIL McNEIL is the author of the bestselling *The Only Boy For Me,* and edited the *Magic* anthology with Sarah Brown last year. Her second novel, *Stand By Your Man,* will be published in 2003. Gil is a consultant at Brunswick Arts, and a Director of Piggy-BankKids Projects. She lives in Kent with her son.

SHYAMA PERERA is a writer, broadcaster and mother of two and lives in London. She has written three novels: *Haven't Stopped Dancing Yet, Bitter Sweet Symphony* and *Do the Right Thing.* Her next work of fiction examines the world of genetics and the ethics of making babies.

MALCOLM PRYCE was born in the UK and has lived and worked abroad since the early nineties. He has held down a variety of jobs, including BMW assembly-line worker, hotel washer-up, aluminium salesman, deck hand on a yacht travelling through Polynesia, and advertising copywriter. He currently lives in Bangkok. He is the author of the novels *Aberystwyth Mon Amour* and *Last Tango in Aberystwyth.*

JOANNA TROLLOPE is the mother of two daughters, the stepmother of two stepsons and now a grandmother. She is the bestselling author of ten novels, the most recent of which is *Girl From the South.* She has been married twice and now lives alone – except for a

Labrador the size of a sofa – partly in London and partly in the Cotswolds.

PENNY VINCENZI began her career as a junior secretary for *Vogue* and *Tatler*. She later worked as a fashion and beauty editor on magazines such as *Woman's Own*, before becoming a contributing editor for *Cosmopolitan*. She is the author of two humorous books and eleven novels, the most recent of which is *Into Temptation*. She is married with four daughters.

MARINA WARNER is a novelist, historian and critic. She has written award-winning studies of mythology and fairy tales, including *From the Beast to the Blonde* and *Fantastic Metamorphoses: Other Worlds*. Her latest novel is *The Leto Bundle*, and a collection of stories, *Murderers I Have Known*, was published last year. She is now writing a study of ghosts, *Spiritual Visions*.

DAISY WAUGH is a journalist and the author of three novels and a travelogue, *A Small Town in Africa*. She is at present working on a fourth novel, to be published in 2004. She has two small children and lives in London.

ARABELLA WEIR, author and comedienne, is best known as the creator of the catchphrase, 'Does my bum look big in this?', which is also the title of her international bestseller. Her third novel, *Stupid Cupid*, is being made into a film, for which she wrote the screenplay. She is currently working on a fourth novel, *Or Is It Just Me?*.

TOBY YOUNG is the author of *How to Lose Friends & Alienate People*, an account of the five years he spent trying – and failing – to take Manhattan. To date, it has appeared on bestseller lists in Britain, America, Canada, Australia and New Zealand. It is being made into a film by Channel 4.

A Note on the Type

The text of this book is set in Linotype Sabon, named after the type founder, Jacques Sabon. It was designed by Jan Tschichold and jointly developed by Linotype, Monotype and Stempel, in response to a need for a typeface to be available in identical form for mechanical hot metal composition and hand composition using foundry type.

Tschichold based his design for Sabon roman on a fount engraved by Garamond, and Sabon italic on a fount by Granjon. It was first used in 1966 and has proved an enduring modern classic.